Praise for Into the Hollow

"Beautiful. Raw. Tender. Gritty. The cherry on top of the crème of Young Adult fiction."

—Sunniva Dee, #1 international bestselling author

Into the Hollow

lynn vroman

OWL HOLLOW PRESS

Owl Hollow Press, LLC, Springville, UT 84663

This book is a work of fiction. Names, characters, places, and incidents are products of the author's imagination. Any resemblance to actual people, living or dead, or to businesses, companies, events, institutions, or locales is completely coincidental.

Into the Hollow
Copyright © 2018 by Lynn Vroman

All rights reserved. No part of this publication may be reproduced, distributed or transmitted in any form or by any means, without prior written permission.

Library of Congress Cataloging-in-Publication Data
Into the Hollow / L. Vroman. — First edition.

Summary:
Seventeen-year-old Freedom Paine vows to protect her young brother when her father takes them to hide in the hollows of Appalachia, experiencing the simple, wholesome goodness of finding first love, enduring the harrowing realties of life in rural America, and discovering herself along the way.

ISBN 978-1-945654-16-9 (paperback)
ISBN 978-1-945654-17-6 (e-book)
LCCN 2018944925

Steve, Victoria, Katherine, Olivia, and Rhys, this one's for you.

CHAPTER 1

Free

a + b = c
In Theory, Anyway

The last present Daddy gave me was a gun.

Not a minute after I unwrapped the used .22, he took me out back to shoot rusted targets lined on the woodpile. After missing the first shot, I hit every can. Even though misery clouded his eyes then, Daddy beamed and set up more so I could do it again. And I did, the cans falling to the snow-covered ground with every blast of the gun. *Ain't you a natural, Free?*

That was my eleventh birthday, almost seven years ago, but the memory of my father's words gave me confidence, especially now. They played in my mind as I peered into the scope, not moving. This shot had to count; we couldn't spare the ammo for a second one. *A natural, a natural, a natural...*

"Shoot him, Sissy."

"Quiet," I whispered. We lay prone atop a bed of rotting vegetation, probably covered with ticks I'd have to pick off both of us at home.

Deep breath.

His neck stayed in my sights, the shotgun barrel propped on a fallen hickory branch, my cheek against the cold stock.

Steady.

Stop shaking, dammit!

I prayed for luck and pulled the trigger. *Boom!* Heavy wings flapped, kicking up dirt as gobbling echoed through the morning fog.

"You got him!" My brother ran to our kill, the rest of the flock escaping into the thicket.

I grinned when he tried to lift the gobbler by its legs, and looped the shotgun strap on my shoulder. "You doubting me, Little?"

"Never," he said, the early chill turning his breath to smoke. He attempted to pick up the bird again, failing. It probably weighed more than he did.

"Good thing." I stood and brushed off my jeans before collecting our supper from Little's struggling hands. "C'mon. We'll get Daddy to cook him up while we're gone."

"Can we shoot another one tomorrow?"

"Sorry, buddy. This here's probably the last hunt. Not much ammo left."

"Oh." He hurried after me as I led us out of the woods. "Can we have potatoes, too?"

"None left."

"Darn."

I loved how he spoke. He didn't have the sharp twang like Daddy and me. Little's clean voice brought Needles, California, to Poplar Branch, West Virginia—America's dirty secret. At least that's how I saw our hiding spot in Middle of Nowhere, Appalachia.

I pointed to some rocks before he tripped over them. "Hey, remember the ginseng around here? That root we told you about?" At his nod, I continued, "Well, Daddy got himself a nice haul last night. If all goes the way I expect, food won't be a concern for a while."

His footfalls were loud, sounding more like a full-grown man than a skinny five-year-old boy. "Will we get our lights on, too?"

"No electric here. Already told you."

A pause. "When are we going to stop camping, Sissy?"

"Soon." I guided Little down the steep ravine toward the road.

Camping. What Daddy and I had told him four months ago when we arrived at the shack we lived in now. Every time he asked when we'd be going home, I'd tell him the same thing.

Soon.

The only lie that fell from my lips and hit his ears.

Once we made it to the narrow road, Little pulled out the blue calculator I bought him before we left California. As he typed, the burn scar running along his left palm by his thumb flashed, and I had to hide my wince behind a smile.

"Okay, what's six thousand two hundred and twenty-seven times one hundred and forty-two?" he asked, concentrating on the calculator with his brow scrunched.

I thought for a minute as we shuffled along the road, moving aside when a line of fracking trucks rumbled past. "You make it too easy. Eight hundred eighty-four thousand, two hundred thirty-four."

He squealed, skipping a few steps ahead. "That's right! That's right!"

"Of course it is." I laughed as he tapped more numbers, giving another problem I answered just as fast. My passion had amounted to nothing except a fun trick to amuse Little, but I'd be a human calculator if it made him happy. I'd be anything.

"All right, enough for now." I pulled his hood up when a gust of wind blew it down. "You know what? As soon as I get the sang cashed in, I'm taking you out for pizza."

"Really?"

"Really."

"Can we have soda, too?" he asked, stuffing his calculator back into his coat pocket.

Soda, not *pop*, and something we never wasted money on. But there were always exceptions. "Pizza wouldn't taste good without it."

A smile lit up his face.

I lived for his smile. I swear I'd die for it, too.

He clasped my hand. "You're my favorite."

"Right back at you."

He said that instead of "I love you." I had no idea why he said it, but I enjoyed being his favorite. He was mine too, after all.

"Now, we—" I glanced up as we neared our house, and the warmth his happiness gave disappeared when a newer pickup truck pulled into the driveway behind our beat-up Buick.

"What, Sissy? What's wrong?"

"Nothing." I crouched in front of Little when we reached the yard and tweaked his nose as the truck's engine revved beside us. "Go on in and wash up with the pot of water on the stove. Careful not to get burned, you hear?"

His blue eyes finally left the shiny red truck and met mine. "Who are they?"

"Nobody you need to worry about." I stood on legs begging to give. "Get to it. And save some water for me. I don't feel like going to the well again this morning."

"Should I get Dad?"

I shook my head. "Let me see what they want first."

"Are you sure?"

"I'm sure."

"Okay." He eyed the truck once more and ran to the porch, jumping over piles of scrap metal and old toys.

I hated that he couldn't lock himself inside. Dry rot had claimed this place probably before I was born, and a good kick had enough power to send the door—and the walls—flying into the living room.

After Little made it inside, I dropped the bird away from any garbage and shrugged the shotgun strap off my shoulder. Took a deep breath. Then went to the truck.

They won't know it's not loaded, Free. Don't panic.

Tinted windows hid the occupant, but that wouldn't intimidate me—on the outside. Inside, vomit begged to splatter the door panel. I tapped the window with the tip of my gun, and when it rolled down, I aimed at the bulbous nose of an older man. "Can I help you with something?"

He smirked, showing off a nice set of dentures. "Well, I hope so. You know who I am?"

"Can't say I do." I inched the barrel closer until it almost touched the man's face.

"Put your gun down, girl. I just want to talk to you."

"I'll keep it where it is if you don't mind. What do you want?"

He turned away long enough to grab something from his passenger seat. "You recognize this?" He tossed a floppy gray hat out his window, the thing landing at my feet.

I refused to give it my attention. "No. Why?" *Please leave, please leave, please leave...*

The man's watery eyes turned to stone. "You tell your daddy if he wants to steal from me, he better be ready to pay the price." He shifted into reverse. "You make sure to give him the message, let him know you and I had a conversation."

He backed out, his fancy truck not bothered by the ruts in the driveway. When he disappeared down the road, I sank to my knees.

Not good.

What the hell had he gone and done this time?

I stuffed the hat in my back pocket and stayed there, my eyes shut against the gray and fog and cold, wet filth seeping through my jeans.

My mind went to work:

Eight hundred ninety-two divided by sixty-eight...

Times twenty-five...

Minus two hundred point forty-three...

One hundred twenty-seven point fifty-one.

Keep. Calm.

I opened my eyes and stared at our shack—a home that wasn't any kind of home. If Daddy had done something to jeopardize—

The ginseng. Goddamn ginseng.

The turkey went in one hand, shotgun in the other. Every step toward the porch ignited my anger, making it hard to see past it. But Little wouldn't witness the rage. He'd been through enough without me losing it in front of him.

"Who was it?" The door hadn't closed before Little tugged on my wrist. His face, naturally pale and full of freckles, whitened more, making his orange hair appear fluorescent. My little carrot. He had belonged to me since the day his mama gave birth to him.

"Someone Daddy knows." I set the gun down on the way to my knees. "Don't go outside for a while without Daddy or me, okay?"

"Why?" His eyes were older than they had a right to be.

"Just listen to me." I cupped his cheek. "You know I'd do anything for you, right?"

"I'd do anything for you, too, even hurt bad guys."

Don't cry.

"I don't need you to hurt bad guys. I need you to get ready." I stood, clenching the turkey until its leg bones dug into my skin and added, "Remember, Little, wherever you go, I'm right behind you. No matter what." My promise to him.

"And I'll hold out my hand so you never get lost." His promise to me.

"I'm counting on it. Now, you go on and get dressed. Check yourself for ticks. I'm letting Daddy know we're leaving soon."

"What should I wear?"

"Your black pants and my gray sweatshirt."

"But those pants have holes in them."

All three pairs of pants he owned had holes. "Only in the knee. Hurry, can't be late."

As soon as our bedroom door shut, I stormed through the living room, furnished with three old lawn chairs arranged near the wood stove and a couch with no discernible color, to the bedroom beyond it. No need to knock. He slept sounder than a corpse.

I stared at him, sprawled out on the stained mattress. His shaggy beard and filthy clothes made him look vulnerable. Even the grime caked under his fingernails, evidence of his digging, hit me in the heart. But dammit!

He knew better.

The turkey landed square on his chest, feathers and blood flying above him.

"Hey!" Daddy shot up, and the bird fell to the floor as he swiped at his chest. "What the hell you doing, baby?"

I pulled his hat from my back pocket and flung it at him, saying nothing.

I didn't need to.

"Damn." He reached for it and sat on the edge of the bed. "He come here?"

"Who is he?" I wouldn't crack. I wouldn't.

"Duffy Sloan. Owns a stretch of land up a piece." Daddy met my scowl, his brown eyes, so much like mine, full of contrition. "Byron works for the guy on and off, told me about a few honey holes."

"Why you listen to that jackass is beyond me." I sat next to him, the squeaky springs protesting the extra weight. "And why the hell you leave your hat there?"

"Heard dogs and got spooked. The thing flew off on the way out the woods."

I shook my head. "This Sloan guy probably has trail cams all over the place, and… Byron, Daddy? He'd turn in his own kid for ten dollars."

"Byron let us stay here, didn't he? And what choice do we got? Your check barely covers food." He took my hand and squeezed. "If I could find a good hole, a patch that would give enough sang…"

He used to have a great job in the mines near Bluefield, an hour from here and where we used to live. But he gave it up to start over in California two weeks after my eleventh birthday. Exactly thirteen days after Mama died. He couldn't risk it, though, going back to his old boss to gain real employment. Not now.

So, ginseng—Daddy's answer for money.

"You can't be stealing. If he goes to the cops…"

"He ain't going to no cops. These boys handle their own up here." He held our joined hands against his heart. "What should we do? Use them smarts God gave you and help me out."

"Would he let you slide if you gave back the sang?"

He chuckled and said, "Not likely."

"Can he prove it was you without the hat?"

"I didn't see no trail cams, Free. I'm thinking all he's got is Byron's word."

"Which isn't worth a thing around here."

"True."

I took a minute to think, but the answer was obvious. Sometimes the line between right and wrong became so thin it disappeared.

"I'll take it into Dillinger's before work. Get rid of it," I said, finding him grinning. "You think you dug a pound?"

"A tad under, maybe."

That would give us a good amount of cash, and I'd risk this Duffy fellow's threat for it. Once. "Don't do it again."

"I swear."

Little ran into the room, his smile on full volume. "Guess what, Dad? Sissy's taking me to eat pizza and soda!"

"That's great, little man." Daddy released my hand and caught Little in his arms, kissing the top of his head. "What would we do without our Freedom?" He sighed and said to me, "We gotta stay here for a while longer."

I nodded, rubbing Little's back. "Wish we could go back to Needles."

Silence. Then: "You know we can't."

CHAPTER 2

Free

Think + Feel = Attract

Our blue 1986 Buick Regal, with rust eating at the back passenger door and torn beige interior, was our most prized possession. It substituted as our house for a while in California after Daddy lost his job. It got us back to West Virginia without a hitch, too.

Thankfully, it never broke down. Daddy said it was a gift from God. I chalked it up to luck and Daddy's wherewithal to have new tires put on before everything went to hell.

God forgot us a long time ago.

I checked the rearview mirror as I started the engine. "You know this car's going nowhere until you buckle that belt."

Little wrinkled his nose and reached for the stained strap. "The seatbelt smells."

"Well, that's what happens when you get old." I backed out, trying to avoid the bigger ruts in the driveway. "Are you going to scrunch your face up when old age makes me stinky?"

"You're only seventeen."

I hit the road and shifted into drive. "I won't be seventeen forever. Someday you'll be changing my diapers like I changed yours."

Nose wrinkle. "Gross."

"Gross?" I reached behind to tickle him. "How about I tickle you until you pee your pants. That'd be gross."

"Stop! Stop!" he said, giggling and squirming away from me.

I laughed and returned my hand to the wheel with a glance at the plastic bag on the passenger seat. Selling the ginseng sort of made me feel like a drug dealer, but the risk was worth it.

Daddy came up with dreams like sang digging all the time. *One sang season, Free. Just one, and we'll be millionaires.*

Yes, Daddy was a dreamer, something I loved about him, and most of his dreams worked out better than this one. His dream of escaping Mama's ghost moved us out of West Virginia to a fresh start in the desert heat of Needles, California. We were happy there for the most part. Happier when Daddy met Laura. Then Little came along, and happy turned into heaven.

But Laura started drinking. Postpartum depression, her doctor had called it. She called it a mistake, her Landry Allen Paine Jr. mistake. Alcohol didn't erase him the way she'd hoped.

Thank God.

Anyway, at least one part of my father's dream turned out right. *We'll find ourselves a place where those bastards can't track us. They ain't never tearing my family apart, Freedom. I promise you that.*

They hadn't found us. Not yet. We were still hidden. Still together.

"Sissy?"

I shook my head. *Don't think about it.* "What is it?"

"There's that boy again."

Little didn't need to tell me where to look; the boy who lived a mile down the road always caught my attention. Sometimes he'd be carrying a bucket of coal and coming out of the woods across the road. Sometimes I'd find him sitting in front of his house in an old lawn chair, writing in a notebook. His light brown hair needed cut, and he was skinny and too tall, but there was something about him.

Today, he ambled along the road, reading from one of those notebooks he always carried and not paying attention to us as we drove past. Those times when he did glance up and smile made my day brighter, I hated to admit.

Little tapped the back of my seat with his foot. "Should we see if he needs a ride?" Same question he asked every time.

My same answer: "Not today."

We turned at the stop sign in Davy near Mim's.

I grew up thinking Mim Alcott and Mama were sisters. They laughed the same, had the same long brown hair, and would finish each other's sentences. When Mama got sick, Mim stayed by her side in the hospital—and fought with Daddy for the place next to Mama's bed after the doctors said there was nothing left to do.

Mim was the only person I told about what happened in California. I didn't trust anyone else, not that we had any kin around here to trust. Except for Byron Mumford, Mama's younger brother. The house we lived in? Mama grew up in that dump. When Daddy went to Byron to ask for help, my uncle called Mama a traitor because she let some city boy whisk her away to Bluefield, where she became "highfalutin'."

But kin's kin, Byron had said. *And kin always stick together.*

If Mama was watching over us, I bet she cried. She never wanted her daughter to live in the holler. And now we hid there.

We parked behind Mim's car—on cinder blocks and undrivable. Her someday project, she called it. When Mim didn't have to wait tables at Abel's Diner down the street, she'd watch Little for me. The five hours I worked in a shift, she said he stayed inside reading books or drawing pictures. Sleep too. As rundown as her house was, at least she had comfy beds, running water, and heat. Four-star accommodations.

Mim's three boys, close to Little's age, ran to our doors, laughing and yelling for us to get out. I asked Mim once who their daddy was. All she told me: "No one worth wasting breath on."

"All right, Little," I said, cutting the engine. "Hop out."

"They're loud," Little said, half annoyed, half nervous.

"They're boys. They're supposed to be loud."

"I'm not loud."

"Because you're an alien from outer space."

"Am not."

"Are too." I winked at him and opened my door. "Let's go."

I high-fived the trio I nicknamed Huey, Dewey, and Louie. They laughed, and the oldest recited their names back to me like he always did: "No, Free! I'm Scotty, this is Albert, and he's Jaimie."

Little refused to say anything, as usual.

"Hey, y'all." Mim greeted us at the door and bent to kiss Little's cheek as her boys played behind us. "You two go on in. I'm gonna get these wild things working on their chores."

Saturday mornings here were loud and perfect. Her kids fought, laughed—chores somewhere between half-assed and finished. A Saturday morning as a Saturday morning should be.

"Thanks, Mim." I hugged her. "Really. Thank you."

"Ain't no need to thank me." She patted my back before heading down the porch steps. "There's a couple donuts left on the table if y'all are hungry."

As soon as she said the words, Little ran into the house, heading straight for the kitchen. I ran behind him.

We were always hungry.

After we ate, Little rested on the couch, lost in another book Mim had borrowed from the library, while Mim and I sat at the kitchen table as her boys "cleaned" around us. The cacophonous symphony three rowdy boys performed didn't hinder her ability to have a conversation in the least.

"He should be in school," Mim said, lighting another cigarette. "A boy reading like that at his age? Why, he could be a scientist, lawyer…whatever he wants."

"Not possible right now." I picked at leftover crumbs on my napkin, savoring specks of cake and sugar melting on my tongue.

Mim took another hit, polite enough to tilt her head when she blew out the smoke. "You should be in school, too."

"That's not happening, either."

I hadn't been in school since May, when I was a different person—a junior in AP classes with the dream of going to MIT to study mathematical economics. I was definitely on track until life blew up. Now I worked in a grocery store with no plans beyond making enough money to put food in our stomachs.

Mim kept smoking her off-brand cigarette and thankfully changed the subject. "You ain't showering?"

I zipped my flannel to hide the mud stain on my T-shirt. "Not today."

Another hit. More smoke blown over my head. "Why not?"

She had a knack for seeing things. Why her three boys never acted like other kids around here. Mim had rules, and her boys followed them as if they were scripture. Rule number one: tell the truth, even if it hurt.

Truth: "I have to go to Dillinger's before work."

"Landry digging again, is he? He actually find something this time?"

"He did." A sugar crumb melted on my finger before it reached my tongue.

"Where?"

"Some honey hole Byron told him about."

Mim tapped out her smoke in a dirty plastic ashtray. "Byron? Dumb." A pause. "Where, Free?"

I concentrated on the napkin, crinkling it. Ripping it to pieces. *Five hundred forty divided by six point five...* "A farm, I think."

"Whose farm?"

"Duffy something or other."

"Duffy Sloan?"

...eighty-three point zero eight.

"That's right."

"Oh, sweet Jesus!" She covered my hands, stopping my napkin destruction. "He ain't a man to cross."

"No big deal. When he came over this mor—"

"*He came to your house?*"

I nodded.

She clenched my hands tighter, her knuckles whitening. "Listen to me, Free. You listening?"

My scalp tingled and my lips went numb. I opened my mouth. Closed it. Another nod.

"You tell your never-thinking daddy—"

"He ain't stupid, Mim."

"You tell him to find his money elsewhere," she said as if I hadn't interrupted. "I don't care who he steals from, just... not from Duffy."

I turned to Little. He wasn't hungry or cold, and he wasn't wondering why we couldn't go home, this moment as complete and perfect as Saturday mornings.

A memory, the one I could never seem to forget, flashed in my mind while watching him. The day Laura left for good. Left after Daddy threw her to the ground when we caught her burning Little's hand on the stove while yelling, "Mistake! Mistake!" I could still hear his skin sizzling as he screamed for Daddy to help him.

No, I wouldn't let anyone hurt him again. And I'd never, ever do anything that'd take him away from me. Daddy wouldn't either. Our escape from California proved that.

"Okay," I said. "I'll tell him."

Two hundred forty-six dollars was all Dillinger gave.

Not a fair price, but a boost that would help fill the gaps my paycheck couldn't cover. I pressed on my coat pocket—comforted by the folded bills despite the real threat of Duffy Sloan—as I pulled into Gifford's Grocery. Mim and Mama worked for Mr. Gifford when they were my age, which was why I got the job. The pay wasn't much, five dollars an hour under the table, but it was still money, and Mr. Gifford was nice, always letting me take outdated food home on Saturdays.

I parked where I usually did, at the back of the lot, and got out—stopping short of going inside. Through the spotty window, displaying sale posters and store hours, I saw my neighbor. Mr. Gifford spoke to him next to a pallet stacked with canned food.

Sweat moistened my underarms. *Why didn't I shower?* Of all days to skip it.

Another feel of the bills in my pocket.

You can do this, Free. Own your smelly armpits.

I opened the door and went straight to the register.

"Morning, Freedom!"

Ugh.

Always smiling, always courteous, and always using my full name, my boss came over with the boy. "You remember me telling you I hired a new member to our team?"

No. "Sure."

Up close, the boy wasn't as cute as I'd painted him in my mind. His nose slanted to the left, obviously broken once or twice, and he slouched as if his shoulders weren't strong enough to support his long arms. But his eyes were oceans surrounded by tired circles.

Say something to him, idiot!

"Okay, well…" Mr. Gifford ushered him closer. "Cole Anderson, meet Freedom Paine."

"N-nice to meet you." I stuck out my hand, hoping my palm wasn't too sweaty.

He clasped it, his palm thankfully as damp as mine, and let go after a couple seconds. He then lifted an eyebrow like those guys in movies. One deep arch, high over his right eye. "I know you. I mean, not know you, but know who you are, anyway." His voice dipped, the tone not soulful or profound. Average. Perfectly average.

I wiped my hand on my pants. "I-I don't think so."

"No, yeah, I do." His face reddened. "You're staying in Mumford's old place. I see you sometimes."

"Oh."

He noticed me?

That shouldn't have mattered, especially after Mim's warning about Duffy, but it did.

"Well, all right," Mr. Gifford said. "Now that we're acquainted, let's get to work." He gestured to the storeroom. "Stock what I showed you, Cole. Get going on those pallets in the back after."

"Yes, sir," Cole said to Mr. Gifford, who was already walking into his office. He then faced me and grinned, showing off a crooked eyetooth. “Nice meeting you, ah, Freedom? Is that your real name?”

I nodded. “F-Free.”

“Free…” His twang surprisingly made my name sound better. Maybe it was the way he pronounced his words, as if he were careful to say everything the right way. “I like it.” He turned toward the aisle, saving me from making a bigger fool of myself.

Stuttering, Free?

CHAPTER 3

Free

$C_xH_y + O_2 \longrightarrow CO_2 + H_2O$
Balancing Combustible Reactions

I stood next to Cole in the storeroom, shame blossoming under my skin.

That dark, ugly feeling didn't care about the food Cole and I waited for. No, it attacked me because I forgot. Forgot Duffy's threat. Forgot Little and Daddy. Forgot because a boy with ocean eyes sneaked glances at me for five hours—as I had done at him.

"I don't have much today, but what I got's yours to split." Mr. Gifford gestured to a small mound of bread, a few boxes, some dented cans, and one bag of cookies piled on an empty stack of pallets.

Those cookies were Little's, and I'd fight the object of my recent thoughts to get them. They'd be an apology for the crime my brother would never know I had committed today.

"Thank you, sir," I said, my voice thin.

"Yeah, thank you." Cole stepped closer to the food. "Are you sure? We can take this stuff?"

"Absolutely." Mr. Gifford winked my way. "Y'all are doing me a favor. Saves money on the trash bill."

He'd given the same silly excuse to me when I stood in Cole's shoes four months ago. Not a lick of it was true, but I hadn't argued. Did I say he was nice? Mr. Gifford was more than nice.

Cole lifted a can of peaches. "I…"

Don't feel sorry for him. Don't look at his face.

"Nothing needs said, son. Take what you want." Mr. Gifford waddled to the front, adjusting his suspenders as he began talking to the second-shift people, kids from high school whom I never spoke to.

First thing I grabbed were the cookies. Chocolate chip, Little's favorite. Cole didn't argue or complain; his attention remained on the peaches.

I plucked some bags from a box next to me and handed him a couple. "Here."

He lifted his head, his eyes floating in unshed tears.

Oh, man.

The urge to hug him and tell him everything would be all right, give him some kind of promise and keep it, overwhelmed me.

No! Just…no.

"Does he always do this?" Cole tucked the can into a bag, not moving to take more.

"Every Saturday morning shift." Which was why I always begged to work them. I took his bag and filled it for him, adding the cookies. Two hundred forty-six dollars would buy Little fresh ones. I packed food in a few more, handing them over.

"You sure?" he asked, accepting the bags.

"No big deal." I gathered the leftover food into a couple more of my own, not nearly as weighted down as what I gave him. "I have a few bucks this week to buy more."

His stomach let loose a deep growl, and his cheeks flamed when he pressed against it. "Ah, thanks."

I nodded and pretended not to hear his stomach as I finished filling my bags. It was nothing to be embarrassed about, anyway. I'd been there. I was always there—as if the stomach discovered food was a certainty and begged to have it sooner.

Cole hefted the bags over his shoulders and smiled at me. "Heavy. Gonna be a long trip home."

Nope. Five miles wasn't too long of a hike. "I'd give you a ride, but…um, I got some things to do."

If he would've said something ignorant, I'd have been relieved. Easier to erase a jerk from the mind.

But he kept smiling.

"No problem." He shook his bags. "It's worth it." His crooked tooth made his smile nicer.

Shame, shame, shame.

"I'll see you around?" he asked me. He then tipped his chin at a newer employee as she hung her coat. She said hello to him without a word to me on her way back to the front.

"Sure, whatever," I said when he gave me back his attention.

"When do you work next?"

"Monday afternoon."

"Hmm, I don't work till Tuesday night. You here then?"

"No."

"You don't talk much, do you?"

If I could stop sweating… "I talk."

"Doesn't sound like it." From the fold-out table we used for breaks, he collected his notebook and stuffed it into one of the bags. "I best get going, but…nice putting a name to your face, Freedom Paine."

I almost gave in and offered a ride but closed my mouth. The last thing I needed were the complications that came from being kind.

When I handed Little the secondhand-store bag after he buckled his seatbelt, I expected happy bounces. Not tears. He examined the pants I bought him as if they held secrets, his fingers tracing each worn-out stitch, each crease.

"Little?" I adjusted the rearview mirror. "You okay?"

He nodded.

"Are you sure?"

Another nod.

I stepped on the gas after the crossing bar lifted, and the Buick lumbered over the railroad tracks. "You don't look okay."

"Because," he said, his voice as small as his body. The voice he used when trying to be brave through tears. "Thank you for the jeans, Sissy."

The road blurred, my eyes stinging. "You never have to thank me. It's my job to take care of you."

"I want to take care of you, too."

"You do, Little."

"I can't buy you pants without holes in them."

"You can when you're older."

"But—"

"Enough, all right?" I cranked the radio to hide the frailty in my voice. The pants were a better penance than stale cookies. "We're not sad tonight. We're eating turkey, and then you're reading me the book you've been lost in all day."

I peered in the mirror long enough to see him switch his attention to the book Mim let him bring home for the night. "But I've already read half of it."

"Well, you'll have to tell me what I missed."

"Okay, but you might get scared."

"You'll protect me." I spared him one more look.

He hugged the book and his pants to his chest, a soft smile on his lips.

Simple things. What I wouldn't give to have a life full of them.

As we headed up the steep, narrow road toward home, we listened to music and ignored the dilapidated houses that sometimes sat next to nicer ones and people milling around in their garbage-filled yards. Not everything up here was ugly; there was beauty too. Leaves capped poplar, hickory, and beech trees in every peak and valley, creating a color splash only a fall in West Virginia produced. Most of the hollers *were* breathtaking, and the people living in them decent folks. God just overlooked Poplar Branch.

One old church covered in chipped paint a couple miles from our house still captured Little's interest without fail. Not so much the church, but the sign in front of it: "Sinners Wanted."

"I don't like that sign, Sissy," he commented every time we drove by.

"I know." I ran out of explanations months ago after he first noticed the blocky red letters painted on plywood.

We rounded the corner near Cole's trailer in time to see him climbing his steps. My cheeks warmed as I slowed down, and flared when the Buick's motor caught his attention.

"He waved at us, Sissy!"

"I saw."

He waved. Nothing more. The gesture shouldn't have given me the impulse to stop and apologize for not offering a ride home.

What is it about you?

We pulled into our driveway to smoke curling from the chimney, thanks to the stove pumping out warmth we usually anticipated. And when I opened my door, the smell of turkey from the pit behind the house made my mouth water. The only damper on an otherwise perfect afternoon? The rusted truck parked in my spot.

Little got out and tucked his hand in mine. "Is that another mean man?"

"No, just a stupid one." I squeezed his hand. "Take those bags in and get ready for supper."

He did as I asked and ran into the house. Sometimes he listened without a bunch of follow-up questions.

I made fists at my sides, digging my nails into my palms, as I trudged around back. Daddy sat on an old tire, staring into the flames while the turkey roasted on the spit. Next to him, Byron stood with a steaming leg to his mouth, devouring our supper in the disgusting way he did everything. I didn't like the jackass when I was a kid and still couldn't stand him.

"What do you think you're doing?" I snatched the leg from his bony fingers and tossed it into the fire. I'd rather let the flames enjoy it than him.

Byron raised his fist. "You—"

Daddy jumped to his feet. "Now don't be hitting my girl. Ain't no call for it."

"Maybe you should teach her respect, then." Byron lowered his hand. "Taking food right from my mouth…"

"It's not yours," I said.

"It ain't mine? I thought we was kin."

The man didn't resemble Mama except for being short and thin. His front teeth were missing, along with most of his mud-brown hair, and his pupils were so dilated I couldn't tell what color his irises were. Black, I decided. A solid sheet of black and nothingness.

"What're you here for?" I turned to Daddy. "And why you letting him stay after what he done?"

"I…" Daddy started.

"Y'all got it wrong, Free." Byron raked a dirty hand through his hair, his anger replaced with a sincerity I could see through from a hundred miles away. "Why would I rat? I had a stake in it, too."

My hand instinctively went to my pocket, the wad lessened by six dollars for Little's pants. "What do you mean?"

"I told him where to dig, and Landry here agreed to give me a cut of the earnings."

I wanted to rip off his weathered cheeks and toss them into the fire with the sizzling turkey leg. "You're getting nothing. Tell him he ain't getting a cent of it, Daddy."

My father stroked his beard, not saying anything.

What?

"Daddy?" Shock made my voice airy. "Tell him."

"I can't." He avoided eye contact, even after I moved to block his view of the fire. "I gave my word."

"No." I shook my head. "I'm not giving that rat a thing."

"I got kids, too, girl." Byron spoke as if his tongue were too thick, his teeth trapping his S's. "You ain't the only one who gots to eat."

I glared from my father's regret-filled face to Byron's irritated one. "You want paid for ratting him out?"

"I ain't ratted no one out!" He gestured to Daddy. "This dip-wit done left his hat there, and I think Duffy set up a trail cam."

Liar. *Liar, liar, liar!*

"How'd Duffy know where to look if you didn't tell him?"

Byron kicked at another tire, his attention on the rusted rim. "How the hell should I know? And it's your own daddy's fault! I told him to go legit, sell for Duffy."

"Sell for him?"

"Pills and shit. More money in that than digging around in the man's dirt for a bunch of wild roots."

No way in hell. "He's not a drug dealer," I said through clenched teeth.

"And because of it, he done got himself in trouble."

I stepped forward. He wasn't big; I could take him. "*Because you—*"

Daddy held me back. "I owe it. Give him half of what you got."

"*Half*?" I struggled in his hold without any luck. "No. Absolutely not."

"You heard him. Half." Byron held a hand in my face when I opened my mouth. "You do me wrong, and I'll kick your asses out of this house." He narrowed his eyes. "Maybe call the law. I'm smart enough to know y'all are hiding something."

Daddy's fingers squeezed my upper arms, and I felt his beard scratch against my ear. "Give him the damn money," he whispered.

Choices.

No, choices didn't exist for us anymore.

I cleared my throat. "All I got is two hundred."

"No way!" Byron spat on the tire, a string of brown chaw juice landing with a splat against the rubber. He pointed to Daddy. "You said you dug almost a pound. Has to be worth twice that."

"Well, I got ripped off," I said. "But Dillinger didn't ask no questions, and I didn't complain when he gave me a price."

Byron considered me with his sunken black eyes. Then, "Christ on a crutch. Dillinger's nothing but a cheapskate."

"At least he took it."

"Give it here, then. Hundred bucks."

I shrugged from Daddy's relaxed hold. "I left it in the glove box."

"Why you leave so much money in the car? It ain't safe 'round here."

"Apparently it's not safe anywhere," I mumbled as I shoved past him.

When I reached the car, I jumped in and hunkered down before pulling the wad from my pocket. Two hundred forty. I bit my lip to stifle a sob. Little wouldn't be getting his pizza.

After counting out Byron's share, I locked the extra forty in the glove box for real and went back to the fire. Forty dollars was two weeks of food if I spent it right.

"Here." I dropped five twenties at his feet. "Take it and go."

Byron collected the bills from the mud, calling me everything but my name. Watching him squat without pride gave me some pleasure. Some.

"If my boys were as disrespectful, Landry, I'd take a switch to their asses."

"If *your boys* had the chance," I answered, "they'd do the same to you, you pill-head!"

Byron took a swing—and Daddy yanked me backward, away from Byron's fist.

"You're nothing but a rude little she-devil!" Byron stuck the money in his front pocket and stalked to his truck, yelling behind his shoulder, "Your daddy won't always be around! You best remember that."

As his truck grumbled from the driveway, I turned and gave my father all the rage I could muster. "Half?"

He stared into the fire. "I should have told you."

"You think?" I snatched up the pot sitting on a rock next to the flames. "Everything you do… *All* the stuff you do…" I pulled meat from the turkey carcass as I yelled, taking the other leg for Little.

"Free, listen. I—"

"No." I stood. "I'm done listening to you."

I left him there, staring into the fire, to eat supper with Little. Maybe he'd find answers in the flames. Or maybe some common sense.

CHAPTER 4

Cole

Mystery Girl Has a Name

I finally knew her name.

Freedom Paine.

For months, I'd wondered about the girl who drove the shitty Buick and the boy she always had with her. Wondered why the hell they'd squat at that sonofabitch Byron's old place. A few of my summer notebooks had headlines about my mystery girl with questions underneath I wasn't brave enough to ask. And the first time we meet, she fills bags of food and gives them to me? Takes cookies from her own and puts them in mine?

Charitable, and not at all what I imagined her to be. Her family stayed to themselves, never once acknowledging me, or anyone else as far as I knew. But as much as this new development intrigued me, I was never so happy to see the tan siding of my trailer. My sore shoulders seriously wanted to release my arms.

Our place sat in the middle of a small plot that appeared hollowed out with a spoon. Rocks, rocks, and more rocks, with a cliff for a back yard. Dad had to lift the trailer a few years back when flooding got bad. It now balanced on cement slabs, with cinderblock stairs leading to the front door. It wasn't worth a thing, but it was home, and it had electric and indoor plumbing, a luxury as far as I was concerned.

As I took the first step, I heard Free's car. The loud-ass grumble was hard to miss now that I'd heard it a bunch. I turned and waved.

Odd, but I felt a bond with her after she filled those bags, like we shared the same secret. Her knowing I needed the food should have embarrassed me. Not with her—the pretty girl with whiskey-colored eyes and one-word answers—because she obviously needed it too.

Whatever. Probably just wishful thinking.

I opened the door to the grainy sounds of a cartoon on TV and Mama bickering with Hannah. The living room always had a layer of oily dust coating everything and smelled like sulfur thanks to how we rigged the coal stove. The exhaust pipe hung out the front window, anchored with chicken wire. Not exactly safe, since not all the fumes escaped outside, but like Mama's complaining, the smell and crud were familiar enough to ignore.

"What you got there, Colie?" Mama stopped griping at my sister long enough to acknowledge me. "What's in them pokes?"

"Hold on a minute. I need to put them down before my arms fall off." I trudged to the kitchen, plopping the bags on top of old papers, dirty plates, and Mama's ashtrays. When I found the cookies, I went to the old television balanced atop a TV tray and sat cross-legged in front of it next to Kaycee. "Look what I got."

My niece turned to me. "Cookies?"

"Yes, indeed. All for you." I lifted the package in the air when she reached for it. "Only if I get to have one."

She giggled as she struggled to reach the package. "Gimme, Colie!"

"Not until you promise to share with your uncle. Or are you the Cookie Monster?"

"I promise, I promise!"

"Are you *suuurrrreee*?"

She crawled into my lap with another giggle and rested her head against my chest. Kaycee was the spitting image of Hannah when she was younger, with light brown hair, big blue eyes—and innocence. Mama used to show us our baby pictures and always commented on how pretty Hannah was. Always "was." Never "is."

"You're a silly," Kaycee said, reaching up to tap my cheek.

"You're a sillier." I patted her cheek in return before opening the package and handing her one.

"Hey!" A boot hit my back. "I *said*, what you got there?"

I turned to Mama glowering and Hannah smiling. They looked alike. Not in the sense they had the same hair color or face shape, but by the way the pills had eaten at their skin. They reminded me of apple people—those faces made from dried apples, wrinkly and thin. Neither had their teeth, the drugs stealing Mama's forever ago and Hannah's before she turned twenty. Both were young, and both appeared close to sixty.

"Damn, Mama! Why're you hitting me?" I rubbed my lower back, my aching shoulders complaining.

"Tell me what them pokes are."

I tried hard not to roll my eyes. The bags were clear plastic, easy to see what was in them. "Food."

"Food?"

"You know, stuff you eat." I set Kaycee on the threadbare carpet before going back to the kitchen to put things away.

Hannah came over and rifled through the bags. She'd kicked her pill habit when she found out she was pregnant with Kaycee at seventeen. She only fell off the wagon once, a year ago. But she hopped right back on it again, and I was proud of her. A shame her teeth had to pay for past mistakes. "Where'd you get money to buy all this? It must've cost at least fifty bucks."

"It didn't cost anything," I said.

She snapped her head toward Mama then back to me, and whispered as if the FBI tapped our trailer, "You steal it from somewhere?"

"It was free." *Free*...Dang. I couldn't say the word without thinking of her.

"You best not be stealing from nobody, boy. I already got one son in the jailhouse, along with a husband."

"I'm not stealing, Mama. Mr. Gifford gave it to me."

She reached for her cigarette case on the coffee table. "That how he plans to pay you? With food?"

"Would it be so bad if he did? At least we'd get to eat." We only had a full fridge the first week of the month. The rest of the foodies were usually gone right after the one shopping trip. Mama sold them for her "medicine."

She lit up and sucked until her thin lips disappeared. Her eyes watered as she blew out gray smoke. After another drag, she said, "You think I enjoy watching you kids go hungry? I try my hardest."

I hated dealing with her when she cried, especially when she was high. Her tears made me madder. "You could always stop buying your pills."

Silence. Like the silence in a funeral home at the beginning of viewing hours.

Then, "We're running out of coal."

She never argued when I veered the conversation in this direction. The direction of her failure and her kids having to suffer for it. My words were all the punches I had against her and this trailer and the empty fridge and so many other things. But I wasn't a total douche. I always stopped attacking before she hit the mat.

"Yes, ma'am," I said.

"Hear there's fixing to be a mean storm come Monday. Best get it before." Mama tapped out her cigarette, the sharp clang of ashtray hitting the table telling me how hard my punches were. "I'm turning in. My back's been aching something fierce."

She acted like a suffering doe, one that needed put out of its misery.

"Cole," Hannah whispered as Mama stumbled down the hall. "Why do you got to make her feel bad?"

I shoved groceries into the cupboard with a little too much force. "She deserves it."

"No, she's sick. Maybe give her a break sometimes."

"I'm only giving her what she gives me, Han."

"Yeah." Hannah pulled at her hair, breaking off the frayed ends, and avoided eye contact.

"What is it?"

"Well…"

I ignored the desire to stomp my foot. "What, Hannah?"

She finally looked up. "Shad came by today. Dropped off some pills."

I swear the can I held dented as I squeezed. "How'd she pay for it?" I already knew the answer—we had zero cash.

"You know how, Colie." Hannah studied her daughter, who acted innocent and happy and perfectly oblivious. "Daddy'll make sure Shad answers for it."

"He'll make sure Mama answers for it, too." Her actions would get her hit and worse. People talk, and I guaranteed they were talking about Mama and Shad's payment plan.

"Nothing to worry about now, I guess. Daddy won't see the light of day without bars in front of it for a few more years."

"Did you at least get Kaycee out while that prick was here?"

"Uh-huh. Took her to your spot and let her play in the leaves." She smiled. "She left you some flowers."

"Sweet of her." I glanced at my niece. *So innocent.* "Make sure Kaycee doesn't eat all those cookies. She'll get sick."

Hannah planted her hands on her hips and pursed her lips, as thin and sunken around the gums as Mama's. "I know how to take care of her."

"Really?" I pointed to the sippy cup next to Kaycee with Mountain Dew in it. "That's not good for her to drink."

"Ain't nothing else in the fridge."

"Buy milk instead."

"Pop's cheaper, Colie."

I dug into my scalp, frustrated. "I know it."

"Besides, we was brought up on the same stuff, and we turned out fine."

"You honestly think we're *fine*?"

"As fine as anyone can be up here."

Right.

Without even thinking about it, I reached into my back pocket for my notepad, the one I'd had since my tenth birthday:

Idea 1078

Join the Circus

"How're you escaping now?"

"Circus. Wouldn't be much of a change." I put my notepad away and nabbed a box of cereal from the stash I'd brought home. My supper for the night. "Hey, I got some homework and things to do. Make sure y'all eat, one of those cans of soup or something."

She giggled like her daughter, the sound too young for her puckered face. "Mama's baby telling me what to do…"

"Somebody has to."

"You going to church tomorrow?"

Mrs. Anvil, the resident do-gooder in the holler, picked us up for church every Sunday. She also took Mama to the Wal-Mart in Bluefield first of the month and brought our mail to us from the post office in Davy. Good woman, but her kindness wouldn't change our predicament.

"'Course." I hugged her. "See y'all bright and early."

A half hour later, I sat on my mattress with my back against the wall, jotting down details from the day.

My room, the one I used to share with my brother Richie, was the nicest in our dump. I kept it neat even though my mattress soaked up moisture from the subfloor when it rained. Dad had to tear out most of the floors after the floods, but he put new plywood down. My stuff was stacked on crates, and my clothes were folded in a dresser Mama bought at a yard sale. Richie's mattress butted up to the wall on the other side, all his things piled neatly on top of it. I could be poor all day long, but I refused to be disgusting.

Anyway:

First Day of Work

- *Mr. Gifford (Santa Claus of McDowell County)*
- *Free food!!!!!!!!!!!*
- *Save for apartment*
- *Create a savings plan*
- *GET APARTMENT*
- *Met Mystery Girl*

I smiled for the first time since I got home. Free deserved a headline all her own.

I peered up from my notes to stare at the wall. Not just any wall, with its paper-thin paneling, but *the* wall, with pictures of the new prison on 52 and mugshots of Dad and Richie. I pinned an old mugshot of Mama above them.

The wall was why I studied and turned in my homework. Why I took Intro to Journalism in the ninth grade and was now the co-editor of the high school paper. Why I never touched Mama's pills or drank the homemade moonshine she had stashed underneath the kitchen sink. Anything to stay on track for graduation and not end up like my dickhead brother or my waste of a father.

Not so hard. At least, I told myself that when Kaycee cried because she was hungry and pressed on her stomach to help the pain, and when money got so tight the need struck to ask Duffy Sloan for a job selling heroin, which my dad and Richie had done for him. They sat in jail because they refused to snitch on the bastard. Smart of them.

I reached on my dresser for an older notebook and cracked it open. Three months' worth of headlines and questions and theories about my mystery girl littered every page. Guess I used her as an obsession to keep me on the right path, too.

And now she had a name.

CHAPTER 5

Cole

Mystery Girl: The Search for Answers

She wouldn't be talking to friends in the halls of Mountain View High before first bell, wearing a dress or leggings or whatever most girls wore. Not Free, with her flannel coat, worn jeans, and Pearl Jam T-shirt. No, she wouldn't be here. I had already searched for her last week, on the first day of school.

That didn't stop me from giving it another shot.

The warning bell rang as I rounded a corner of the wing I hadn't checked, the seventh- and eighth-grade wing. If Free were in seventh or eighth grade—which I prayed she wasn't because that would've made some of my thoughts about her perverted—she wasn't heading to class. More relieved not to find her here than disappointed, I hiked my bag higher on my shoulder and jogged to the senior wing.

All morning between classes and until lunch, even though my brain said "She's not here," I kept my eyes open. Still no Free.

Damn.

Seniors ate at the same time, fitting in the cafeteria easily. In ninth grade, our class was a hundred-twenty strong. This year, eighty-seven showed up. Those other kids hadn't moved away—hardly anyone left McDowell County. They just ended up somewhere else. A few spit out babies, like Hannah. Others got caught up in things that became more important than education, like Richie.

Deacon Mallory, my best friend since kindergarten, sat across from me, devouring his goulash and talking around mouthfuls. "Why're you so quiet?" he asked after a gulp of chocolate milk. "You ain't said more than two words all day."

Deacon was a cliché. Muscles rippled like mountains under his dark skin that matched his dark hair and eyes. He was the star quarterback with a cannon arm, and scouts were already interested in him. He always wore the right clothes, too, like the sweatshirt and jeans I had on, clothes that were his last year. The jeans were a little short since I was two inches taller, but my boots—also ones he wore last year—covered the high-water action. He never made it a big deal, just tossed me a bag of stuff, usually a week before school started. And I helped him study, his issues with reading and writing sometimes getting in the way of learning.

Yeah, Deacon was a cliché, minus the asshole part. He'd do anything for me, and I for him.

"Hello? You aiming to answer or stare at me with that weird grin on your face?"

I swallowed a bite and shrugged. "Got a bunch on my mind is all."

"Like?" He frowned. "Everything okay at home?"

"Same."

Deacon tapped his fork on his tray. "Then spill it. You got good stuff or bad stuff?"

Everything in life was either good stuff or bad. At least, we thought so.

I watched the cafeteria line grow longer as kids came in. "Maybe both?"

"I ain't gonna like this, am I?" Deacon acted like my older brother even though I had him by six months.

"It's dumb," I said. "You'll laugh."

"I *want* to laugh. Tell me."

"Well…" I peered over his head to see Jess coming our way, along with Deacon's girlfriend Amy, the other two who completed our usual group. "I'll tell you in a second."

"Huh?"

I pointed with my fork. "Girls."

"Hey, guys!" Amy sat next to Deacon, and he turned his head in time for her loud kiss against his lips.

Jess sat next to me and set her tray of salad, an apple, and Diet Coke by mine. "Hey, Cole," she said, sitting too close and smiling too wide. "You get your story written?"

"Yeah, no." I'd spent the rest of the weekend writing about Free—totally worth the cram session I'd be having next period. "I'll finish it in English."

"You better. Sheckler wants it on the first page for next week's run."

"I didn't realize kids smoking in the bathroom was news," I said. "Hasn't it been happening since the invention of cigarettes?"

"You're supposed to write about vaping, not smoking."

"Same thing."

"It's not, and he wants it, along with the consequences if students get caught." She rolled her eyes. "We've officially become his lackeys."

Jess was my co-editor cohort for *Mountain View News*. She was awesome at the job—and a little scary, according to underclassmen who had to get her approval for their stories. We worked well together, mostly because she pushed me to work harder and I convinced her to be nicer.

"Nothing like hanging out with Mountain View's snitches," Deacon said, laughing.

"Shut up." Jess opened a packet of ranch and squirted it onto her lettuce. "Anyway, how'd you like your first day, Cole? Told you Mr. Gifford was easy to work for."

Jess had gotten me that job, for which I was grateful. Gifford's Grocery was a place lots of kids wanted to work, but you had to know somebody who knew Mr. Gifford. As soon as Jess's mom got her in, I pounced, using the friend card. The big difference between us was I needed this job. She worked because her dad demanded she learn responsibility before he bought her a car. It'd have been nice to deal with her "problems."

"He's pretty cool." I wouldn't mention the food he gave. Some things didn't need to be shared.

"He definitely is." Jess moved her salad around her plate, making food mountains instead of eating it. "I saw you talking to that girl. I think Mr. Gifford calls her Freedom? That her actual name?" Her voice pitched high on Free's name, and the way she now stabbed at her helpless lettuce caught everyone's attention.

Great.

Deacon's eyes lit up, and he rapped his knuckles on the table, nodding with his tongue pressed against the inside of his cheek so it bulged out.

I scowled at him, an excuse to avoid Jess's jealousy. I'd made the mistake of kissing her at a party in June. Not too smart of me, but since then, she acted weird, like us being friends wasn't enough. "Will you stop? Your cheek's gonna shoot across the room."

Deacon pressed his tongue harder, his left cheek now twice the size of his right one.

"Who is she? Are you interested in her? Where does she live? She go to Riverview? She don't go here." Jess fired question after question, a trait that made her a great reporter.

Amy looked up from her phone and wriggled her eyebrows, making the ring in her left one bounce. "Are you actually interested in a girl, Cole Anderson?"

Deacon kept nodding his stupid head. Dick.

"No. I—" I shifted to Jess, feeling my face heat up. "I don't know—to all your questions."

"Including the 'are you interested' question?"

I scratched at my hair and kicked Deacon under the table when he snorted. "No, not that one. I—" Geez, she was a machine gun full of rapid question fire. "Stop treating me like one of your interview subjects."

She lifted her fork to her mouth and then lowered it without taking a bite. "She looks like a holler girl. Who wears that much flannel?"

What? Oh, hell no. I swear I was going to turn green and smash things. "I don't know her, and I'm not interested in her. And you're right; she *is* a holler girl. Want to know how *I* know that?"

She shook her head, her eyes wide.

Whatever, I was telling her anyway. "Because she's my neighbor."

Jess bowed her head and fidgeted with the hem of her sweater. "I didn't mean anything by it."

"Ain't no need to worry yourself. We hillbillies done got ourselves thick skin," I said, thickening my accent and scratching my temple as I crossed my eyes.

"Cole—"

"She's a girl I was being nice to." I gathered my stuff and stood. "That's it."

She touched my wrist. "Cole. I *am* sorry, okay?"

"And I forgive you." I groaned when she kept staring at me with those hopeful eyes. "Not like you'd let me stay mad, seeing as you're completely annoying."

She smiled, her shoulders relaxing. "No, I'm tenacious. You work today?"

"Not till tomorrow." I tipped my chin at Deacon, and he collected his things after giving Amy another kiss, her black lipstick, as black as her dyed hair, smearing his lips. "We'll catch y'all later, okay?"

"Well, now," Deacon said on the way to the dish pit, "is this Freedom girl what's got you quiet?"

"No." We emptied our trash into the overflowing bins and tossed our trays on the counter before heading to the hall. "Yes." *Damn it.* "I don't know. Maybe."

"Can't say I'm disappointed about your 'no, yes, I don't know' problem." When we got to our lockers, he added, "About time you had that problem, anyway."

"Whatever."

Deacon laughed. "*Whatever*," he mocked.

I'd never really dated for a reason, mostly for fear of ending up a daddy, and I still had no plans to do so. No, I didn't want to date Free. Just figure her out.

"Let it go, all right?" My most recent notebook slipped out of my locker when I opened it.

"Ooh, new secrets, huh?" Deacon lunged for it.

"Knock it off." Always faster, I snatched it off the floor and turned away from him to flip to the page where I left off last night:

- *Why did she move to Poplar Branch? (!!!!!)*
- *Who was her family? Paine (not familiar)*

- *Byron Mumford allow squatters at his kin's home? (not likely)*
- *Why isn't she in school?*

The faster I cleaned her out of my head, the better. She had to become just another face like most girls I'd had a cursory interest in. Another face with whiskey eyes and lips I sort of wanted to kiss.

Yep, I'm doing it.

"Hey." I shoved the notebook into my backpack and pulled out my copy of *The Grapes of Wrath* for English. "Can you give me a lift into Davy after school?"

"Sure. Why?" Deacon drew out the last word, filling it with the dare to lie.

"I, ah…I gotta see about something."

CHAPTER 6

Free

$a = F_{net} / m$
Finding Acceleration

I thought about Little reading to me last night and how he gave me math questions, smiling when I answered correctly. Daddy occupied my thoughts, too—mostly as guilt for not listening every time he tried to talk to me about Byron. But Cole hadn't crossed my mind while I worked the register and stocked shelves Monday afternoon. Not until I saw him climb out of an old pickup in front of Gifford's after my shift ended.

A gasp escaped when he caught me staring as the truck sped off. I shook my head, trying to wiggle him loose from my mind, and refocused on stuffing two bags of food, including chocolate chip cookies, into my trunk. All this stuff only took twenty-two bucks of the sang money, and it'd last most the week. I'd become awesome at making a dollar stretch.

"Hey."

I jumped and cracked my head against the lifted trunk lid. "Ouch!" Without looking behind me—because I only had to hear his voice once to recognize it—I slammed the trunk closed and rubbed the tender spot on top of my head. "You make a habit of scaring the daylights out of people?"

"You *can* speak in full sentences. I was a little worried last time we talked."

I felt my face turn to fire, and sweat gathered under my arms. This nobody boy shouldn't cause me anything except irritation. But I wanted to see his eyes again, get the full effect of his oceans.

"So…" he started.

Turn around! My body refused to listen to my brain. I concentrated on a few people strolling down the sidewalk, on the abandoned factory building across the street. The distant sound of the train. *Say something…*

"I'm not going away, Free."

"What do you want?"

He came up beside me, bending so I had to see his face. "Do I have to want something to talk to you?"

"Isn't that why people normally talk to each other?"

He grinned. "I don't think so."

"I do," I said and moved around him to get in the car. He followed. "And if you don't want nothing," I continued, "then I hate to disappointment you, but I got *nothing* to say."

"For some reason, I think you have a lot to say." He held his hands to his mouth and blew on them, the cold making his knuckles red.

"You'd be wrong." I opened the door. "Move."

"Jesus, Free." Cole backed up. "I just… I want to know you."

"You don't need to know me." I fumbled in my pocket for my keys and got in.

He caught the door when I tried to shut it. "You're not in school, are you?"

My sweating went into overdrive. *No questions, no questions!* I started the Buick, and as it roared to life, I tried to shut my door again. He wouldn't let me. "Let go!"

"Wait! You have a kid or something? The boy I always see you with? Is that why?"

I felt the blood drain from my face.

My horror must've come through because he let go. "Shit. I'm sorry. I—"

"Cole!"

We focused on the store, where the same girl he acknowledged on Saturday yelled for him.

"Damn it," he muttered and stepped away from my car. "Hey, Jess."

"I thought you didn't wor—"

I shut my door on their conversation and took off, kicking up pebbles that smacked against the Buick's sides in my hurry to leave. When I stopped at a red light on the way to Mim's, I closed my eyes.

Six thousand, eight hundred forty-nine…

"Why are you mad, Sissy?"

"I ain't mad."

"Yes, you are. You're driving funny, and you're not talking. You're mad."

"No."

"Yes. Mim said you look mad too."

"Don't you worry about me." I adjusted the rearview mirror to find Little gazing out the window and sucking on his bottom lip. "Little? Don't worry."

"I don't like it when you're upset."

"Well, I don't like it when you're upset, so let's
okay?" I maneuvered around a big pothole, the mud
barely wide enough to avoid it.

"Okay."

I caught his image in the mirror again. He still stared out the window but no longer sucked on his lip. Progress. "I bought you something today."

"What?"

"It's a surprise, for after supper."

"What's for supper?"

"Let's see, I got corn flakes, peanut butter, or if you're willing to wait, I can boil some beans in chicken broth. Your pick."

"Did you get the little green beans? The one's what taste good in broth?"

"I sure did."

He clapped his hands and giggled. "Beans! Beans!"

When he was happy, I wasn't angry anymore. I wasn't scared of Cole or anybody else getting too close to my truth. I was Little's Sissy, the one who made him clap and giggle. "Beans it is."

"Hey! Look." Little tapped on his window. "The boy. Do you think he'll wave at us again?"

Nope, I wouldn't get mad as we approached Cole walking alongside the road. We had driven past him tons of times, and I was in a big car with steel doors keeping me in and him out. *You have a kid...?*

I had a weight heavier than a baby of my own.

When we made it closer, Cole whipped around, saw us, and stalked into the middle of the road. I veered to the left toward the mountain, and he moved to block me. I wouldn't chance moving to the right—that side led down a steep ravine.

So I stopped.

And laid on my horn.

He didn't budge.

I continued to blare my horn, the sound creaking and old and struggling to keep up with my hand as I pressed and pressed.

He continued to not move.

Little's seatbelt unclicked a second before he came forward, his tiny body fitting between the front seats. "Stop it! Stop honking at him. Stop! Stop!" He grappled for my hand on the wheel, his face pale and bottom lip quivering.

Crap. I lifted my hand from the horn. "Sorry."

"Is he a bad person?"

By the time I was done with my brother, he'd think every human being on Earth was out to get us. "No, no, he's not bad."

"Then why?"

I watched Cole through the windshield. He held his bag strap with both hands, shrugging it higher onto his shoulder.

I sighed and reached for the handle. "Stay here."

"Are you going to leave the car running?"

"Yes."

"What if it slips gear again?"

I turned off the motor and pushed in the emergency brake. "There, safe and sound. Don't be crawling up front, you hear?"

He nodded and leaned back in his seat with his gaze fixed on Cole and again sucking on his bottom lip.

I jumped out and faced our roadblock, who still hadn't moved. My feet sank into the mud as I stepped closer to him, cold gunk soaking my tennis shoes. *Just perfect.* It'd take forever for them to dry. "Are you trying to get yourself killed?"

He grasped onto that strap hard, reddened knuckles turning white. "About what I said…"

"Forget it. It's no big deal."

"Yeah, it is. I hurt you."

"You didn't hurt nothing. Pissed me off, more like."

A small smile curved the side of his mouth. "Well, sorry for that, then."

"All right." I crossed my arms. "Anything else?"

"Sure, a book of things, but not now." His shoulders relaxed as he walked to me. "I meant what I said. I want to know you."

I backed up until I hit the car door. "I'm not worth knowing."

He continued toward me. "Huh, yeah, I kept telling myself that all weekend when I couldn't stop thinking about you."

Oh, wow. "W-well, it seems you need to tell yourself with more conviction."

"Maybe." He gestured to Little. "Who's this?"

This conversation had to be over. Now. I opened the door and got in. "Don't worry about it."

"Does he need a ride, Sissy?" Little's voice floated out loud enough for Cole to hear.

"Sissy?" Cole peered at Little, smiling his smile. "As in sister?"

"You catch on quick." I grimaced at Little. "And, no, he don't need a ride." I shut the door and started the car, wrenching it into drive a little too hard. Stomped on the gas a little too fast. The tires spun a little too much, and mud splashed up a little too high.

This can't be happening!

I pushed on the gas until the pedal hit the floor and rocked my body as if the motion would help get us unstuck. *Don't do this!* Not when Cole stood feet away, grinning as he wiped flying mud from his cheeks.

"Move, move, move!" I hit the wheel after one last assault on the gas pedal.

"Sissy?"

I closed my eyes, let the numbers calm me down, and turned to my scared brother. "Yeah?"

"Will we be okay?"

"Of course."

"Are we stuck?"

I groaned. "Yes."

"Maybe the boy can help."

Ugh. I cranked my window down.

"You seem to be in some trouble," Cole said.

I bit back the sarcasm on my tongue. "It appears that way."

"You want some help?"

I. Hated. This. "If you don't mind."

"Not at all." He opened my door. "Slide over."

"I didn't say I wanted you to drive."

"And I'm not standing behind this thing to push while you keep pounding on that gas pedal like a maniac."

Hmm. *Trust him not to steal the car and drive us over the ledge or stay stuck here forever?* This sucked. After another groan, I moved to the passenger side. "Fine."

"You're welcome." He wasted no time moving the seat back a few inches—then released the emergency brake.

I palmed my forehead. *The emergency brake!*

Instead of gunning it like I had, Cole slid the gearshift into reverse, backed up a bit with some pro steering, and then shifted into drive. Soon, the Buick broke free and coasted forward. He didn't ask for a ride home; he just drove. Everyone remained quiet. Words would've probably broken whatever silent truce Cole and I formed, anyway.

When we stopped at his house, Cole turned to Little and stuck out his hand. "Cole Anderson."

Little grasped Cole's hand. "Litt—I mean, Landry."

"Nice to meet you, Landry." Cole pumped Little's hand a couple times and let go.

"How'd you get us unstuck?" Little asked with the same awe he had every time I answered one of his calculator questions.

Cole winked. "Let's say I know my way around cars."

Little giggled and covered his mouth. *Oh, sure, he's totally hilarious.*

Cole gave me his attention. "So…"

"Thanks, really. But I ain't in the market for new friends."

He grinned his crooked-toothed grin. "Neither was I, but sometimes you find what you didn't know you were looking for."

Cole got out before I could answer and jogged up to his house. All I could do was watch him until he disappeared through the door, uncomfortable with the warmth filling my insides.

When I pulled into our driveway, Little shot out. "Dad!" He met our father, who tramped out of the woods with the shotgun and a grim face.

I got out as Daddy dropped the gun to swoop Little into his arms, his frown disappearing. "You have fun today, little man?"

"Yes! Again! Again!" Little squealed, and Daddy obliged.

"Hunting?" I asked while my brother laughed and squirmed in Daddy's arms.

"Yeah." He set Little down, avoiding eye contact with me.

"See anything?"

"No. No, I didn't see nothing."

CHAPTER 7

Free

y = m1*x + b1
y = m2*x + b2
Two Intersecting Lines

W*hen I couldn't stop thinking about you.*

Cole's words repeated in my mind, making my face heat up. I pressed on my stomach. They floated in there too, loosening the knots.

And as loud as shame screamed at me to forget them for the last few days, I couldn't.

I'm doing this!

I brushed my hair one last time, my hands shaking with excitement, then pulled on the best sweater I owned—a red knit with snags in the left sleeve.

"Where're you going, Sissy?" Little asked as I came out of our bedroom. He and Daddy sat by the stove, a crate upturned between them with cards on the surface. They played Go Fish, the game we used to help Little with his math. He wanted to be like me one day and "do numbers," as he described it.

"Just a walk." I pulled on my shoes and unhooked my flannel off the nail in the wall by the door.

"Can I come?" Little bounded up, already searching for the old rubber boots Mim had given him.

"Not this time, okay?"

His cheeks sagged as if I'd spent the last half hour yelling at him. "Why?"

"A girl's gotta have her time, boy." Daddy stroked his beard. "Like us men."

Little tilted his head, giving me his most serious, cutest expression, a forty-year-old trapped in five-year-old adorableness. "You need time?" he asked me.

I almost relented, almost used Little as an excuse to listen to the shame. "Maybe some." I zipped my coat and opened the door. "Be back before you know I'm gone."

On the way down the muddy road, rain fell lazily, the weather too warm for the droplets to freeze, but cold enough to feel like an ice bath. It was the perfect excuse to tuck tail and run. I kept moving, though. Around the bend, only a mile away, his trailer would appear. If he saw me, I'd have to come up with an excuse for traipsing around in the rain.

What do I say? I touched my smile with cold fingertips.

By the time I turned the corner, the rain had let up, and Cole's trailer appeared as a sore on the mountainside. I slowed down, stealing quick peeks at his door while kicking up glacial mud that soaked clean through my sneakers.

Just go knock on the door!

I took one step toward his yard and stopped when it got hard to breathe. No, I couldn't. Maybe he'd see me and come outside.

He didn't.

I continued down the road, faster and on the verge of tears. Embarrassment burned my face. His words sounded distorted in my mind now and turned to sludge in my stomach.

Shame: *Told you not to go! Told you!*

I lifted my gaze from counting each rock, every pebble, trying to ignore the tears leaking warm paths down my cheeks. Dammit! Too far.

Not far enough.

Reluctantly, I turned toward home. My stomach tightened at the thought of passing Cole's house again. Maybe I'd sprint the last mile home. I inspected my feet, wet and cold and begging for the wood stove. No running.

As I neared his house, I picked up speed. Liking Cole was ridiculous, exactly what my guilty conscience had been harping on. I didn't have the luxury of being—

And there he was, his attention on his feet and carrying a bucket.

I stood paralyzed and studied how his shoulders slumped from the weight of what I assumed was coal. How black his hands were, the soot smudged on his coat and cheeks, too. How tall he was and how he had filled the Buick's seat and driven with the confidence of someone older. How he said he wanted to know me.

He lifted his head, and a flash of surprise brightened his eyes. *Oh, no.* He'd figure out that I came here for him. Me, alone, near his house. I pressed against my fast-beating heart. Maybe he hadn't meant what he said. Maybe he realized I wasn't worth the time.

He set the bucket down, his eyes never leaving my face. "Hey," he said, coming closer.

I shut my slack mouth and swallowed. "Hi."

"You okay?" He was inches from me now, his height suddenly more noticeable.

"I'm fine."

"Then why're you crying?" He reached up with a coal-blackened finger and drew a line down my cheek.

I stumbled back a step. His touch felt like a wasp sting. Not in a bad way, just… a jolt to my system. Foreign. Good. *Really* good. I covered my cheek and shook my head. "I-I'm not."

He held his wet index finger to my face. "You are."

"No." *Work, feet!* I wanted to barge past and yell at him for bringing attention to it. And I wanted to step into him. Feel his coal-stained finger again.

His tongue darted out, bright pink against the soot covering his face, and he licked his bottom lip. Then he reached for my hand. "C'mon."

I hesitated.

"Trust me." He smiled and kept holding out his hand.

Exhaling, I finally gave him mine. His touch felt warm this time, and just as good. "Where?"

"There." He tipped his chin toward the woods, across from his house. "I have a place."

It was dumb to follow an almost-stranger into the woods. I followed him anyway.

We trekked along the steep path in silence, dead leaves crunching under our shoes. Cole never let go of my hand, and I didn't want him to. At that moment, I'd have been fine if someone soldered our hands together.

The sky had brightened by the time we stopped at a crude shelter made with sticks and rope, a bouquet of decayed flowers on the ground in front of it. Cole let go of me and sat underneath the canopy on a rock. "It's not much, but it's dry and private. Built it a couple years ago."

I curled the hand he'd held into a fist, holding onto the tingling in my palm a while longer, and sat on the rock beside him. Its cold surface bled through my jeans. "No, it's nice. Yeah, I like it up here."

"Thanks." He picked up some of the dead flowers, breaking them apart.

"I wanted to thank *you*, actually, for the other day."

He smiled, and the cold wasn't so cold anymore. "That why you're walking by my house?"

I grinned. "Maybe."

"Damn, if that's all it took, I wish you'd get stuck more often."

"And you'd be there every time to save the day?"

He concentrated on his crumbling flowers. "If you'd let me."

What was it about his words? They could be a drug.

"Free? Can I ask you a question?"

And his words also had the power to remind me of reality. "I wish you wouldn't."

"Why're you living here?" he asked, ignoring what I'd said.

"I—" I stood. "I shouldn't have… I need to…"

Find a way to say a full sentence and get out of the woods!

"Wait, stop." He caught my wrist and stood, too. "Sorry, don't leave. *I'm sorry.*" Cole hunched until his eyes captured mine. "No questions? None?"

I shook my head.

"Not even your favorite color? That top secret, too?"

"No, sure, it's no secret." I tugged on my wrist until he let go. "But I don't want to… I can't…" If I could just say what I needed to say without sounding like the liar I was.

"What is it, then?"

"What're you talking about?"

He raised an eyebrow, the same way he did when I first met him, like he practiced arching the right one at the perfect pitch. "Your favorite color?"

"Oh." I smiled. "Green."

"Food?"

"Um…fried chicken, I guess?"

For the longest time, he asked me surface questions, and somehow, he managed to get me to sit on the rock again while he interrogated me.

What's your favorite animal?

Have you ever broken a bone?

What was your best friend's name in kindergarten?

He went on and on until he knew everything there was to know about me without knowing anything at all. As I sat in the woods with Cole Anderson, all I had to be was Freedom Paine, lover of horses, the color green, and Stone Temple Pilots.

Of course, he gave me his answers right after I gave him mine:

My favorite color is fluorescent pink, duh.

I hate dogs, but roaches rock.

Deacon Mallory's been my best friend forever; he'd whoop my ass if I broke up with him.

My laugh felt rusty at first, but after a while, I had no desire to leave that nook under the trees.

During a pause, he pulled a notepad about the size of a deck of cards, and in danger of decaying like those flowers, from his back pocket. It had "Escape Plans" scratched on the cover. After writing something with a pencil he also took from his pocket, he put it away, acting like he hadn't done a thing.

"Escape plans?" I asked, gesturing to his jeans. Maybe he had one or two in there for me.

He rubbed his hands on his jeans, leaving dark streaks behind. "Yes, ma'am, with over a thousand ideas on how to do it."

"What'd you come up with just now?"

"Become a time traveler."

I laughed. "That what all your ideas are like? Impossible?"

"Some are better than others." He itched his temple. "It's just for fun, you know? But I have real escape plans, don't you worry. Working at Gifford's is gonna help get me an apartment in Welch come graduation."

"There ain't much of anything in Welch either, Cole."

"I've spent my whole life with nothing." He kicked at the dead flowers. "Having nothing's not what I want to escape from, anyway."

I scooted closer to him. "What're you escaping from?"

He shook his head. "I'll tell my secrets if you tell yours."

Fair enough. "Keep it to yourself, then."

"I think I will, if you don't mind." Cole stood as he scrutinized the darkening sky. "It's getting late."

"Hey." I got up, too. "I have another question for you. It's not personal. At least, I don't think it is."

Ah, his perfect, perfect eyebrow. "Shoot."

"What're you always writing? In your other notebooks."

"You *do* pay attention to me. I'm flattered, Freedom Paine."

I felt my cheeks warm. "Just tell me."

He opened and closed his mouth, stared above to the colorful leaves still grasping their limbs, and then pinned me with his oceans. "You really want to know?"

Maybe not. "Yes."

He brought his thumb to my bottom lip. "Headlines."

I stepped away from his thumb and sucked in my lip for a second. It tingled stronger than my palm. Wasp sting. And a sensory overload I wasn't sure I could handle. "Headlines?"

"Uh-huh. Surprised?"

I nodded and touched my lip. *Tingle, tingle, tingle.*

"You'd be more surprised if I told you what most of my headlines have been about lately."

"You're not gonna tell me?"

"Not yet. C'mon." He reached for my hand again.

God, this boy...

I slowly gave it to him, and he curled his fingers over mine, giving a light squeeze before heading back down the mountain.

On the way, he continued to ask his weird questions, making me laugh and *almost* forget how heat raced from my fingertips to my shoulder. It felt odd, this contact with Cole. Odd that it began to feel natural. Safe. Once we reached the road, he didn't stop. Not at his house, and not to grab the bucket of coal still waiting in his yard.

"Where do you think you're going?" I asked, not bothering to remove my hand from his. I wanted to hold on to that Cole warmth for as long as I could.

"I'm walking you home."

"I know the way."

"Yeah, I do too." He kept going. "I want to see you again."

"When?" The question came out before I had a chance to pull it back in. My plan was only once. Until I found out his "favorite" color. How he was co-editor of the school paper, which explained why he wrote secret headlines in a notebook. How his main goal was to be the first in his family to graduate high school.

"Tomorro—shit. Wait," he said. "I have work tomorrow."

"What time you off?"

He glanced down at me, his right eyebrow doing its movie-star arch. "Why?"

"I could come get you or whatever. No big deal."

"Yeah?"

"Sure."

He stopped, and it took a second to realize we'd reached my house. "I get off at seven."

Giddy and I had never been well acquainted, but I wanted to bounce on my freezing, wet feet. "I'll be there."

"Well, all right." He let go of my hand and strode backward long enough to say "I'll be waiting for you" before heading to his house.

When I floated inside, high on Cole, I barely noticed Little tugging on my sleeve. "You were gone a long time, Sissy!"

I studied his innocent, anxious face, and my throat tightened. I'd be buying him more cookies soon. "Sorry, buddy."

"And what's that black stuff on your face?" He pointed to my hand. "It's on your fingers too. Did you fall in the mud?"

"Um…no." I used my sleeve to wipe my cheek and found Daddy in the same chair I'd left him, a knowing frown curving his lips downward. I ignored it. "Y'all eat?"

Hours later, as I lay in bed holding sleeping Little, Cole Anderson invaded my mind. I bit my lip when the phantom heat from his hand touching mine lingered on my skin. What I wouldn't give to read his headlines, find out if the inside of the boy next door was as addicting as the outside. If his words on the page were as warm as the words whispered from his mouth. Warm as his skin next to mine.

The front door creaked, and my body went on alert, all thoughts of Cole forgotten.

I checked the wind-up alarm clock on the floor next to the bed. 2:24. *Darn it, Daddy!* Without waking Little, I crawled from the bed and squinted out the window. Yes, it was dark, but I saw him.

Daddy headed to the woods, the silhouette of the gun strapped to his shoulder easy enough to make out in the dim moonlight.

What're you up to now?

CHAPTER 8

Cole

Girl in Hiding

The clock in every class slowly *tick, tick, ticked* past each number, annoying the ever-loving piss out of me. I barely slept last night, Free so clear in my mind I couldn't close my eyes without seeing her. I'd been half tempted to skip school and go to her house this morning, beg her to spend the entire day with me. But I did the time, handing in my homework, taking a physics quiz, and helping Deacon with his *The Grapes of Wrath* essay during lunch. It was hard to concentrate on it, though, seeing as how I felt his eyes burning holes in my forehead.

"What?" I asked him.

"Good stuff or bad?"

"What're you talking about?"

"The way you've been preoccupied today, acting all strange and stuff. Something's up."

I took a quick sip of chocolate milk. *Play it cool. Don't let him see too much.* He'd never let me hear the end of it. "Free's getting me after work."

"No shit?"

I grinned. "No shit."

"Details, dude. As soon as your ass enters this building tomorrow."

"We'll see." I pointed to Amy and Jess approaching the table. "Subject change, all right?"

Deacon did his dumbass cheek-bulge thing and nodded.

By journalism, last class of the day, I was ready to jump out the window. Jess sat beside me as we marked stories, her red slashes and cranky notes left in the margins funny as hell. She gossiped while she ruined the day for budding writers and again subtly asked about homecoming.

"I'm not going, Jess, with you or anyone else. Stop asking."

"You know what?" She threw her pen on her desk without another word and went to ask for a bathroom pass.

I sighed and gave my attention to a sophomore handing me her story. A relieved smile traced her lips when Jess stormed from the room. I couldn't blame her. In a good mood, Jess was tough, and after my angry friend threw her pen, she showed today wasn't a good-mood day.

Time moved even slower at work. I made the best of it, stocking shelves and joking around with Carrie, a junior from Riverview. I concentrated on making Jess not pissed at me too. It only took about an hour for her to stop shooting fireballs from her eyes. Not too bad, I'd say.

At exactly 6:53, everything fell into background noise when Free's Buick coasted past the front windows, her headlights flashing into the store.

"Cole? You listening?" Jess asked.

"What? Yeah." I finished bagging Mrs. Peelcott's groceries, smiling at her as she took her things and left.

"What'd I say?"

"Uh…"

She rolled her eyes. "Thought so."

"Sorry. What was it again?"

"Nothing important." Jess pointed out the window—to the rusted Buick in the parking lot. "Hey, that's the Freedom girl, isn't it? What's her story?"

"Don't know," I said, focusing on the car. *Roll down your window!* After waiting all day, I just wanted to see her. Almost needed to.

"Carrie, she go to your school?" Jess asked.

"Nope." Carrie snapped her gum. "Only ever see her leaving here as I come in."

"She's homeschooled." Huh, that lie came out a little too easy. I faced Jess, guilt heating my face.

Her lips turned down in a sour grimace. "Thought you didn't know."

"She's my neighbor. We talk a little."

"Oh," she said, eyes downcast. "I forgot."

"Feel lucky you *can* forget it." She needed reminded sometimes that the ten miles separating our houses was the breadth of a continent. I flagged down Mr. Gifford. "Can I head out, sir? My ride's here."

Mr. Gifford waved his clipboard toward the back. "You get them pallets unloaded?"

"Yes, sir. Every last one."

"All right." He headed toward his office. "About closing time anyway."

Jess frowned. "Your ride?"

Uh-oh. "Yeah."

"That's convenient."

All that work to make her forgive me wasted in seconds. "Jess, come on." Lame, but I had nothing else.

"Whatever. Have fun with your *neighbor*." She turned her back to me, shoulders stiff and sending frigid vibes my way.

I looked from her to Carrie to Free. As bad as it made me feel, the choice was simple. "I'll see y'all later."

I grabbed my coat and backpack from the storage room and tried hard not to run to Free's car. As I got closer, I noticed her watching me, the smile she wore yesterday gone. No worries. I'd just do everything possible to give it back to her.

Her brother's orange hair didn't come into view until I opened the door. After a grin aimed at Free, I turned to offer Landry my hand. "How's it going, Landry Paine?"

Where Free had lost her smile, Landry's mouth was stretched wide as he took my hand. "Hi, Cole Anderson."

I pumped his hand a couple times before facing Free, who drove out of the parking lot toward the road leading to Poplar Branch. "So, what's on the agenda today, kids?"

"Daddy wasn't home when I got there," she said.

"Okay, and…?"

She paid too close attention to the road. "And I have Little with me. I'm thinking I'd drive you home? Maybe do this again another time?"

I'd waited for her like Christmas morning, and no freaking way would I let her blow me off. "Nah, now's good."

"But my brother—"

"Is more than welcome to hang with us." I turned to Landry again. "Got anything in mind? I'm game for whatever, except eating spinach. I draw the line at spinach."

He giggled, and in my peripheral, I noticed Free's lips turning upward. *Score!*

"We can go to our house," Landry said. "We have cookies."

"Cookies? Well, why didn't you say so?" I zipped my coat, the Buick's heater core not working all that great. "Cookies are way better than spinach."

Free nodded. "Sounds like as good a plan as any." The stress tightening her cheeks lessened with her smile.

No, she was better than Christmas morning.

Idea 1079

Patent Mystery Girl's Smile

As soon as we parked, Landry ran inside their house. "I'll get the cookies ready!"

"Stay away from the stove!" Free hollered as we got out.

When she looked at me, really looked, her gaze softened and her cheeks pinked. I wanted to take credit for her new color, not let the cold have it. Behind the over-sized flannel coat, worn jeans, and tired eyes, she was beautiful.

Should I reach for her hand? Probably not. I didn't have the excuse of guiding her through the woods this time, and no sense in risking her rebuilding that wall of hers if I tried without a reason.

I tucked my needy hands inside my coat pockets. "I guess we better get in there before he eats all the cookies."

"Oh, right." She started for the porch. "Come on."

We sat around the stove, a couple of lanterns on upturned crates our only light, and played Go Fish, ate stale cookies, and laughed at Landry's impression of Free when she pumped water from the well. At how he swore she could knock over buildings with her groan when he needed the outhouse in the middle of the night. Well, Landry and I laughed. Free sort of had a scowl-smile thing going.

After a while, Landry pulled out a calculator. "Watch this!" He rattled off an equation to Free, and she gave the answer a few seconds later. Landry held his calculator for me to see. "She's a human calculator!"

Had to admit, I was pretty impressed. "You get it right all the time?" I asked her.

"Of course she does," Landry answered.

She ruffled his hair, her face flushing. "I have me an admirer."

"You have more than one," I said. Her cheeks flamed brighter, and before she could reconstruct her wall, I spouted, "What's the square root of thirty-four?"

"Five point eight three and then some." She gave me a knowing smile. "Am I right?"

I shook my head, laughing. "I have no idea."

Landry went on and on after about how awesome his sister was and how she could shoot turkeys dead first try. "And someday she's going to a faraway school to do numbers—I forget what it's called. When we're done camp—"

"Little!" Free stood so fast her chair toppled over. "Enough, okay? No more stories."

Landry's lips instantly puckered.

Free cursed under her breath and crouched in front of him, rubbing his arms. "Sorry. Why don't you get your book? I'll bet Cole wants to hear about your castles and knights."

His eyes fixed on me, tears brimming in them. Poor kid. "You want to hear a story?"

"Sure, pal. I love castles." When he ran into a room off the kitchen, I peered up as Free straightened. I knew that frown. It was the same one she gave when asked questions remotely below the surface. "I won't ask you. Promise."

She closed her eyes. Pain shadowed her face, like it was rooted so deep, the leftover had no other choice but to settle on her skin. "I wish things were different, you know?"

"All the time." I encircled her wrist, guiding her to Landry's empty seat in front of me, and didn't say anything when she opened her eyes to reveal liquid. I traced my index finger down her left cheek, her jawline, her right cheek, wishing I could wipe away her misery. By the time I reached her bottom lip, my hand shook.

She remained motionless, concentrating on my eyes as I did hers. I cleared my throat to speak when cold air gushed through the front door and washed the moment away.

A man stood in the entryway with a shotgun. "Who the hell are you?"

Free jumped up to stand in front of my chair. "He's Cole, Daddy. My friend."

No way was I going to let her protect me. Did he hurt her? Was that the secret she kept from me? Rage flared in my gut. I rose to my feet, nudged her to the side, and held my hand out to her father. "Cole Anderson, sir. I live about a mile down the road."

He stared at me. "Ain't it time you be getting home, Cole Anderson?"

"Ah…" I lowered my hand as he brushed past me, Free at his heels until they disappeared behind a door down the hall.

I stood there, watching the door with Landry beside me, a thick book in his arms. In seconds, loud yells leaked from the room, the uninsulated walls not blocking much. One thump, one loud smack, and I was going in there.

I caught some of their argument, like her father shouting, "You can't trust these white trash sonsofbitches!" and Free countering with, "You trusted Byron!"

Moments later, Free stormed from the room, giving Landry a frown before facing me and gesturing to the door. "Let's go."

Silence filled the minute it took to get to my house. When she stopped, she wouldn't take her eyes off the windshield. Her lips moved in what looked like silent numbers. *One, two, three…*

"Are you—Will you and Landry be okay with him?"

"Of course."

Should I believe her? Did I have much of a choice? "Can I see you again?"

"I don't know." More silent counting.

"Please." I felt her slipping away, water running through my fingers.

She turned to me, her eyes wide. "You need to get out," she whispered.

I had to listen. Somehow, I knew if I didn't, she'd fall apart. When I clambered out, my joints stiff, I pleaded one last time before closing the door on her. "Promise me this won't be the last time I see you."

She shifted into reverse. "Told you. I'm not worth knowing."

"Yes, *you are*."

"Shut the door, Cole."

I sighed and backed away, shutting the door with my foot.

Then she was gone.

CHAPTER 9

Free

Knowing ≠ Learning

My birthday fell on the day after Christmas, but December 26 wasn't for celebrating anything. Not only because it was the eve of my mother's death, but because of my father, too.

When men in dark suits came to collect Mama's body, he wailed so loudly I hid under my bed. I'd never forget the sound, a wounded animal caught in a trap. After, he refused to leave his bedroom. He wouldn't even come out for Mama's funeral. A few nights passed before I was brave enough to check on him. He was in the corner, curled into a ball with the used .22 he had given me days before.

My last birthday. My last Christmas, too.

I lay in bed and stared at the ceiling, listening to Little's soft snores next to me. When my mind wandered to *that* time, sleep never came. No, it gave me space to think. Daddy had lied to me about hunting, including where he'd gone tonight. And he chased away Cole, making me remember friends were a liability. I screamed at him, accused him of being careless. Accused him of ruining our lives.

But my thoughts flooded with *that* time when I lost Mama and almost lost Daddy. When I had to pry the gun from his hands and beg him not to leave me, too. When he cried and repeated sorry until the word turned into a moan. When the next morning, he stopped crying and became the dreamer. *We're leaving, Free. We're gonna sell everything and move to wherever the Lord takes us.*

I buried my nose in Little's hair, inhaling his scent. He smelled like Landry Allen Paine Jr.—the perfect smell.

Thank God Daddy became a dreamer.

I slid my arm from under Little's head and cocooned him in blankets before tiptoeing from the room to find Daddy sitting by the stove, lost in thought.

I sat next to him. "Hey," I said, holding my hands to the fire. The place always smelled like wood smoke, hiding the musty decay underneath.

He glanced my way. "Can't sleep?"

I shook my head. "I keep thinking about her."

Her was code for *Mama*. Neither of us said her name aloud; it still hurt too much. Daddy taught me how to hunt, shoot, and play Sudoku at eight—when I realized how perfect numbers are, how they always give a solution. Mama showed me everything else: how to make cookies, read the clouds, the importance of "real music" after digging out her old CDs—Stone Temple Pilots, Nirvana, Rage Against the Machine, and so many others. She showed me I was the most important person in her life.

"I miss her, too." He folded his hands in front of him. "Sorry for tonight. That boy."

I pinched my thigh, focusing on that pain instead of the hurt inside. "It's fine. You're right."

"Don't make it any less bad, me being right. Does it?"

"Guess not." We concentrated on the stove for a moment. "Where've you been going, Daddy?"

"We can't stay here."

"Doesn't answer my question."

"It does."

I shifted to study his profile, his shaggy hair and thick beard. He used to be clean-shaven. Mama had told him she loved his face, always brushing her hands across his cheeks. The best memory I had of Bluefield was when Daddy would come home from work with coal dust coating his skin and clothes. If Mama's CDs were playing, he'd sweep her into his arms while she stroked his dirty cheek, admiring him as if he were the only person in the world. They would dance in slow circles, even if Kurt Cobain blared in our living room, demanding "Teen Spirit." And he'd tell her he loved her—all the time: *Love you to the ends of Earth, Annie. Always have, always will.* Her death made him cover what she loved so he wouldn't have to see it anymore.

"Daddy? Don't do anything stupid."

He bowed his head. "She'd be mad I brought you here."

"Daddy…"

"She never wanted her daughter raised in Poplar Branch."

"*Please*."

"I wanna take y'all somewhere special. Where it's warm and we don't have to worry about food."

I clenched my hands in my lap. "That place don't exist. Not for us."

"It does. We just need a little cash to get us there."

I kneeled in front of him and pressed on his thighs, willing him to see me and not his new fantasy. "Tell me you're not selling drugs for Duffy."

"I got morals, believe it or not."

"And all *I* got is you and Little. You understand that, right?"

"Trust me, Free." He lifted his gaze to mine. "You need to trust me."

CHAPTER 10

Cole

Mystery Girl Runs

I didn't say a word to Free all morning. She hadn't acknowledged me since that night at her house, driving past me for the last few days without a look in my direction. No problem. If she needed time to realize I wasn't the enemy, I'd deal with it. But the effort it took to act as if she weren't working alongside me today caused sweat to saturate my light blue T-shirt, now dark blue. I could only blame *some* of the extra perspiration on lifting boxes of canned vegetables and crates of lettuce.

By the time Jess and Carrie came in at the end of our shift, I had to force myself not to drag Free to the back. I couldn't wait any longer. She'd talk to me now, dammit.

I nodded to Jess. "How's it going?" I asked her, trying to keep my eyes off Free as she cashed out her last customer at the other register.

Jess tucked her purse under the counter. "All right. You?"

"Not too bad." Not too great either.

"You talk to Deacon?"

"Not since yesterday."

"We're hanging out at my place tonight, Netflix and pizza." She hesitated. "I can come get you after I'm off if you want."

"Maybe." I turned when I heard Carrie take over Free's register, Free already on her way to the back. "Give me a second, okay?" I ignored Jess's frown and hurried to catch up.

"Hey," I said, tapping my shoulder against Free's when I reached her side.

She stiffened. "Hello."

"How've you been? Good?"

"Fine."

Her apathy wouldn't deter me. I *did* stand in front of her moving car.

I collected my empty backpack from the break table and lifted it higher when she gave it her attention. "Easier to tote stuff home," I said.

She nodded and angled away from me as Mr. Gifford hurried in with another crate of food, plopping it down on the pallets next to the rest. "I'm pressed for time, but y'all know what to do."

Free found some plastic bags after Mr. Gifford huffed back to the front and filled them without a word.

Where to start? "So…"

My voice activated her hyper-drive, and she scooped groceries faster.

Damn it. "What happened, Free?"

"No idea what you're talking about."

"Yes, you do."

She ignored me.

Nuh-uh. Bull. Shit. We started something, and whatever she was hiding, I wanted to know—so I could show her it didn't matter.

I stuck two dented cans of soup into my bag. Paused. Okay, time to venture into her off-limit zone. "You related to Byron? He's the last Mumford left up there, and—"

"Stop." She straightened and held a hand in my face. "Just stop it. I ain't answering."

Backfire. Her angry words didn't make me regret I'd asked her. It was the tears filling her whiskey eyes, the way her full lips pursed.

"I'm sorry." I dropped my backpack, the cans in it clunking against the floor. "Last thing I want to do is upset you."

"I can't do this." She jabbed a finger toward my chest. "You don't get it! This friend thing you want to push on me—I don't want it. How many times do I need to tell you? You don't know me. You don't know *anything* about me."

"But that's exactly what I want, to know you—as friends." I stepped closer and stopped when panic widened her eyes. "I'm not trying to get with you or anything, I swear."

Free gathered her bags and stormed past me. "I'm full-up on friends. Don't need another." She turned before heading out front. "Please. Leave me alone. I should have nev—"

"No, don't say it." I narrowed my eyes at her. "Don't you dare finish that sentence."

"I'm…*I'm sorry*, Cole. I am. Concentrate on saving for your apartment." She gestured to my jeans. "Your bizarre escape plans, too. Forget about me, okay?" She then made her own escape through the front door, head bent and shoulders slumped, the world using her back as a resting place.

Freedom Paine.

Her name said it all.

I dragged myself to Jess's register. "What time you coming to get me?"

I turned the corner toward my place, my backpack heavy with food. I had taken more from the pile after Free left. I might have gone girl crazy for a split second, but I didn't go senseless. I needed that food. And an hour and a half was a long enough—cold enough—trek to talk myself out of Freedom Paine, especially when she drove past me. Again. While it poured freezing, ball-shrinking rain. Maybe I'd made her out to be more than she was. I mean, all she did was give me cookies.

And witnessed me cry over charity food and not say a word about it.

And allowed me a glimpse of her surface while I held her hand.

And picked me up from work and showed me a little more than her surface.

God, I wanted her out of my head.

Screaming leaked outside as I stepped to the first cinder block. *What the hell?*

Hannah whipped the door open before I could turn the knob and pulled me in as Mama raged in the kitchen. "She's at it again, Colie."

"What'd she take?"

"I got no idea, but she's been carrying on for an hour now. Letter come in the mail from Richie. Said he might be home soon." Hannah's sunken face crumpled more when Mama threw pots and pans into the living room, screaming incoherently about Dad and Richie. "I can't calm her for nothing. She already done punched me in the face."

"All right, dammit." I dropped my bag by the door and went to persuade Kaycee out from behind the couch. She lifted her arms, crying and repeating "Why is Mamaw doing that?" in her scared voice as I carried her to Hannah. "Go into your room and lock the door. Don't know why you didn't do it in the first place."

Tears fell from Hannah's eyes. "Mama kept flinging stuff at me, and I couldn't get Kaycee to come out from her hiding spot."

As if proving her point, a frying pan arced across the room, narrowly missing Kaycee's head. "None of y'all are worth a thing! Not your good-for-nothing daddy or Richie or…"

I had no clue what Mama said after, her words turning into trilled venom.

I propelled Hannah toward the hall. "Go!"

When my sister made it into the room she shared with Mama and Kaycee, I inched into the kitchen with my hands up.

Same routine.

Same goddamn routine.

Idea 1080

Invisible Man

"Now, Mama…"

CHAPTER 11

Cole

Friends Seek Solace at Cliff

Amy and I sat on the bleachers, watching Deacon's practice. We did that sometimes, usually because we had plans to go to the cliff, a place Deacon and I found when we were in fourth grade. That was before Deacon's mom stopped letting him come over to my house—right after Dad got arrested the first time.

Amy offered me some of her candy bar, and I shook my head. She shrugged, biting off a chunk. "Deacon says Richie's coming home," she said around a mouthful.

"He *might* be coming home. Depends on his parole hearing."

"You think he'll make parole?"

"Hope not."

"I hope not, too," she whispered.

All I'd been to my brother for the two years before he got sent to the clink was a convenient punching bag, and my friends knew it. They'd seen the swollen eyes, the broken noses. Gifts from Richie Fuckhead Anderson.

Silence filled the space between us while we watched Deacon throw one ball after another, the next farther down the field than the last. The cheerleading squad practiced too, away from the players. Amy used to be a part of that. This year, she'd quit. I think it was because her home life had gotten worse after her dad's hours were cut. He was lucky, though. Most miners around here lost their jobs completely.

Amy swallowed the last bite of her candy bar and stuffed the wrapper into her bag. "Jess said you don't talk to that girl no more."

I flashed a smile as fake as Amy's hair. Her naturally blond hair looked fine to me, but this past summer she'd cut it almost as short as Deacon's and dyed it black, another thing she'd done after life got bad for her. "How would Jess know?"

"Because she watches you like a stalker." Amy tapped my knee with hers.

I cringed. A stalker. What I almost turned into. I had avoided Free for a week, though. She wanted me to stay away, and so I did. Whatever. Nothing I could do about it. "No, I haven't talked to her."

"What's her name again? Something different, right? Jess calls her 'that girl.'"

I examined my reddened hands, rubbing them together to combat the cold. "Freedom."

"Yes!" Amy snapped her fingers. "Great name. You know anything about her?"

I rubbed harder. "Not much."

"Well, did you ask her?"

I tipped my chin at the notebook between us, the pages flapping with the wind. "What do you think?"

"How am I supposed to know what you write in there? Christ, that info's more classified than the CIA."

She had a point.

"Yeah, yeah, I asked her."

Coach Nate blew his whistle in time to avoid the rest of Amy's interrogation, and Deacon came running toward us from the end zone, yanking his helmet off on the way. "Hey, y'all!" He winked at Amy and nodded in my direction. "You got my keys?"

I pulled them from my pocket and dangled the keyring in front of him.

"Awesome. Go get her started."

"On it," I said, climbing down the bleachers.

Amy followed but stopped to hang over the low cement wall separating the field from the bleachers to give Deacon a pretty X-rated kiss. I kept going. The last thing I wanted to stick around for was their grope-fest.

The four of us had always been close, an exclusive club formed in first grade. Deacon and I partnered up with Amy and Jess one day at recess, and Jess had deemed us "best friends forever!" after we played tag until Mrs. Kepler called us back inside. Somehow, her declaration stuck. But in tenth grade, Amy and Deacon crossed the friend line. After the initial surprise of seeing two of my best friends kissing, it became natural, like they'd been that way all along.

"Wait up!"

I turned to Amy speed-walking toward me. Her cheeks were flushed, and a soft smile ghosted her lips, our conversation obviously forgotten.

Good.

Freedom was hard enough to forget.

"Will you come away from there! You're fixing to get yourself killed!" Amy dragged on Deacon's arm without success.

He stayed on the rocky ledge, yelling loud enough for his voice to shoot back at us.

"Deacon Mallory!" She tugged again.

And he continued to howl at the gray sky, ignoring her.

"Fine! Suit yourself, you damn fool." She plopped down next to me, our feet hanging over the edge of our cliff, high above the valley below. Deacon stood on the other side of her, still hollering like a crazy person with his head back and arms wide.

Our spot gave the view of the world. Mountains reached heaven, and trees bursting with fall leaves covered their sides in colorful blankets. No rundown shacks, no trash-infested yards. No muddy roads or abandoned factory buildings or clapboard houses ready to cave. Deacon could scream as loud and as long as he wanted, and we'd still be hidden from everyone. Safe from whatever waited for us at the end of the mile-long path that began near my trailer.

Deacon sat and heaved without saying a word. Going away to college scared him, the reason he came here a lot lately. Even *if* he got a scholarship, he'd have a hard time getting through classes—because he'd have a harder time asking strangers for help. It'd mean admitting to someone besides Amy and me that he couldn't read that great.

Here, Deacon didn't have to tell us again why he had to yell. We knew. Same reason I would yell after Mama went crazy or when food ran out before the first of the month. Or when Amy's dad came home drunk and beat up her mother.

Sometimes secrets hurt too much to keep inside.

CHAPTER 12

Free

$\lim_{x \to a} f(x) = l$ and $\lim_{x \to a} g(x) = m$ Limits

Daddy spent much of Laura's pregnancy convincing us it was a good thing, a miracle. Laura hadn't seen it that way, and neither had I. I planned to hate whatever popped out of her stomach. At school, I'd get into fights, take my anger out on innocent faces. My grades slipped, too. When Daddy had to come in and listen to my school counselor tell him I was troubled, I sat in the hall and cried and hated him for starting a new family with a woman who wasn't Mama.

But then he came.

Daddy brought me into Laura's hospital room with a proud grin and a puffed chest. Laura stared at the television above her bed, eyes already empty, and her parents sat off in a corner. I hadn't much cared about Laura's obvious apathy or her always kind parents. What stopped my heart was the squirming bundle Laura's mother held, so small it fit along her forearm.

"Come on, Free," Daddy said, pressing against my back. "Come meet your new brother."

I didn't budge from the doorway. "But… he's so little."

The bundle made a warbled cry as if answering to my voice. His sounds were strong enough to form tears in my eyes as I shuffled to a vacant seat, hesitating before holding my hands out for him.

Laura's mother rested her bundle in my arms. "Careful, now, honey. Support his head."

I nodded, my voice locked behind emotion I couldn't understand—until I had Landry Allen Paine Jr. in my arms. Little. While I admired his face and counted all his fingers and toes, even counting the downy orange hairs on his head, I fell in love for the first time. It hurt. And it made me whole.

From that moment, he was mine.

Mine to feed and bathe when Laura refused and Daddy had to work.

Mine to sing to and rock while Laura drank or disappeared and Daddy went out in search of her.

Mine to watch sleep, my hand always going to his chest to make sure he breathed.

Mine.

And I was his.

As Little and I lay in bed this morning, before the sun peeked through the window, his soft snores played in rhythm with my heart. I felt that punch; I always did while watching him sleep, as if every day was the day I'd fallen in love with him.

The cold wind stole through the walls, its howl laughing at our attempts to hide from it. And I pressed my hand against Little's chest as he snuggled closer to me in his sleep.

"Where're you going?"

Daddy spent the entire night gone, as he had for days, doing God knew what, and as soon as I came out of my room this morning, he said he was leaving again.

"I'm taking the next step, Free. The very next step."

He ran his dirty fingers through his beard and paced near the stove, ignoring the baked beans in a pot on top of it, boiling and bubbly. The heat made me sweat. Daddy spent the time waiting for me to emerge from my room building the fire too hot and warming food he didn't plan to eat. Wasteful. He hadn't changed his clothes, either, mud caking the knees of his camo pants and sleeves of his matching flannel. His digging clothes.

"Do you really have to take the car, though? It don't got much gas."

He laughed like I said something funny. "Bet your ass I do, and it gots enough to get me where I need to go."

"But today's food day at work. If I miss, we'll have to use more of the sang money."

He gripped my shoulders, and I could smell the forest soil on him. "You won't be going to work again. Not here, anyway. We're leaving. Tonight." He let go and hurried into his room.

Oh, no. He wasn't getting off that easy. I kicked at Little's broken crayons scattered on the floor and marched after him. *Here we go.* Another dream to follow. Excitement started sizzling in my veins. "You serious?"

"Never been more serious in my life." He ripped through his clothes, always unfolded in a basket next to his bed, and pulled out his only pair of jeans and another flannel. "We hit the load, baby!" He hooted and jumped up and down.

"You…What'd you do?"

He peeled off his hat and threw it next to his clothes on the bed. "We can't stay here, not no more. It ain't good for you and the boy."

I swallowed, my throat as dry as summer in Needles. "Drugs, Daddy?"

"Told you I wouldn't touch that junk, and I haven't. Ginseng, like I said we'd find."

"Where'd you get it?"

He floated those dreamer eyes over me. "You're too grown for your own good."

"Answer."

"Free." He pulled me into his arms. "You have to trust me. We got no choice."

"I always trust you." Usually, anyway.

"Good."

I brushed an itch on my nose against his dirty shirt. "Then if you ain't gonna to tell where, show it to me."

He let me go and gave his I-have-a-secret grin. "Show you what?"

"You know what! Show me our ticket, Daddy. I wanna see it."

He laughed again and dragged me outside to the Buick. "I loaded it while you was sleeping." He popped the trunk. "Go on, now. Take a gander."

I stepped around back on tingling feet and—Oh, wow. Resting on a bed of black garbage bags had to have been at least ten pounds, if not more, of gorgeous, three-pronged ginseng roots. Dirty, veiny gold.

"My God," I whispered, but the curse screamed inside my head.

Daddy shut the lid, smiling big and giddy. "Told you."

I smoothed a hand over the dented metal of the trunk. "How much is in here?"

"Enough to get us far away from here and set us up in a decent place."

"Where's that?"

"We'll find out once we get there."

My excitement fizzled some. "That's not a plan."

"It's what I got right now." He gestured to the woods across the road. "This ain't living, Free. If we keep going like this… Dang. Maybe Little'd be better off with—"

"No." The word slipped out, acidic and burning, as I pressed my fingers harder into the metal. "No, Daddy. We can't do that. We can't!"

He stared at me with a face full of doubt.

"*No*." I held my hands in prayer because I was praying. Praying for my very heart—who still slept in our bed. "*Please*. All we done would be for nothing!"

"All right, all right." He patted the air. "I hear you. Go on in, see to your brother. We ain't gonna have much time after I cash this in. Pack everything important, and y'all be ready." He started for the house.

I ran after him, careful to miss the rusted car parts in the yard. "Take us with you!"

"It ain't safe. And don't ask me why, 'cause you won't like the answer."

I didn't ask again where he found the sang; he pretty much already answered. "How long will you be gone, then?"

"A few hours or so."

If he stole from Duffy or another person, that person was probably rightly pissed and searching shops, including Dillinger's, for any recent big hauls. "You should probably go to Kentucky, sell to a dealer there."

"Don't you worry." He tapped his temple. "I got it figured out."

"Can we stop by Mim's before we leave?" I asked as he gulped a few bites of beans, hissing when he burned his mouth. "Let her know we're okay?"

"Maybe." He set the pot down, his spoon clanking against cast-iron, and headed into his room, already peeling off his filthy shirt. "Just be ready."

"We will be," I said, staring at the pot. Little and I would eat beans for breakfast. We might be leaving, but that didn't mean we had to waste food.

He came back out in minutes, dressed, still cruddy, and with the shotgun in his hand. "Loaded this with the rest of the ammo. Keep it by the door, just in case." He set it next to our wood pile.

"Yeah, sure. Okay."

Daddy hugged me. "It's all gonna work out, baby. You'll see."

I squeezed him hard. "I believe you."

Two hours passed, and he didn't make it home.

Little woke up in tears because he wet the bed. I dressed him in fresh clothes, gave him breakfast, made him brush his teeth, and then sang to him until he stopped being upset.

Another hour.

I went into Daddy's room and stuffed his things in garbage bags like I had ours.

Three more.

I packed what food we had left in more bags and set them by the door, next to the shotgun.

Afternoon turned into night.

I built up the fire and made Little and myself a can of soup for supper.

Night fell into dawn.

The next morning, Little sat by me near the stove, his coat next to him on the floor. "Where do you think he is?"

"He'll be here soon. Don't worry, okay?"

"Okay."

Okay. I went to check our things for the hundredth time and dug out some crackers, tea bags, and two mugs.

"Here. Don't eat too fast." I handed him the crackers and grabbed an old towel to wrap around the pot handle, pouring water into each mug. The well behind our house wasn't the cleanest, but if I boiled the water, we could drink it without getting sick. I had pumped enough for tea and for us to wash before Little woke this morning.

I set my brother's cup next to his chair and slumped into mine, blowing on my tea and soaking in the heat. He ate quietly, taking small bites and chewing until the crackers had to have gone liquid before swallowing. While he focused on his breakfast, I focused on the stove and tried not to let panic color my mind. Maybe he went to Kentucky like I suggested. Plausible.

"Sissy?"

"Yes?" I sipped my tea to cover my frown.

"Where are we going?"

Another sip. "Don't know yet."

"We're still camping?"

I drank until bitter tea burned the back of my throat and nodded.

"Will we have lights there?"

"I hope so."

"Will we see her there?"

His mother was *her* to him, like mine was to me, but for different reasons. His told him more times than I could count that he was a mistake. Her biggest, ugliest mistake. Mine loved me more than breathing.

"Do you want to see her?"

He bit into a cracker, the muffled crunching loud inside the quiet shack. "No."

"Well then…"

"Sissy?"

"Yes?"

"I like camping with you."

I tilted my head to find him staring at the fire in the stove window and swinging legs too short to touch the floor. "I like camping with you, too."

He smiled. "You're my favorite."

"Right back at you." I reached for his hand and laced my fingers with his. They felt like fragile shells, those delicate silver dollars found in the sand at beaches. He'd lost weight since coming here; his ribs protruded against his skin. Guilt always bit at my heart when I held him against the cold at night.

I let go of his hand and swiped at a tear on my cheek. "Hey, Little?"

"What?" He balanced his crackers in his lap and reached for his tea.

"Will you read to me?"

"Okay."

Hours later, the sun faded, leaving faint streaks behind. The way the sky glowed, with red and orange on the horizon, used to make me happy when we lived in Bluefield. Mama said it was God's way of promising a perfect next day. I stared out the screen door, willing her words to come true.

Nothing changed outside from when I stood here a while ago, everything the same. The same mud and decaying, manmade things. The same fall-colored haven across the road. The same rot battling the same struggling beauty.

And no Daddy.

Little stood beside me, wrapped in a blanket. "He's not coming back."

"He is."

"What if he left us?" His voice went small and shaky. His brave voice. "What if he thinks we're mistakes?"

"No, Little." I fell to my knees and brought him into my arms, hulking blanket and all. "You're not a mistake. *You're not.*"

His sobs wet my neck. "Then why?"

I couldn't give him my fear. I couldn't say *Daddy's in trouble.* So I carried him to bed and held him close as his body quaked. "You're not a mistake, Little," I whispered, stroking his carrot hair. "You're my everything."

Headlights flared through the bedroom window, interrupting the pitch black, and the Buick's motor grumbled through the gaps in the walls.

Thank you, Lord!

I wriggled out from under the covers, careful not to wake Little. The Buick's lights guided me into the living room where the stove had burned to embers. Another engine roared into the driveway, this one newer, a hum next to the Buick's cough.

Oh, no. *No, no, no!*

One step toward the door. Another. I didn't want to see who the other engine belonged to, but the fire ants attacking my nerve endings told me what I already knew.

I picked up the gun, its weight heavy in my trembling hands.

Took a deep breath.

Cursed God and His morbid desire to punish us.

Opened the door.

Their headlights blinded me as if I were on a stage. My audience didn't speak, but I felt their eyes on me, leeches sucking on my skin. I lifted the gun and pointed at nothing.

"Daddy?" My voice didn't sound like mine. It was too young, too scared.

A door opened and slammed shut; grunts and engaging guns followed. Sounds from at least three people. A thousand people. "What I say about your daddy, young lady? You forget to give him my message? I sure do hate to chew my cabbage twice, but I suppose I should give it again."

Anything I had considered saying stayed trapped in my tightening throat.

This was how I'd die, with my own words choking me.

"He done gone too far this time." Gravel crunched, and footsteps grew louder near the porch until Duffy's shock-white hair glowed in the headlights. "Can you hear what I'm saying to you?"

"Get off my yard." *Too young, too scared.*

He laughed as he came closer, now right in front of me with one booted foot resting on the first step. "You got moxie." He signaled behind his head, and two men with rifles sidled up to stand behind him. "But if you keep aiming that gun at my face, it might get you and yours killed."

I stared at them, beyond them. "Where's he at?"

"Put down the gun, girl."

"Where is he!"

Duffy planted his hands on his hips and spat, never taking his eyes from mine.

Everything tilted: the men, the yard, the *fucking* headlights. "Did you—Is he dead?"

He spat again. "Not yet."

What do I do?

A muffled cry came from my bedroom window. I rushed to it, blocking Little's view, and dropped my gun. "Please," I pleaded.

Duffy stepped onto the porch and peered over my shoulder. "Younger brother, worried, I'd guess. Shame what your daddy puts y'all through."

I pressed my back against the window until the glass complained. This—*this*—was gut-wrenching, death-inducing. "*Please*."

He watched me, waiting for something. Whatever it was, all he had to do was ask, and it'd get done. Anything. Little's sobs leaked through the window, louder now and unraveling me, amping up the sounds of the engines, the blinding sheen from the headlights.

"This is y'all's last warning." He pointed to the window. "Next time he steals from me, I'm taking it out on you and that boy. Make sure you tell him this time."

I nodded, and kept nodding as the two gunmen returned to the Buick and yanked my father's limp body from the back. *Oh, God!* All the blood. His face no longer looked like his face. He wasn't moving, not one twitch.

Little's sobs turned panicked when they dragged Daddy up the porch steps and through the front door, dropping him with a dull *thump*.

"Now, y'all have a good night," Duffy said after the two men headed for his truck. He snapped his fingers. "Oh, and, ah, it'd be best if we kept this between us." He spat one last time on the porch, splashing my bare toes with it, before strolling to his truck as if he'd just left Sunday sermon.

I waited there until his headlights disappeared, the Buick's still shining and motor still groaning.

Little beat on the window. "Sissy!"

"It's okay." I didn't turn to face him. Couldn't. "It's all right."

The sound of his pattering feet. A pause. "They killed him! He's dead. Dead! Dead! Dead!"

"No." I forced my legs to move to the door, the Buick's headlights following me inside.

Little was on his knees by Daddy, his tiny hand lifting our father's. "What's wrong with his hands? What's wrong with him?" His face blanched to the color of sun-bleached bone.

I crouched beside him to inspect Daddy's hands—and had to swallow the puke rising up my throat. His fingers were slick with blood and loose skin, every fingernail pulled from their beds. "Go back into the bedroom," I told him with as much calm as I could find.

Little kept crying, kept showing me Daddy's hand.

I lifted my brother, holding him while staring at our father, who still wasn't moving. "Little, are you listening to me?" I whispered. When he nodded, I took him into our room and continued, "I need you to stay in here while I take care of Daddy, okay?" I put him on the bed and bent in front of him. "It'll be all right."

"It won't." Tears ran down his cheeks, and his body shook.

"It *will.*" *Stay calm, stay calm.* But I could already feel shock freezing my insides. I had to force words past my chattering teeth. "I have to go out there now. Sit still until I come get you."

He searched behind me, out the window. "Will the bad men come back?"

"N-no, they're not coming back."

His gaze fell on mine as he pressed his left hand to my cheek, his scar rough against my skin. "Don't leave me."

"Never ever, Little." I kissed the top of his head and left the room, closing the door behind me on the way back to Daddy.

I rested my ear against his chest. The *thu-thump* of his heartbeat allowed me to breathe.

"Daddy?" I smoothed bloody, matted hair from his forehead. "Can you hear me?"

Nothing.

I lifted his shirt to see his stomach and hissed through my teeth. Bruises so black and purple the headlights were enough to show them as clear as if it were daytime. I scrambled to his left side and examined his ankle. His foot dangled from his leg, only skin keeping it connected to his body.

I stifled a moan. *Stay. Calm.*

He was alive—but that was all. Nothing here would help him. Not me, not this shack with no clean water or electric. I went to his shoulders and reached under them, trying to drag his heavy body toward the headlights. He barely moved, only groaning with the short distance I'd managed.

I straightened and took in everything around me. *Think!* What could I—

That's it! My only option in the world. I ran to my bedroom and swept Little into my arms, carrying him out to the car, not bothering with shoes or coats or sanity.

"What about Dad? We can't leave him!" Little struggled when I heaved him into the back, the upholstery coated with Daddy's blood. It smelled metallic, strong.

I gagged. No. *Ignore it!* "We're not leaving him." I forced Little to sit and buckled him in. "Don't move, you hear me? Don't try to get out of this car."

I shut his door and got in, yanked into reverse, and pressed on the gas. We drove barely a mile before I slammed on the breaks and put the car in park. "Stay here," I told Little, and jumped out. Rocks and trash cut my feet as I raced for the three cinder blocks to the front door. I pounded until outside lights came on and the door swung open.

Cole stood there in sweats and a T-shirt, his oceans wide. "Free?"

I lost it. Cried and cried and cried and attempted to speak. "Please… My dad… I—My house…"

He said nothing, just nodded and went to snatch shoes from a mat by the couch. A small woman glowered from me to Cole, yelling at him as he sat to put on his sneakers. I had no idea what she said, the screaming inside my brain too loud to hear. All I could focus on was Cole's fingers tying his laces in quick knots. Then his back as he headed down a hallway before returning a second later pulling a hoodie over his head.

He clasped my hand. "I'll drive."

CHAPTER 13

Free

$$d = v_i \cdot t + \frac{1}{2} \cdot a \cdot t^2$$

Free Fall

I concentrated on Cole's wrists. Not out the window. Not on my brother. If I saw Little's fear or our house around the bend, I'd shatter.

His wrists. Only his wrists.

None of us said a word as Cole pulled into my driveway and cut the engine. I looked up at his face, cast in shadows. Nothing sounded better than giving in and letting him handle everything. This boy I hardly knew. This boy who was the closest friend I'd made in over a year. I wouldn't, though. Give up. Little depended on me to be as strong as Cole's wrists.

His chest moved with a deep breath before he turned to face the back, a smile barely lifting the corners of his mouth. "Hey, pal."

When Little didn't answer, Cole covered his folded hands. "Your sister and I are gonna check things out, but I want you to stay here, all right?"

"Don't leave me." Little's voice had no emotion, like the plea had been set on repeat before his mind checked out.

"We're not leaving you. We'll be back in no time; you'll see." Cole let go of Little and nodded to me as he opened his door. "C'mon."

I reached for the handle and hesitated. I wanted to stay in the car, too. Hide here until we woke and this night disappeared.

Cole covered my hand the same way he had Little's. "*Come on.*"

"Okay. I…Okay." I slipped my hand from under his and wiped my eyes. "The headlights, you need to keep them on so we can see."

Cole flicked them back on before we got out. He took my hand and picked a way through the yard with the least amount of garbage, my throbbing feet thankful. "What am I walking into, Free? Your dad… is he in there with a gun, drunk, or… what?"

My breath hitched. "Daddy would never hurt us."

His hand tightened around mine. "Is he…?"

Little's voice blared inside my head: *Dead! Dead! Dead!*

"No."

"Good. That's good." He took the porch steps two at a time, leading me as if I were a floating balloon behind him. When he opened the screen door, he froze. "Shit."

Daddy lay where I left him, the headlights faintly revealing the massacre that used to be his face. He groaned a gurgling sound. "F-Free?"

I hurried to Daddy's side. "I'm here."

Cole swallowed a scream, the echo of it breaching the quiet. "He—We need to get him to the ER."

I nodded, brushing Daddy's cheek, and winced when he gave a pained cry. "I can't lift him on my own. I tried, but…"

"Okay, ah, all right. Yeah." Cole went outside and said through the screen door, "I'm gonna back the car to the steps."

While Cole revved the engine, I bent to whisper in Daddy's ear, "We're taking you to the hospital. Everything'll be fine."

"No h-hospital." His swollen lips hardly moved.

"We don't have a choice." Tears dripped from my cheeks to his earlobe. "You'll die, if not."

"No."

A car door slammed and then another. Cole talked to Little, using that high-pitched voice everyone used when lies and fear spouted from their mouths. "As soon as we get him help... Keep your eyes closed no matter what you hear..."

I heard the creak from the back left car door opening before Cole tromped up the steps. "Free?"

I peered up to the strain on his face.

"We need to get him into the back seat."

"How?" I couldn't think anymore. Couldn't find any solution to any problem.

"You're gonna have to grab his legs." Cole moved to my father's head and bent to reach under his shoulders. "I'll tote most his weight."

I scrambled to do as Cole ordered but stopped when my eyes fell on Daddy's left ankle. "His ankle's broken."

"You *have* to lift him. I can't do it by myself."

I tried to hold Daddy's calves, my grip slipping. "I can't." My tears came faster with each failed attempt to clutch him in another spot.

"Free? Look at me."

No, I had to find another way. I had to. Unintelligible things spilled from my lips, a string of useless words. Pleas. Promises.

"Free!"

A sob escaped when I lifted my gaze to Cole's.

"We'll be fast, I swear, but you need to do it."

I glanced at Daddy's ankle, his foot hanging there, and took a shaky breath before grasping above the break. He let out a tortured scream as I lifted with Cole and passed out before we got him to the car. A blessing. As Little hummed in the front seat,

Cole scooted into the back and pulled Daddy in by his shoulders while I pushed until my father lay sprawled on the seat.

Cole shut the back doors. "Get in," he told me.

Cole drove, and Little continued humming in my arms with his hands covering his ears and his eyelids shut so tight the delicate skin bunched. I held him close, not buckling seatbelts, as we took off down the hill. I kept telling lies in his ear in that high-pitched fear whisper. Cole remained quiet, concentrating on the pothole-filled road. He tapped on the wheel, the tapping not hiding how his fingers shook.

The hospital was at least twenty-five minutes away. Twenty-five minutes of Little's humming, Daddy's silence, and Cole's tapping, the kind of tapping that yelled *This isn't okay!*

I closed my eyes and searched for numbers, for something to calm me down. Nothing.

By the time we made it into Davy, I wanted to scream and punch and fight, the silence from the back too loud. What if he was already dead, and we drove in this quiet not knowing it? When the signs for Davy Hospital appeared on street corners, I curled Little's trembling body tighter to me, wishing he'd fit inside.

Cole parked at the ER entrance, left the motor running, and rushed through the automatic glass doors. The calm he'd held on to vanished as he pounded his fists on the front desk and pointed frantically toward us. The man behind the desk picked up a phone, talked for seconds, and followed Cole to the car.

"We're going to take care of him now," the man said after he opened the back passenger door.

I nodded, keeping Little as close as possible.

The man's face was smooth and kind. He stayed in control while the world around me burned to ashes. "It'll be all right."

I nodded again, holding Little closer, his humming right next to my ear, his eyes sealed shut.

A trail of others streamed from the doors, two pushing a stretcher. They gave each other commands as they pulled Daddy from the back to the gurney then rushed inside.

I watched them disappear through a set of double doors, not acknowledging Cole when he got back in. He parked in a spot close to the entrance, hopped out, and came around to open my door. “Here, give him to me.”

“No!” I jerked away from him. “No,” I said with less venom. “I have him.” I stepped on the cold pavement and moaned against the pain in my heel.

“Dammit!” Cole gripped the door and blocked my second attempt to get out. “You can barely walk on your own. Let me have him.”

“*He’s mine*.” I was a feral mother, a rabid bear.

“I’m not trying to steal him from you.” He lowered until we were eye level. “Your feet are a mess.”

I searched his oceans for deceit but found compassion. Worry.

Fine.

Fine.

I whispered into Little’s ear, coaxing him to let go of me. When he did, Cole gently lifted him into his arms and tucked Little’s head in the crook of his neck. Daddy’s blood smeared the back of my brother’s shirt and pants. “All right, Landry. All right, now.”

I limped behind them through the ER entrance. Cole immediately took Little to the kids’ section, where cartoons played on a TV above a table stacked with books and toys. The kind man had returned to his desk and now watched me with sad eyes. I went to him, trying not to hobble. “When can I see him?”

Tom, according to his name tag, doused me with all the compassion I could stand. “He’s beat up pretty bad, miss. It might be a while.” He reached in a drawer to his right. “Meantime, can you give me some info? His name? Does he have any allergies you're aware of?"

He rattled off a few more questions while I stared at him, saying nothing.

"Miss? At least give me his name. Please."

I found my brother watching television as Cole stroked his back and pointed at the screen. "Landry Paine Sr."

"Can you tell me what happened?"

The fluorescent lights caught Little's carrot hair just right, making it flame. I could already feel him being pulled away from me. "He got jumped."

"That your brother over there?" A pause. "You're both covered in blood."

My attention drifted to Little's soiled shirt. "It ain't ours."

They came shortly after like I knew they would. Two deputies. I had made up my mind when I gave Daddy's name away. In a panic, I made the wrong decision.

As calmly as I could, I nudged Cole, who sat next to me with my sleeping brother still in his arms. "I need you to do something."

"Anything."

I kept my eyes on the cops as they spoke to Tom, who pointed in our direction. "I need you to take Little out of here."

"Why?" He pointed to the deputies. "Because of Smith and Christie?"

I nodded and felt fresh tears well in my eyes when the cops glanced our way, one talking into the radio attached to his uniform near his shoulder. "I'll explain later, but please. They'll figure everything out soon, and it'll be too late."

"Figure what out?"

I pushed at his shoulder. "*Please*."

His expression turned from confused to worried to resigned in a second. He stood, fitting Little better into his arms. "Where?"

I gave him Mim's name and address. "Hurry. I'll be there as soon as I can."

Cole grimaced at Tom's desk as the two deputies started in our direction. "I know these guys, Free. They won't let me leave."

"*Just try.*"

Without another word, Cole headed for the doors. A deputy stopped him, speaking low enough I couldn't hear. Cole gestured to the outside and whispered back. The deputy shook his head.

All my pieces fell apart.

"What's your name?" the other one asked me, his voice as kind as Tom's face.

I couldn't cry or speak or breathe when the other cop removed sleeping Little from Cole's reluctant arms.

I lost him.

Cole came back to me, defeat sagging his cheeks, as the cop carried my brother through the same double doors Daddy had disappeared behind.

I lost him.

CHAPTER 14

Cole

Girl's Escape Attempt Foiled

Free wouldn't look away from the ER doors. Not when Deputy Smith asked her questions. Not when I wrapped an arm around her waist. She was catatonic, her face so pale her lips blended with her chin.

"Free?" I whispered in her ear when Smith asked for her name again.

She blinked once. Twice. Then sobbed as if she'd finally heard my voice.

I held her so tight my fingertips went numb.

Smith sighed, his face drawn. "I know this is hard, young lady. I know. But the faster you give us some information, the faster we can help."

Free shook her head against my chest. "I can't."

"What about you, son?" Smith rubbed the back of his neck. "Who're you in all this?"

I swallowed. "Her neighbor. She came to me… after."

"And your name is…?"

"I already told Deputy Christie."

"Now you can tell me."

"It's Cole. My name's still Cole Anderson since the last time I said it a minute ago."

Recognition brightened his eyes. "That's right. You're Mike Anderson's kid."

I lifted my chin. "Yes, sir."

"Well, *Cole Anderson*, can you give me some info, then?" he asked, frustration tightening his voice. "Names of this girl and that boy, at least? Did you tell Deputy Christie *that* a minute ago?"

"No."

"Well?"

Her name was her secret. I knew that now, and it killed me. *Please forgive me*. "Freedom and Landry Paine."

Smith nodded and turned toward the ER, leaving us alone.

"I'm sorry." I pulled Free to the chairs and held her on my lap as I had her brother. "So sorry," I repeated, smoothing a hand over her long, tangled hair.

She didn't yell or scream. She didn't move. "I lost him," she whispered. "I lost him."

What could I say? Nothing. Nothing would make this better. I kept my mouth shut and held her.

What felt like hours later, Free lifted her head from my shoulder, her eyes puffy and red. "Do you remember the address I gave you?"

"Yeah."

"I need you to go there. I need you to tell Mim what happened."

I tucked hair behind her ear. "I will."

She looked over her shoulder at Smith and Christie coming out of the ER. "If I don't see you again… Everything you've done…"

"I'll see you again," I said as the deputies drew closer. "*I'll see you.*"

Christie helped her to her feet and asked if I had a ride home. Before I could answer, Free spoke to them for the first time. "He brought us in his car." She didn't glance my way as she lied.

"You have a number where we can reach you?" Smith asked me.

"I don't have a phone."

"Same address as your old man, up there in Poplar Branch?"

"Y-yeah, yes." I shivered now, cold without Free on my lap.

Christie spoke low to Smith, and he nodded. "Get yourself home now," Smith said. "I'll know where to find you."

I watched Christie take Free through those double doors. She limped, droplets of blood coming from her left heel. "What'll happen now?"

"We'll take good care of them, son." Smith palmed my shoulder as if it were an afterthought. "Go on. It's late."

Smith turned, and, while talking into his shoulder radio like he was part of the secret service, he disappeared behind the doors. My eyes darted from the ER to the desk guy to the exit. Why would she lie about the car? Did she think I'd be waiting at the front doors with the engine running?

"They're safe now," the desk man said.

I nodded but didn't move.

"I promise you, they'll be *fine*."

No they wouldn't be. But damn. Not a thing I could do just standing there like a fool.

I dug the keys out of my front pocket on the way to the exit. The parking lot lights, the cold air—it all turned hazy as if this were one of those dreams where I floated naked in a crowded room and could do nothing about it.

I got in.

Started the car.

Listened to the loud, groaning engine.

Stared at the ER entrance.

Waiting for her.

If she had wanted me to be her getaway driver, I'd have done it.

I waited.

And waited.

Escape plan number one? Become Superman. Cliché and unoriginal, for sure. But trust a kid brought up in the holler: it'd take Superman's powers to escape it. He'd have been able to help Free. Not some skinny kid from Poplar Branch, whose talents consisted of writing messy words in notebooks and fixing old cars.

Because she wasn't coming.

I pulled out of the lot and drove to the address she gave. If I couldn't save Free from whatever was going on with her brother and her beat-up dad, I could at least pass on her message.

I parked behind an Olds on blocks. In the dark, with the moon as a piss-poor guide, the thing appeared as a formless metal blob. But I knew cars. I understood them as well as the words I wrote, and I could tell the make and model by the curve of the rusted bumper and taillights. Seeing an immobile car on stilts wasn't anything new around here, though. Standard lawn decoration.

No inside lights came on when I knocked. I lifted my fist again, pounding a little harder this time. Still no lights.

You couldn't get lost in Davy if you wanted to. This was the place. Had to be. Unless Free gave the wrong address. Damn, that'd be bad.

Finally, a light.

Another.

I stood straighter, exhaling. An outside light came on, and a woman peeked from the side of a curtain covering the door window. She narrowed her eyes at me, and I could hear her say, "What do you want?" through the thin windowpane.

I cleared my throat. "Free told me to come. She… she's in trouble."

She let the curtain down, and a second later, the door swung open. The woman whom I assumed was Mim had dark, straight hair in a messy ponytail over her shoulder and wore a green terrycloth robe. "What kind of trouble?"

"She…" Where to start?

"You're Gina and Mikey Anderson's boy, ain't you? From Poplar Branch."

"Yes, ma'am. Cole." I'd given my name to more people tonight than I had my entire life.

Mim peered over my shoulder. "Why're you driving Free's car?"

"She gave it to me."

"Bull."

I held up my hands. "No, yeah, you're right. She… The cops, she lied to them."

She didn't blink once. "You got to the count of five to make sense before I call the law on you."

Shit.

"One."

"Wait! I—"

"Two."

"All right, fine."

I told her everything. How Free came to my door without shoes. How her dad's ankle dangled from his leg. How his nails were all pulled out.

God…his fingers.

How I drove them to the hospital and the deputies showed up.

I stood on Mim Alcott's porch and talked and talked. My voice grew hoarse, and my cheeks were wet by the time I'd explained how Free cried against my chest, repeating, "I lost him." How she cried and how I couldn't do anything about it. This woman became my priest to whom I told my sins and final fears.

She rubbed my arm, her unblinking eyes now blinking rapidly, lashes pointy with tears.

"So that's it." I dried my cheeks with my shirtsleeve. "That's all there is."

"Okay, then." Mim nodded once and turned, leaving the door open as she walked inside.

Whether she meant it or not, I took the open door as an invitation to follow. At that moment, she knew me better than my own mother. That gave me the right to come inside and beg her to make this better.

Mim went to a wall phone in the kitchen, her mumbling rant about Landry Paine being a no-brained idiot reaching my ears.

"What're we gonna do?" I asked.

"*We* ain't doing nothing." She dialed a number, cursed, slammed the receiver onto its cradle, and picked it up again.

I stepped forward, my soles squeaking against the linoleum. "But—"

She rested the receiver between her ear and shoulder and reached for a notepad and pen on the counter by the toaster. "Go home, Cole. There's nothing you can do now except pray."

"No, no, we—"

She turned her back to me and spoke in low tones to whoever answered on the other end.

"Ms. Alcott?"

Her back heaved with a deep breath. "Hold on." She faced me again. "What?"

"Will they be okay?"

"I don't know." Her voice broke. "I just don't know."

I didn't answer any questions Mama and Hannah hit me with as soon as I walked through the front door. Mama stumbled behind me, not willing to take silence for an answer, until I locked myself inside my bedroom. I lay down on my mattress, not bothering to take off my shoes and hoodie, and stared at the mugshots of my family.

Freedom Paine, the girl with secrets. And even after tonight, I still wanted to know them—so I could protect her from them.

"Boy, you best open this door," Mama demanded with slurred words. "I ain't done talking yet."

"I'm tired. I'll explain in the morning." When she was sober and back to the nicer version of herself.

"You little…"

She pounded on my door and ran through her list of names she liked to call me when I pissed her off. I shook my head and focused on Dad's mugshot. His lips curved in a smirk that stank of pride. As if getting put away was a badge of honor. I let out a breath when Mama got bored of yelling and staggered away.

"Colie?" Hannah tapped on my door a few minutes after Mama left.

I stifled a groan. "What?"

"Everything okay with you…and that girl?"

A pause. "Yeah."

"If you need to talk…"

No, I didn't want to talk. I turned out my light and rolled to my side.

CHAPTER 15

Free

$\mathbf{F(I)}^{jr}_{<}\ \mathbf{L}^{sr}$

We lay on an uncomfortable bed in the ER while waiting to see Daddy. Little couldn't stop fidgeting, and the paper sheets crinkled every time he moved closer to me. He smelled like hospital soap. So did I. Nurses had given us scrubs and cloth slippers to wear after we were led into a bathroom and told to clean up. When we made it back to our room, our bloody clothes were gone.

Good.

I sighed and tucked blankets under Little's chin. Why were hospitals so cold? No matter how many thin blankets they gave us, Little's teeth continued chattering. I pulled him tighter to me and again searched the walls for a clock. Still had no luck finding one. Who knew how long we'd been here, but I was almost positive night had turned into morning.

"All right, kids." Deputy Smith opened the curtain in front of the bed. "He ain't conscious, but y'all can say goodbye before we leave."

Finally.

"Thank you, sir," I said.

Little held my neck, not saying a word, as I slid off the bed. I ignored the burning in my left heel where they'd put four stiches, and carried my brother down the hall behind Deputy Smith. When we stopped at Daddy's bed, machines beeped around him and his hands were wrapped in white gauze. Splotches of blood plumed on his bandages, a macabre tie-dyed pattern. Little gasped and smashed his face against my shoulder.

Don't you dare fall apart.

"It's okay, buddy." I rubbed his back and averted my gaze from Daddy's hands. "He'll get better."

Deputy Smith cleared his throat. "I know this isn't ideal."

I nodded and shuffled to Daddy's side. "Little," I whispered. "Come give Daddy a kiss."

He shook his head without lifting his face and held me tighter, his delicate fingers pressing hard against neck.

"Are you sure?"

A nod.

"Okay." I bent to kiss my father's forehead for both of us. "I'm sorry, Daddy. So sorry."

At the sheriff's department, Little and I sat in a room with three plastic chairs and a rectangular table resembling a chemistry table. Two cups of orange juice and two packages of graham crackers sat in front of us, untouched. One mirror covered the back wall. One thick, metal door.

The kind of room claustrophobics have nightmares about.

Little curled into my lap and twined my hair around his finger. "Are we in trouble, Sissy?"

"No, we're not in trouble."

"Why're we in the police room?"

"I guess they didn't have nowhere else to put us."

"How long do we have to stay?"

I kissed the tip of his nose and pasted on a smile. "We've been here ten minutes."

"It feels like forever."

"You thirsty?" I asked, changing the subject.

He shook his head.

I reached for a cup and sipped, the juice too sweet, and gestured to the crackers. "Hungry?"

He shook his head again.

"Tired?"

"No."

"Little." I set the cup on the table. "It's safe here, you know."

He let go of my hair and snuggled to my chest. "I know."

"You do?"

"Yes." He pressed against my heart. "Because you'll always be right behind me."

God. *Oh, God. Oh, God.*

My promise meant nothing now.

"Little—"

A *click* filled the room, followed by the door swinging open to Smith's exhausted face and some woman with blond hair clipped at the sides. She wore kindness like makeup, eyes soft and mouth turned up in a slight smile.

Smith sat across from us, dropping a manila envelope on the table. "This here is Miss Drury. Works with Children and Youth."

She nodded to me. "Hello."

"Hi, ma'am," I said, the polite words hurting my throat.

Little ignored her and turned his face into my neck.

"Miss Drury will be taking Landry out for a minute to let him use the restroom, maybe get him some hot breakfast. Young man?" Smith tapped on the table until Little turned his head. "Would you like something to eat? Fill your belly?"

Little shook his head then cupped my face in his tiny hands. "I don't want to go away from you."

His fingers were icicles against my cheeks, stinging reminders that I had failed him for the thousandth time. "It'll only be for a second, okay?"

He studied my face, his blue eyes piercing mine with his fear and doubt. "Don't leave me."

I nodded, my voice lost to the misery clogging my throat.

His fingers pinched my skin. "Don't leave me," he repeated.

I opened my mouth and prepared to lie when Miss Drury came over. "Come on, Landry. Deputy Smith wants to talk to your sister for a bit."

"No," he wailed and held my face tighter. "*No, no, no*."

"It's okay," I managed, pushing him off my lap. His fingernails left tingling tracks across my cheeks. "It's all right."

"It's not okay! Stop saying it because it's not!" He shrugged away from Miss Drury and scrambled to my lap again.

"I'm sorry, Little." I forced him from me once more. Losing contact with him was like having my arm ripped off. "I'm sorry."

He stood there and cried. "Don't leave me," he whispered a third time.

I shook my head, my pieces ready to explode into nonexistence. "I won't."

"We have a bunch of yummy things to eat with your name all over it." Miss Drury took his hand. "I'll bring you back here in no time." She spoke to him about empty nothings while guiding him to the exit.

Little turned my way when the door opened. He held his hand out to me with tears and hiccups and shaking fingers before disappearing down the hall with Miss Drury.

A sob escaped as the door closed behind my brother, and I had to cover my mouth to prevent more from coming out. I focused on Smith's tired eyes. I was the wrench in his night. The thing preventing him from going home to his no-doubt comfortable bed in his no-doubt cozy house.

Stop. No self-pity. No dwelling on failing Little. Strength, even if it were a disguise masking the ashes. I uncovered my mouth and cleared my throat. "Did you lose the coin toss?"

Smith gave me his undivided attention as he opened his envelope and pulled out some papers. "Coin toss?"

I gestured to the mirror. "Christie. Did he get to leave after you pulled the short straw, or is he behind that mirror, ready to be good cop to your bad?"

Smith laughed, a sort of sleepy, surprised chortle. "Good one."

"Which is it?"

"Option one." He pointed at the papers, his smile drifting into a frown. "We have a lot to talk about, Miss Paine."

I shifted. "I suppose we do."

He folded his hands on the papers, his wedding band glinting in the dim light. Without his hat, he appeared older. Silver weaved through his dark hair, and his hairline struggled to stay close to his forehead. He could've been someone's grandfather. I wondered if he was this nice in his real life. If his family was happy when he came home from a job dealing with people like me. "Let's start with who attacked your father."

I studied his weary, light eyes, saying nothing.

"Do you know the person or persons involved?"

More silence.

"Freedom. You staying quiet ain't helping nobody."

And talking would make it worse. Duffy's threat screamed louder than Smith's kind face. I continued to peer at his eyes, trying to clear my mind of everything but wondering about their color. Green? Blue?

He hefted a loud sigh and searched his papers. "We found something when we ran your father's name."

My back muscles tightened, and I had to remind myself to breathe. I knew this would happen, prepared myself for it the minute I gave Tom the Desk Guy my father's name. Didn't make reality any easier.

"Seems he found himself a spot of trouble in California." Smith shifted a piece of paper for me to see. WARRANT typed in bold letters filled the header. "Kidnapping and failure to appear in court."

I slid my gaze lower on the sheet to see Daddy's picture, an old one of him and Laura while she was pregnant, and Little's pre-school photo.

The second time I'd ever seen my father cry was right before we left California—after the hearing where Little's grandparents won custody of him. He drove directly to the pawn shop and sold Mama's engagement ring for the old shotgun, a box of shells, and gas money. We were going to show them that living in our car was only temporary. That Daddy would find another job. That Little wouldn't be safer with his grandparents.

Everything we'd done to stay together came down to a sheet of paper.

"Where, exactly, in Poplar Branch have you been living?" His voice stayed gentle, concerned, but he kept the warrant visible, a reminder that he had me dead to rights.

I wrapped my hands around my stomach. "Byron Mumford's old place."

"I know the house. Not a place fit for a coon to live." A pause. "Y'all squatting?"

I shook my head. "My mama was a Mumford."

"Where's she now?"

"Dead."

Smith cursed under his breath and squeezed the bridge of his nose. "I'm sorry to hear that. I truly am."

His voice sounded so genuine I believed him.

He leaned forward. "But, Freedom, we have ourselves a real big problem here."

I nodded.

"And once your daddy's up to it, he'll be extradited to California to face these charges. You understand what that means?"

I clenched my fists until my nails dug deep into my palms. "No." Yes.

"He'll be transported back to where the crime was committed." Another heavy sigh. "They're gonna put him in jail."

"For how long?"

"My guess is a year or two."

A year or two. Not too long. Not forever.

"While he's away…" His voice lowered, going gentler than it had been all night. "While he's away, you'll be put in foster care."

"What about Litt—Landry. What about him?"

"We called his grandparents last night. They'll be here in a couple hours."

Everything hurt, the pain scorching. Needles poked into raw flesh.

I lost him.

Tears fell unchecked, and it took all I had not to crawl under the table and wail like Daddy had after Mama died. "He… I…"

Smith silently handed me a handkerchief from his pocket.

"Maybe…maybe I can go with him. Maybe they'll let me."

He was shaking his head before I got the words out. "We asked, Freedom. They're afraid you'll take Landry again and run away."

As much as I hated his grandparents for no other reason than taking him—they had always been nice people—they were right. But—

Fear made me sit up straighter. "His mother…sh-she's not allowed to—"

"We know. Her parents said she ain't around, anyway. No clue where she is."

I nodded, not satisfied. Not anything but hollow.

"We have a home for you here in McDowell County. You'll get to go to school, be in a warm house with decent people. Be a kid."

I barely heard him, my mind dull. "I-I have a friend. Mim Alcott."

"She called last night, said she'd take you in, but…" His sighs rivaled the echoed screams in a train tunnel. "She's a single woman with three kids. Part-time job, rent she's behind on, no room for another mouth to feed. The state requires foster homes to…"

I stopped listening. Until he said Little's name.

"…thought you'd like a chance to tell Landry goodbye."

My head snapped up. "Is that woman telling him everything?" I was once again a savage animal protecting her young, bared teeth and foaming at the mouth.

Smith's blue or green eyes were sympathetic as if he understood the wounds my violence hid. "We thought it better if you told him." He thumbed over his shoulder, toward the mirror. "We'll be watching, of course, but you'll have until his grandparents arrive."

My fangs retracted, leaving only the hurt behind. Hours. I had hours to amputate the most important part of me.

CHAPTER 16

Free

F - L = 0

Little sat across from me, a plate of breakfast, computer paper, and crayons between us. We didn't touch the food, the scrambled eggs turning hard and dark yellow. I scooted my chair closer to the table while Little drew—the woods and a turkey flock flapping their wings. For the last hour or so, while he colored and asked math questions, I tried to tell him, tried to dig courage from deep under my cowardice to admit I'd failed him.

"Sissy?"

I blinked. "Yes?"

"Will you talk more?"

I studied him, his carrot hair and pale skin, committing everything to memory. "About what?"

He kept his attention on his picture, making lines for the sky, repeating them mechanically as if he didn't realize the crayon was still in his hand. "Don't care."

You will care! You'll care and you'll hate me.

"Do you remember where we lived before here?"

Little shrugged, still drawing those blue lines. "Yeah, home."

I focused on his hair. God, I'd miss running my fingers through it while he slept. "Did you like it there?"

Another shrug. More lines. "Not her."

"Right, but besides her, did you like it? Do you remember your grandparents?"

His lines darkened as he pressed harder on the crayon. "I think so."

I covered his hand, forcing him to stop. "Look at me, Little."

He shook his head. "Are we done camping?"

"We're done."

"Are we going home?"

"Not exactly."

"Then what?"

"Come here," I said. "Come sit on my lap."

He didn't move. "Are we going home, Sissy?" His repeated question was an accusation, like there were a million other things he demanded underneath.

I forced myself up and moved around the table, gathering him into my arms and sitting in his chair. When I had his weight on me, I took a selfish moment to lock the feeling away. This would be the last time I'd feel whole. "You are. But… not me."

His cries were quick and excruciating. He wrapped his arms around my neck and pressed his face against my heart, sobbing and pleading with me. "You promised. You promised!"

"I know," I kept repeating. My voice came out in a spiraling, wailing moan.

I rocked, wishing the motion would throw us backward, back in time before coming here, before living in the Buick. Back to before Daddy and I made all the wrong decisions—

Wait.

Wait a minute.

We wouldn't say goodbye. Never goodbye.

"Little. Listen to me, okay? Listen real close."

He continued to cry, but at least he stopped repeating his heart-puncturing words.

I pulled back to meet his swollen eyes, mine feeling as large and puffy. "I'm not going home—not yet. But I will, you hear me? This is only temporary."

He wiped the back of his hand under his eyes as hiccups shook his chest. "How?"

I found a red crayon and brought his turkey picture closer. "Let me show you." I drew on the upper right side, near his orange and yellow sun.

He rested his cheek on the table as I wrote. "December 26? Your birthday, Sissy."

The day I had stopped celebrating. Until right now, this very moment.

"Yes."

"Why?"

"It's our magic."

"Our magic?"

I circled the date with a black crayon. "As soon as this date comes, I'll be on the road to California, and I won't stop until I'm at your house."

Little ran his fingers over the waxy numbers, his hiccups dwindling to heavy breaths. "You'll stop camping and come home?"

This boy. This perfect, beautiful boy whom I lied to. "Yes, Little. I'll stop camping." I went on to tell him how many months until the magic date. A little over three. Folded the picture and stuffed it into his hand and explained exactly how many days it would take me to get to him. Told him I wouldn't stop to sleep.

He stiffened on my lap, clutching the picture until the paper crackled in his grip. "Are they giving me to her?"

"No, Little, no." I squeezed his thigh and kept my voice unafraid—the total opposite of the inside. *Please don't let this be a lie!* "You'll be staying with your grandparents, and they got a nice house and a back yard with those prickly cactus plants. A gray cat, too. You remember, don't you?"

He nodded. "But you'll start driving right after Christmas, in the Buick?"

"Yes." I brushed hair from his temple. "Make sure you look for me."

"And you won't get lost? Even if you don't see my hand?"

My insides turned to acid-dipped tentacles, twisting and closing up my airway. I brought his cheek to mine and took in his smell, the texture of his skin, the feel of his breath against the side of my nose. "I won't get lost."

Less than an hour later, he was gone.

"Okay!" Miss Drury tapped a few more times on her keyboard. "That covers it."

We spent the last hour at a desk in the main room with her asking me questions about where I lived in California, how we lived there, the name of my school, if I had any relatives because they found none on my records.

I answered on autopilot:

Needles—like they didn't already know.

Needles High School, where Daddy had been a janitor for about a year until he got fired for missing too many days. Days he'd spent taking care of Little when his mama went missing and I had school. We rented a small house a couple of miles from school grounds that we lost about the same time Daddy lost his job.

No relatives I knew of except a set of grandparents I had never met somewhere in West Virginia. Daddy's folks refused to speak to him after he went "slumming" and married a girl from Poplar Branch. I had no idea if they were still alive.

I didn't mention Byron Mumford. Neither did she.

And I missed Little so much the pain ate away flesh and bone.

"That all you need from me?" My foot ached. My head ached. My eyes. My legs. I had been awake for over twenty-four hours, and whatever adrenaline rush I had before drained to empty.

She nodded. "I'm sorry for all you're going through, Freedom, but we'll take good care of you."

I stared out the window over her shoulder.

"And Jolene, ah, Mrs. Mabry, takes in a lot of our kids." She hesitated. "You'll like her."

Our kids. In a matter of hours, I had become a ward of the state of West Virginia.

Her warm palm covered my ice-cold hand, startling me enough to give her my attention. "It'll be great," she said. "Just great."

I swear sympathy had become a color since stepping into the hospital. Smith's eyes weren't green or blue. They were sympathy. Light sympathy, same as Miss Drury's.

"Freedom?"

Speak of the devil. I turned to face Smith behind me. "Yes, sir?"

He wore his hat again, hiding his receding hairline and shadowing his sympathy eyes. "We have some deputies fixing to go to the Mumford place, check things out. You have anything you might want us to get? Clothes, personal items?"

I took my hand out from under Miss Drury's and nodded. "They're in some bags by the door."

"Y'all planning a trip?" He was still digging.

"No." And I was still not answering.

He sighed his heavy sigh. "I'll drop your things at the Mabrys' later on today."

After he left, Miss Drury and I waited for this Jolene woman in the lobby. My eyes stayed glued to the glass exit door. I wanted to leave this place where Little was pulled from my arms. As his grandfather took him from me, Little lifted his turkey picture: *I have our magic, Sissy. I have it.*

"There she is." Miss Drury's voice gave off that high-pitched, I'm-about-to-lie tone. "Mrs. Mabry is so concerned about you. Why, when I told her…"

I don't care!

I don't care!

A woman spilled out of one of those dark blue minivans resembling a rocket ship from the front. Despite her weight, she moved like a waddling sprinter, at the door in seconds. A man lagged behind her, skinny and scowling with a cigarette dangling from his mouth. I stood straighter and took a breath. *Here we go…*

"Is this her?" Jolene asked Miss Drury as soon as she came inside. She blended with half the middle-aged women around here. Curly, over-processed blond hair. Thick makeup, but not thick enough to fill in the creases on her forehead and cheeks. Polyester, flowered blouse and too-tight jeans.

"Yes, ma'am," Miss Drury said, moving to shake Jolene's hand. "And let me say how much we appreciate you taking her on such short notice."

Jolene nodded. "You see this a lot, I'm afraid. Poplar Branch ain't no place for kids, infested with drugs and low-life nobodies." She tipped her chin in my direction, her blue-shadowed eyelids lowering some. "I want you to understand, young lady, me and Mr. Mabry done gave our lives to the Lord, and He's called upon us to take care of His misbegotten children."

"Thank you?" I peered over her shoulder to whom I assumed was Mr. Mabry. He stayed outside, turning his scowl toward the gray sky. "Both of you."

I wanted to disappear into the air and manifest on Little's new doorstep.

"God's grace is thanks enough." Jolene held me by the wrist as if I were five years old and guided me to the van after a quick goodbye to Miss Drury. Mr. Mabry—Kenny, she'd called him—brought up the rear. As soon as she opened the side door, stale cigarette smoke stung my nose, and when Kenny started the car, gospel music blared from the speakers.

Too tired to cry and too empty to care, I snapped on my seatbelt and closed my eyes.

Nine thousand twenty-two times four hundred...

PART II

CHAPTER 17

Cole

Girl Missing

"Where the hell'd you find this?" Deacon pounded on the Buick's roof after I parked beside his truck and got out.

His loud, familiar voice almost made me crack, but nah. Embarrassing myself in front of Mim last night had been more than enough. "It's Free's."

A grin sneaked to the corners of his mouth. "Is that so? She your girl now? Did y'all…?" He pumped his left index finger in and out of his cupped right hand.

Hell no. Free wasn't a lewd hand-gesture girl. "You're such a dick." I trudged toward the school, backpack slung over a shoulder and wearing the same clothes I had worn last night. Except for the sweatshirt, which was balled on my bedroom floor, covered with blood.

"Hey, man! Hey!" Deacon caught up with me, adjusting his ball cap to sit lower on his forehead. "What'd I do?"

"Nothing." I stopped and ran a hand through my hair, my eyes gritty with exhaustion. "You haven't done anything. It's just… I had a night last night. A bad one."

Deacon narrowed his eyes. "Richie make it home?"

My best friend, always the hero, even to me. He'd been itching to take on my brother since the last time Richie blackened my eye, a week before staties pinched him and Dad for selling. I was sure Deacon could take Richie now—and surer that I couldn't, which sucked to admit.

"No, not yet."

Deacon's shoulders dropped some. "It got something to do with your mystery girl and that ugly-ass car, then?"

"Yeah, ah…" I tilted my head toward a bench underneath a bare-limbed poplar tree, away from the kids rushing in before first bell. "Over there."

Deacon shrugged. "Lead the way."

By the time I purged my guts, skipping the crying and rambling that came out when I had confessed to Mim, Deacon's eyes were wide and his jaw was slack.

"Sucks, you know?" I said, picking a dead leaf apart. "She's gorgeous, smart, and some sort of… of…"

"Felon? A criminal, maybe?"

I shook my head. "I was gonna say secret."

"A secret felon."

"Sure, whatever." I dropped the leaf and stretched out the kinks in my shoulders.

"Look, just keep me in the loop." Deacon stood. "I'm not about to let a bunch of white trash jump you for being guilty by association."

"*I'm* one of those white-trash folks, remember?"

"But you smell better and still got your teeth."

I laughed. "Silver linings, I guess."

"Exactly." He pointed to the door with a grin. As we walked, he said, "You need some cliff time?"

More than anything, I'd love a chance to yell at the entire world. "Nah, not today. I have some stuff to do after school."

"You need me to come with you?" Deacon's voice dipped low. *Geez.* Sometimes it felt like Amy and I shared a boyfriend.

"I can handle it on my own." I wiped snot from under my chilled nose, the fall cold attacking in its usual lazy way. "I *am* a grown-ass man, for Christ's sake."

He clapped me on the back as we entered school, the first bell ringing politely in the halls. "There's nothing manly or grown about you."

And I patted the top of his head. "Except for the two inches I got over your stumpy ass."

"Except for that. Jerkoff."

Optimism was a dangerous thing. It could always backfire at the last second, give a reminder that pessimism—realism—was a better mindset to have. Whatever settled in the half-empty glass tasted better. But sometimes, if I stayed positive, it seemed good stuff prevailed over the bad. The latter swelled in my chest on my way to work after leaving Mim's.

Before I started my shift, I sat at the break table and pulled out my notebook:

Hope Remains for Missing Girl

- *Powers-that-be denies Mim guardianship over Free.*
- *Bonus: Free's in a foster home in McDowell County (Here!!!!).*
- *Whereabouts of Landry sr. and jr.: "Not for me to tell you."*

"Hiya, Cole." Mr. Gifford rushed to the back, blotting what looked like spaghetti sauce from the front of his shirt with a towel. Smelled like sauce, anyway. He gestured to it with a smile and reddened cheeks. "You wanna come help me clean my mess? Got broken jars and sauce everywhere on aisle four. Looks like a bloodbath out there."

Reluctantly, I closed my notebook and stood. "Yeah, sure. Be there in a sec."

"Appreciate it."

As Mr. Gifford went for the mop and bucket, I put my stuff away and donned an apron. Dang, I couldn't stop grinning, even while I sopped up nasty tomato sauce and broken glass.

Here.

Somewhere in my tiny part of the world, Free still existed.

And I would do whatever it took to find her.

Idea 1081
Avenger

CHAPTER 18

Free

$Pr(E) = \frac{n(E)}{n(S)}$
Measure of Intelligence

Cigarette smoke wafted above our heads as if the minivan had a carbon-monoxide ozone all its own. Another girl, Sarah, rode with me on the way to school. We didn't speak or look at each other, our silence like the silence in California, when Daddy would drive around looking for a safe place to park the Buick at night. The gospel music droning from the speakers couldn't hide that sort of desolate silence—it was how defeat sounded.

We drove into a parking lot as busses pulled into another next to us. No matter where the location, school was school, with half-awake kids schlepping to the doors and teachers hurrying in with smiles for anyone who took the time to glance up from their shoes. I sort of missed it. The learning part, anyway. Not so much the people part.

"Y'all meet me back here as soon as they cut you loose, you hear?" Jolene tapped out her cigarette before pushing the release button for the side door. "Don't make me wait."

Sarah mumbled "okay" and shuffled out to join the rest of the herd going into the building. I sat there, pulling my flannel tighter around my chest, thankful I had it back. Smith dropped off my things last night, or so Jolene said this morning when she brought the garbage bag into the room I shared with Sarah and two younger girls. We slept in bunk beds, each with a sheet, blanket, and pillow. Not bad. At least there was heat.

One question automatically tripped from my mouth when she woke me up: "Smith say anything about my father?"

Her answer: "They ain't gonna give me that information."

Every minute since waking up I thought of him and Little. The place Little went to was clean, thankfully, better than the shack we made him live in. The only thing keeping me from losing it was the knowledge he didn't end up in foster care with strangers.

But the thought of my father, trapped in some jail…

Christmas. All we had to do was hold on until then. They allowed visitors in jail, right? And Daddy would come up with a plan when he got out. He always came up with something. We'd be together again. I had to believe it.

Had to.

Jolene turned to me. "Freedom?"

I flinched at the sound of my name. "Where…Where do I go?"

"Office."

"Office?"

"Uh-huh. First door on the right as soon as you walk in."

"Ain't you coming?"

"You need me to?"

"Well, don't you have to sign stuff or whatever?"

"Did it yesterday while you slept. They got your records emailed over already." She clicked her fake nails along the back of the passenger seat. "Do you want me to come with you?"

I groaned and waved residual smoke from my face on my way out. "No. I can go on my own."

The door hadn't closed completely before Jolene backed up, leaving me in the middle of the parking lot. I gripped the strap of a borrowed backpack and frowned at kids who sneaked peeks in my direction.

You can do this. One foot in front of the other. I took a step, then another, my stitched heel throbbing. Stopped. Tried to slow my breathing. I scanned the cars and some kids running toward the door. I scratched my arm. My thigh. My skin felt way too tight.

I should've just—

Yes!

I stopped searching the lot; I didn't need to see anything else. Because there it was, in the third row parked by an old truck. Rusted blue body, crack in the passenger side window, and the spot on the back panel where Little and I scratched a game of Tic-Tac-Toe with the key after a particularly boring day while we still lived in it.

The Buick.

I limped to my car, and when I reached the driver's side, I dropped my bag and pressed against the window with one hand and tried the handle with the other. I wanted to curl into a ball in the back and hide away from the world until the day after Christmas.

Open!

The door wouldn't budge, but that didn't stop me from yanking on each handle. Tiny mewls left my mouth, the sounds of a cornered animal—or a psychotic person trying to break into the least attractive car here. In the distance, a bell echoed. I looked up and found no one else outside. Only me and the Buick, stuck in a foreign place without my family.

I bent to retrieve my bag, and blood on the back seat caught my attention. Brown rust slashed tan cloth, a pattern that looked like Cole had scrubbed the upholstery but rushed to get it done. Daddy's blood.

Tears stung my eyes as I closed them.

Five thousand eighty-four times fourteen...

Seventy-one thousand, one hundred seventy-six.

Four thousand eight hundred twenty-nine divided by—

My eyes snapped open.

The Buick parked in the lot meant one thing.

Cole was here.

Flashes from two nights ago filled my head, when he helped without question and how he held Little, and then me when I needed it most.

Maybe he'd help me again.

I'd spent a good amount of time in a counselor's office just like this in junior high, right before Little was born. It was small and next to the principal's bigger, more intimidating office. Posters covered the walls with "inspiring" words about never giving up on the future, and college brochures scattered tops of cabinets in an inconspicuous way.

Behind the desk sat the typical "caring" person only too happy to hear students' deepest fears—so they could pass out a pamphlet on blended families, the dangers of unprotected sex, or other nonsense.

The caring person *du jour* happened to be Mrs. Juanita Callahan, according to the name plaque on the edge of her desk. She had the standard nice face, a Miss Drury face. But unlike my social worker, Mrs. Callahan didn't have that naïve, I'm-new-to-this quality to her niceness. Hers had the I've-heard-it-all wrinkles at the corners of her eyes and creases around her mouth. She appeared about forty with dark, flawless skin and black hair cut into one of those fancy bobs like women on TV.

"Freedom? You can talk to me."

If I sat any straighter, my spine would snap. "Okay."

"Is there anything that *isn't* okay?" She grinned. "You've answered the same for every question I've asked."

I peered out the window behind her. To the fall trees and their dead leaves littering the ground. To the lot where the Buick was parked. Anywhere but at her stare that rivaled Mim's.

"I spoke with some of your teachers from Needles High. By what they say and from reading your transcripts, it's obvious that you're an exceptionally bright young woman. Mr. Jorden said you had your sights set on MIT."

I bit my thumbnail to hide my surprise. This lady actually took the time to contact my old school?

"Technically you're still a junior, since you weren't in attendance during your last month, but your course of study was on track with our senior curriculum here, all AP classes. Impressive."

Silence.

She shuffled through the papers. "I also see you were on the mathlete team and took your SATs."

I shrugged.

"Do you know how well you did on the test?"

No.

"You scored a fourteen ninety, well above average."

For a moment, pride gushed through me. I'd studied hard for the SATs, banking my future on them. Not anymore, though. No test would save my family from our situation.

Another shrug.

"You can ignore me all you want, but I won't stop talking."

I bit and bit until my nail reached below the nail bed. The pain sparked memories of Daddy's fingers, all bare of nails, all mangled and loose skin. Only two nights ago. Two nights and here I was, forced to start a new chapter.

I focused on her no-nonsense brown eyes. “Can you do something for me?”

She folded her hands on papers I guessed were my high school transcripts. “I’ll try.”

“My father… I need to know if he’s okay. Maybe find out where they’re taking him?”

“I don’t think I’ll be able to find out.”

Something about her instant change, how her lips pulled down and sympathy clouded her eyes, allowed my desperation to seep to the surface. I didn’t want her to feel sorry for me; I was tired of people feeling sorry for me. I wanted to make sure Daddy was still breathing.

“Please,” I begged. “No one’ll tell me nothing, and… and they only let us see him once. I ain’t allowed to go back to him either. I got no idea if—”

“All right.” She reached over and covered my clenched hands. “I’ll see what I can do, but you have to do something for me.”

Of course. “What?”

“*Try*, Freedom. I want you to try.” She let go of my hands and sat back. “You put in the effort, and so will I. Deal?”

I shifted and rested my hands on my lap. “What do you want me to do, exactly?”

“Focus on your education. Don’t let that intelligence go to waste.”

“I’m not keen on going through eleventh grade again.”

“I don’t blame you.” She tilted her head to the side. “So, I’d like to put you in senior-level classes. We’ll spend the rest of today testing, and if you perform well, we’ll get you into classes tomorrow or the next day.”

“That it? All I have to do? Take some tests?”

"That's all." She pulled out more papers and a few pencils.

I leaned forward, eyeing what she spread across her desk. Algebra, calculus, geometry. Math? I could do it in my sleep. "Anything else you want?"

"Matter of fact…"

Had to ask, didn't you?

"I want you to come see me before homeroom, every morning."

"For what?"

"To talk."

"Sure." I shrugged. "Why not?"

"Good. Now," she started, and slid the algebra sheet and a calculator my way, "we'll work on math this morning, and if you finish before lunch, we'll move on to English after. Tomorrow, we'll work on science and history, then hopefully have you starting classes by the afternoon."

"Can't wait," I quipped and brought the paper closer.

Three hours later, I'd breezed through the math assessments. Each time I finished one, Mrs. Callahan would give me the next and leave the office with the completed test. We didn't speak while I worked. Meaning, she didn't try to dig below my surface, and I didn't knock her down with more attitude.

"Okay, time for lunch." Mrs. Callahan handed me a slip of paper with a number: 312512. "This here is your student ID number. Punch that in, and your—"

"I know how free lunch works."

"Well, aren't I lucky, what with you saving me from saying two more words and all?"

My face heated. Her attitude outshined mine, and I was too brain-exhausted and hungry to compete. "Sorry, ma'am."

The corner of her mouth tipped up. "Forgiven. And—not that you care—but the way you handled those tests…Mr. Stuben has already graded your algebra exam. You aced it."

I would hope so since I made it through Algebra II by eighth grade. "Who's Mr. Stuben?"

"Math teacher here."

"Oh. Well, what of the other ones?" I sailed through them all, and a part of me felt small for wanting to hear someone acknowledge it. "He get to them yet?"

"He should have them finished after lunch. If all goes right, you'll be seeing him in calculus soon."

"Calculus? If I'm going to be in the class, why'd you make me take the test?"

"Curiosity." She winked. "Torture."

"Funny."

"I think I am." She stood and smoothed her red skirt. "Let's get you something to eat."

Kids didn't crowd the halls between periods like I had expected, but there were still enough to stare at us as we walked by. Mrs. Callahan said grades seven through twelve went here. Like Needles, small and everybody knew everyone. Not a good thing in my current situation. Mrs. Callahan went on and on about Mountain View like we weren't the main attraction in a three-ring circus. I had no idea what she said, catching a word here and there. It was hard to listen when my armpits warmed with wet heat and my knees shook. I almost laughed. After all I'd been through, doing the initiation march down a new school's hallway felt worse than pumping water from the well on a freezing morning.

"Here we are." Mrs. Callahan stopped at the cafeteria entrance. Posters hung on the white brick walls, most handmade and about a homecoming dance. "All seniors eat at the same time."

"For real?" The room was half empty and quiet as far as cafeterias went. Round tables filled the middle with a separate room off to the right, one door marked "Enter" and the other "Exit"—the kitchen and dish stations.

"For real." She waved me inside. "Eighty-seven seniors—now eighty-eight."

"I haven't taken all the tests yet."

"No, but I have faith in you."

"Thanks." I perused the sea of students, searching for oceans.

"Can you remember your way back to my office? Or… maybe you want to take lunch there today?"

I shook my head, already leaving her side to follow the short line toward a stack of trays by the "Enter" door. "I'll stay here."

"All right, then. See you in a half hour."

I nodded, not giving her anything else. I was too busy scoping the round tables for the only friend I had in the universe.

Where are you?

CHAPTER 19

Cole

Missing Girl Found

I'd devoted the entire night to figuring out a way to find her. A waste of time. All I had to do was go into the cafeteria. *Poof!* There she stood, searching the room with a tray clutched in her hands, oblivious to the people staring at her—including me.

"Hey, man. What the hell?" Deacon shoulder-checked me. "You're supposed to walk in, not stand out here like a moron."

"She's here," I said, rubbing my shoulder.

"Who's here?"

I pointed.

"Oh. That her? Your sort-of girlfriend? She's pretty."

"She's not my 'sort of' anything."

Deacon snickered. "So…your *real* girlfriend?"

"Will you shut it?" I pushed hair from my eyes. "You're always running your mouth."

Deacon being Deacon helped me relax, though. Reminded me that I shared the world with more people than the one person standing twenty feet from me.

"Are you gonna talk to her or stare like some crazy-ass stalker?" He shoved me again. "Seriously, dude, you're being pathetic."

"Yeah, yeah, ah…" I glanced at our regular table. Jess already feverishly whispered to Amy while they gawked at Free. *Great.* "What about them?"

Deacon nodded their way. "Got that situation covered. You go find out what's up with your girl."

"She's *not* my girl."

"Whatever." Deacon headed to the table, taking an apple from his lunch sack and chomping into it on the way.

Move!

My stomach protested when I bypassed the lunch line and twisted when I made it within a foot of her. "Hey."

She turned to me, her face pale with dark circles around her eyes. "Cole." My name drifted off her lips like a relieved sigh.

When I spent last night figuring out a way to find her, I also imagined what I'd say when I did. It would be something confident or bold. Power words, positive ones.

"You're here." I cringed. Those two words weren't on last night's list.

Tears floated in her eyes, turning them topaz. "I don't know what to do."

I scouted the cafeteria for an empty table, finding one in the back. "C'mon."

She followed me as I weaved around tables filled with kids I'd gone to school with since kindergarten. Their curious eyes pointed at Free. When I looked at her, I thought her beautiful, a star trapped in a cosmos of duds. What did these people see? Just her old clothes and tired eyes? Probably.

"Thank you," she said as we sat. "Have I said that yet?"

I covered her hand. "You don't have to thank me."

She shook her head, eyes fixed on our joined hands. "Everything is so messed up."

"I know."

"I lost him, Cole. I lost them both."

"I know."

"Stop saying 'I know.'"

"Okay."

She laughed then, a wet, grainy sound. "You have a way with words."

I smiled. "Undercover poet, at your service."

"Poet, huh? Didn't realize poets wrote for newspapers."

"Call me Clark Kent…whose superpower is killing it with the stanzas."

She snorted. "Dumb."

"Thanks."

She lifted her gaze to mine, and I smiled wider. Without taking my eyes from hers, I grabbed the napkin off her tray and blotted her cheeks with it. "You like to play the hero, don't you?" she asked.

"Not always."

"I don't believe you. Add *Leave to Save the World* to your escape plans; I'd believe that idea." She took the soggy napkin from me and wiped her nose with it. "I was doing fine before I saw you. Done crying, you know? Formed the beginning of a plan and everything."

Physics prevented me from moving closer to her, my chair already overlapping hers. Sucked. "Plan for what?"

She folded the napkin into a tiny square, concentrating on the task. "I'm going to them."

"Where are they?"

"California."

California? She might as well have said Mars or Jupiter. Same distance as far as I was concerned. "When?"

"Day after Christmas."

"Why then?"

"My eighteenth birthday." She peered at me with swollen eyes. "I saw the Buick outside."

"Mim said to keep it until we talked to you."

"Could you? I mean, until I leave. They put me in this… this place, and I doubt they'd let me…"

"'Course, Free. Anything you need." I rubbed my palms on my jeans. "Some things need a look. The heater core's going, and the gearshift slips."

She began picking at her food. "Yeah."

Damn it! It'd be nice if just one situation would go as I practiced it in my head. "I'm telling you 'cause I can fix it, at least give it a shot."

Free stopped pushing her mashed potatoes around her plate. "Really?"

"Uh-huh. If Mim's not aiming to do anything with that Olds, I could maybe use it for parts."

"She calls it her someday project." She shrugged. "But I could ask—if I see her anytime soon."

"I'll ask." I winced at how my voice cracked. "I can go after school."

"You can?" Hope filled her eyes. Good. Maybe I actually said the right thing for once.

"Sure. Ah, I can fix old cars. My dad taught me…" *Stop!* Enough word vomit. "Anyway, yes."

She pressed a palm to her heart. "Thank you."

"No problem."

I turned toward Deacon when Free forked a bite and popped it into her mouth. My friends' stares were drilling holes in my back. Deacon mouthed *Are you okay*, while Amy gave her it's-all-right smile and Jess frowned. I shook my head and faced Free again. No, not okay at all.

I had until Christmas.

When her plate was clear, I asked the one question that came out exactly how I wanted: "Will you tell me now?"

She took time swallowing her last bite. "Tell you what?"

"Everything. But we can start with Sunday night."

"Not much to tell."

I laughed, catching the attention of a few tables in front of us. Laughing was better than yelling at the top of my lungs. Since that night when she kicked me out of her life over secrets, I'd been holding on to my temper. And now she had the nerve to blow it off like it was no big deal? *After* she said she was leaving? Fuck that.

No.

"You owe me more, Free. Way more."

"I know."

She gave nothing else.

I stood when the warning bell dinged and lifted her tray, my anger simmering. I didn't care about right words anymore, not when the need for answers took over. "Let's go."

"Where?"

"You tell me."

She stood, wringing her hands. "Oh…um, counselor's office."

The halls were full of seniors going to their next class, and sophomores and juniors heading to the cafeteria. Free waved at a girl who nodded back before bowing her head over books clutched to her chest.

"Who's she?" I asked, steering her around a group of kids.

"Sarah, from…home. I share a room with her."

"Oh." Right. "The place you're at okay?"

"I guess."

We didn't say anything else until we reached the office. "I'll come back at the end of the day," I said, catching her elbow when she moved toward Callahan's door. She wouldn't get off as easily as she had at lunch. I knew exactly what to say now. Questions burned in my throat, and I was tired of dealing with that pain.

She tugged on her arm until I let go. "I won't have much time."

"Look, I can't help if—"

"Jesus, Cole!" Her anger lashed out, triggering mine. "Why is it so important?"

"Because you're important!" The commotion in the office, the kids in the hall, everything disappeared. I didn't give a shit about anything or anyone except for the girl in front of me. "Because I want to know why you're in a foster home." I lowered my voice. "And why your family's in California and why the *fuck* your dad had his nails yanked out."

Stories traveled across her face. Wide eyes, a scowl, complete and utter devastation. I wanted to take back my words then. The way her mask lifted to reveal vulnerability erased my anger and filled me with the need to slay her dragons. It was the same feeling I had when I found her on the road in front of my house. When she banged on my door two nights ago.

"Mr. Anderson. Do we have a problem?"

I lifted my head to see Callahan behind Free with her arms crossed and mouth turned down. "No, ma'am."

"Freedom? Is everything all right?"

She nodded without looking behind her, those tortured eyes all mine. "Yes."

"Are you sure?"

"Yes, ma'am, I'm sure."

"Okay. Well, time to get back to work." Callahan uncrossed her arms. "Say goodbye, Mr. Anderson. You'll be late for class." She left us alone amid everyone else in the main office.

I kept begging Free silently.

"You might hate me if I tell you."

"Never."

"You say that, but…"

"Tell me one thing. One. I'll prove it to you."

"All right." A pause. "My dad got arrested."

"I reckoned that much, Free. And if that's what you're afraid of, I got news for you: my dad and brother's been in the jailhouse for over two years now."

"What a crappy thing to have in common."

"But not rare around here. Why'd they take him?"

She swallowed, her throat bobbing, and whispered, "Kid-napping."

CHAPTER 20

Cole

Mystery Girl Wanted for Questioning

Kidnapping.

Kidnapping?

Holy hell.

"You want us to hang with you until she comes out?" Deacon asked. He, Amy, and I leaned against a row of freshmen lockers near the office.

"Nah, I can handle it on my own."

"When you introducing us?" Amy snuggled to Deacon's side, her goth-punk getup and pale complexion complementing his button-down shirt and dark skin. "I mean, really. You finally like somebody and you're keeping her to yourself."

If only this were as simple as liking some girl. "Tomorrow. But you gotta take it easy with her."

She laughed. "What the hell you think we'll do?"

"Not y'all I'm worried about."

"Jess?"

I winced. "Yeah."

"Give her a few weeks seeing you with Free, and she'll realize she didn't like you that much. Seen her do it before with

Chris Jacobs. Honestly, I think she enjoys the idea of liking someone. The chase."

"If you say so."

"I do," Amy said. "Anyway, why's Free in school now? What happened?"

I shook my head, a not-quite-true excuse on my tongue. "She—"

"Give him a break, Amy. Girls are new to our monk friend." Deacon held out his fist to me and winked in his I-got-you way. "Need to get to practice. We're going to the cliff after. Coming?"

I ignored his comment and gave his fist a bump, thankful he stopped his girlfriend's interrogation. "Hell yes, I'm coming. Meet y'all at the field in an hour."

"Sounds good," Deacon said.

Amy looked up from chipping at her black nail polish and surprised me with a hug. "Looks like you need one of these."

I awkwardly patted her back. "I look that pathetic, huh?"

"Yep!" Deacon snatched Amy from me and tucked her back under his arm. "You got your own now."

Amy lightly punched Deacon in the chest. "Jealous much?"

"'Course not." Deacon tipped his chin in my direction. "Later."

"Yeah, see ya," I said, watching them disappear outside.

My friends were total head cases. Thank God.

I felt a nudge to my side and peered down to find Free, her face impassive. "Surprised you came," she said.

"Why wouldn't I?" I tried not to act like her presence turned me inside out, and waved to Callahan.

She nodded to me with a frown.

"Uh-huh, thought so." I pursed my lips.

"Thought what?" Some of Free's shield fell, allowing curiosity to slip into her voice.

"Callahan has you in her crosshairs."

"That a bad thing?"

I thought of my stint as one of her projects last year when she convinced me to take my SATs. She gave up on me after I stormed out of her office when she got too personal, too close to what really happened at home—where I wasn't the writer. Where I wasn't a goddamn thing.

"Nah, not a bad thing," I said. "She'll just try to save you. Ready?"

She rolled some pamphlets, the paper crinkling in her hands as they became tubes. "You still want to talk after what I told you?"

"About your dad?"

She nodded. *Crinkle, crinkle.*

"Like I said before, you'd be surprised how many people around here have the same story as you."

She moved in closer with an almost-smile when kids rushed the halls, their after-school chatter loud. "There's a horde of kidnappers in McDowell County?"

I grinned and headed outside. "A horde of criminals."

"Daddy isn't a criminal," she said, walking beside me.

"No? Why don't you explain things to me, then?"

She didn't reply, her eyes straight ahead while she tapped the pamphlets against her leg.

Whatever. I'd let her have her silence—for the next thirty seconds.

Once we made it outside, I steered her to the Buick when she tried to veer toward a blue minivan.

"If I don't go over there, she'll get mad."

"Who?"

"Jolene."

"Who's that?"

She rolled her eyes. "Foster mom, Cole."

"Right." I kept my hold on her elbow until we reached the Buick. "This'll just take a sec."

"If you want my story, writer-man, you'll need longer than a second." She crammed the rolled paper into her bag.

"Then just give me the headlines for right now."

"Huh?"

I leaned against the front bumper. "You know, Man Gets Arrested for Dog-Knapping. That sort of thing."

"Okay, fine. Headlines…" She lifted her chin toward the sky. "Man Takes Son Away from Potentially Abusive Situation."

"Your brother?"

"Yes."

"He your real brother? Not some kid from the street?"

"No! I mean, yes, he's my real brother." She pulled her flannel closed and shivered. "Stupid thing to ask."

"Disagree." I touched her cheek and directed her attention from the minivan to me. "What about you? Were you in an abusive—"

"Never."

By the way her expression tightened, I could tell this subject was off limits. Something to ask Mim about. I cleared my throat. "Good. Another."

She huffed and stomped her foot. "Um…Man Steals Ginseng from a Cocksucker."

"Colorful. Who'd he steal it from?"

Her gaze faltered. "None of your business."

Oh, shit. "You've been threatened."

She moved away from the car with another huff. "Stop it. I'm not your story."

Yes, you are. Had been for a while, but I let it go. For now. "Fine. Next topic: find a way to see me outside school."

"How?"

"You're a smart girl, Free." I hid my worry behind a small grin. God knew which crazy asshole in the holler had threatened her. "Find a way."

"Great advice."

"Maybe I'll follow you and break you out tonight."

Challenge lit her eyes. "Maybe you should."

I opened my mouth to tell her that'd be exactly what I was willing to do when Sarah came out of the minivan and hurried toward Free. I gestured to the younger girl. "You gotta go."

Free turned, and her shoulders slumped. "Crap."

Sarah reached Free's side and whispered in her ear before lifting her hand to me. I smiled at her, and her cheeks flushed as she ran back to the van.

"You're going to Mim's?" Free asked when we were alone again.

"Yep. Right now."

"Good. So…see you soon." She turned to the van. The driver—Jolene, I assumed—rolled down her window, letting out a cloud of smoke. She fussed as Free got in.

For a second, I imagined myself striding over there and cussing the woman out. But Free was strong, and she'd survive.

As soon as the van left the parking lot, I pulled out, too.

Time to fill the gaps.

I expected Mim to purge herself of Free's secrets, give me the answers I needed without having to ask the questions. My plan: knock on her door, stare her in the eyes, and say, "I know about the kidnapping."

Did that.

Didn't work.

Mim was the hardest, most tight-lipped interviewee I'd ever come across in three years of interviewing people. When I smiled, she blew smoke above my head and rolled her eyes. When I complimented her hair—I got desperate—Mim said to "use your wiles" on somebody who didn't wait tables all day on swollen feet, handled three boys, and had twenty years on me. Shot. Down. Hard.

She gave me a few scraps, though:

Mystery Girl Slowly Unraveled

- *Mim Alcott and Free's mother were childhood friends. (Mother died of bladder cancer when Free was 11.)* ☹
- *Byron Mumford (bastard), Free's uncle (!!!!), is the reason Landry Sr. ended up half-dead and arrested, as far as Mim is concerned.*

"What about Free's dad," I asked her as I wrote. "What's your opinion on him?"

Boy, did she have an opinion:

- *Landry Sr. is a "no-thinking cloud-head, who couldn't make a right decision if it slapped him in the face and stole his nose."*
- *Free's input: Landry Sr. stole ginseng from "a cocksucker."*

"Anything you can tell me about Landry Jr.?"

"A bit," Mim said.

- *Landry Jr. has an abusive mother in California and he now lives with said abusive woman's parents—as far as Mim Alcott is aware.*
- *It wasn't kidnapping so much as "not listening to the courts when they tried to steal the boy away from the only family he knows."*

I stopped writing for a second when Mim got up to refill her coffee mug. Man, I'd have never guessed Landry Sr.'s story. Pills? Yes. Heroin? Almost definitely. Not a root you had to spend time digging and finding a legit buyer for to make a profit.

When Mim returned to the kitchen table, I continued, "You know who Free's dad stole from? I think they threatened her."

- *"Maybe it's best you leave it alone."*

After that, I scribbled down some thoughts of my own:

- *Why would Landry Sr. risk it?*
- *Byron Mumford (Could be possible suspect)*

He'd been one of Richie's friends—until Byron stole from him. I'd have to keep an eye out for the guy.

I asked Mim one more question:

- *Mim's answer to request for use of Olds: "She don't need me contributing to her wrong decisions."*

I closed my notebook after that and thanked her.

No, Free didn't need anyone helping her, but I would. As I pulled in next to Deacon's truck by the football field, I racked my brain trying to determine exactly how I could help while making sure she didn't do anything she might regret.

Idea 1082

A Rocket to the Moon—Two Seats

Amy gave me the answer a couple hours later at the cliff after I let her and Deacon in on everything. "Well," she said, pulling a blanket tighter around her shoulders, "I only see one answer."

"Which is?"

"You need to go to California with her."

CHAPTER 21

Free

$$\bar{I} = \frac{\Delta q}{\Delta t}$$

Electric Currents

Jolene's house didn't look any better this afternoon. Not that it was disgusting, but it wasn't any place where I wanted to spend much time. Kids half-dressed, some with dirty faces, glanced up from playing with broken toys when we walked in. Two others, obviously in elementary school, sat at the coffee table in the living room doing homework. No excitement brightened their faces. No fear. Empty. Same look Sarah had.

At supper, we sat around a big table, eating boiled hot dogs and macaroni and cheese. Jolene made us bow our heads to pray. Kenny didn't participate, though. He smoked at the head of the table, his eyes pointed to the small, outdated television sitting on the kitchen counter. After we ate, the kids scattered like cockroaches.

There were four bedrooms, three upstairs and Jolene and Kenny's off the kitchen, with one bathroom next to the room I slept in. The bathroom smelled faintly of sewage, and brown stains circled the sink and tub drains. But the toilet flushed, and water ran through the pipes.

I showered before bed, using a suspicious bar of soap. There wasn't a towel anywhere, forcing me to dry off with my flannel before putting on a fresh pair of sweats and a T-shirt.

After dressing, I stayed in the bathroom and pinched my leg a hundred times to avoid losing it. Not because of this house with its empty-eyed kids, but because of a garbage bag. All of Little's things were in there with my clothes. His book and socks and the pair of pants I bought him with the sang money. His blue calculator.

What was left of my last chapter fit inside a garbage bag.

On my way into the bedroom, I overheard Jolene yelling at Kenny downstairs. Not crazy yelling. The demeaning kind. The yelling that made a person sorry for being human. I closed the door on Jolene's voice and lay on my bottom bunk, staring at the top mattress and imagining a rescue by the boy with ocean eyes. How would he find me? Climb on the porch roof and knock on the window like in those movies where the boy saves the girl?

"You awake?"

I sucked in a breath, and my face heated as if Sarah heard my fantasy. "You scared me," I whispered.

"Sorry."

I turned to where she lay on the bottom of the other bunk bed. The room wasn't big. If I scooted to the edge of the mattress and extended my arm, I'd have been able touch the side of hers. "Don't be. Good to know I can still get scared."

"That don't make sense."

"Nothing does anymore."

"Yeah." She scratched above her eyebrow. "Why're you here?"

"Same reason as everyone else, I guess." I shifted to my side, careful to keep my voice low. The younger kids fell asleep a while ago, and last thing I wanted to do was wake them. Sleep was probably their only vacation. "What's this place like? Pretty bad?"

"Depends on what you consider bad," she said softly. "Compared to what I came from? Not bad at all."

I winced, not asking her to elaborate. "Sucks, Sarah. It really does."

"It's life."

"Not much of one."

She pulled her blanket to her chin. "You get used to things."

We stayed quiet for a moment, neither of us obviously good at talking. I forgot how to "friend" a long time ago. The skill required practice, and I hadn't practiced much since California.

"How many kids live here, exactly?" I asked. "I counted eight."

She nodded. "That's right. It changes every so often." She rattled off names I'd never remember. "I've been here for over a year, and twenty different kids have come and gone."

"A revolving door, huh?"

"It's how Jolene makes money."

"Kenny seems like a jerk," I whispered. "He don't talk much."

"He got laid off from the mines a few months back, and he's been extra mean since. Jolene's decent, though, and they don't hit no one." She paused. "Kenny don't touch none of the girls neither. Better than the last place they stuck me."

Oh God.

"Better than most," she said, turning away from me. "Trust me."

I sank deeper inside myself and tried not to blame my father for everything. We hadn't become rich from digging ginseng. We became broken.

I closed my eyes.

Six hundred twenty-two times eighty...

Divided by nine hundred twenty-four...

Fifty-three point eight fi—

The sang money!

I sat up and fished around at the bottom of the bed until I had my bag open. Moonlight glinted off the shiny cover of Little's book, where I put the rest of the money plus another forty dollars. I let out a breath after opening the worn pages to the middle. *Still there!* All hundred fifty-one dollars. Not enough to get to California, but a start. I lay back down and held the book as if it were my brother's sleeping body.

Three months. Three long months.

"Sarah?"

"Yeah?"

I thought of how Cole fit life into headlines. Mine at that moment: Girl's Heart Flees to California. "I'm sorry you have to be here."

Quiet. Then, "I'm sorry you have to be here, too."

"Okay, Freedom, you're almost set." Mrs. Callahan squinted at her computer screen, her reading glasses at the tip of her nose. "I have you in American History first period, calculus second... physics? No, you've already taken that. How about Chemistry II? Then lunch..."

I spent the first few hours of the morning taking tests and must've done all right, since we now worked on my schedule. She could put me in whatever class she wanted. None of them meant a thing to me, a big change from school in California. Stupid to dream. Look where Daddy's dreaming had gotten him.

Daddy...

"You hear anything about my father?"

Mrs. Callahan glanced up from her screen. "I have a friend who's a nurse in pediatrics at the hospital, and I spoke to someone from the sheriff's department." She folded her arms on her desk. "I've left messages, last night and this morning. As soon as I hear something, I'll tell you."

A rogue tingling of respect blossomed in my chest. She upheld her end of the bargain, and by obligation, I had to hold mine. "So what's after lunch?"

She smiled. "You've been paying attention."

"Of course."

"Well, let's see." She returned her attention to the screen. "English, hmm…we have room for an elective last period."

"Just stick me in something," I said, chewing my nail to nothing and bouncing my knee.

"Stick you in something, huh?"

"Don't matter to me what it is."

"Okay." She clicked a few keys. "Psychology? All juniors in that class, but there's a lot of space left."

"Why psychology?"

"Thought it didn't matter."

"It don't." My leg bounced faster. "Be a waste of time, is all."

"Well, that's what we specialize in here, Miss Paine. Wasting people's time."

"Ha-ha."

"Glad you appreciate it." She smiled again, still tapping away on her keyboard. "Okay…done. You're now an official senior at Mountain View High. Congratulations."

"Great."

"No, stop. Please refrain from all the excitement," Mrs. Callahan deadpanned as the printer hummed behind her, spitting out my schedule. She handed it to me.

I accepted it with a grin. She *was* pretty cool. "Thanks."

"Welcome. Now…" She took out a map of the school from a drawer and told me how to get where I needed to be, circling my classes, the cafeteria, gym, auditorium, and so on and so forth. She pointed to my homeroom and a row of lockers, and I glanced at the clock while half-listening to her directions.

Lunchtime.

My heart flipped. Cole would be there, and I tried to tell myself the reason I wanted to see him was to find out what Mim said about the car.

When Mrs. Callahan finished explaining, she folded the map and handed it to me. "All right, time to—"

Someone tapped on her door, one of those polite, hesitant knocks you hear in a doctor's office before the physician enters the room.

"Come in," she said.

When the door opened, relief turned my insides to clouds. "Hi," I said, standing.

Cole flashed me his crooked smile. "Hey."

"Mr. Anderson." Mrs. Callahan waved him in. "Good to see you here again."

Some of the light in Cole's eyes dimmed. "I'm not—I'm here for Free."

"And how do you two know each other?"

"We were neighbors," I said and went to Cole's side, getting as close as I could without touching him.

"Interesting." Mrs. Callahan nodded once to Cole. "Would you be so kind as to walk Freedom to the cafeteria? Maybe help out with her schedule?"

"Yes, ma'am," Cole said, already waving me out of the office. "See you later."

"I hope so." Mrs. Callahan then smiled at me. "Tomorrow, before first bell?"

"I'll be here," I said on the way out.

As soon as we were in the hall, Cole reached for my hand. And I gave it to him.

CHAPTER 22

Free

$f(x) \int f(x)dx$
Integration

So this was Deacon Mallory: dark and gorgeous, wide shoulders, buzz-cut hair, and quarterback of the varsity football team.

Amy was harder to define. Goth, pretty and pale, and interested in knowing my entire story. Weren't goth people s

upposed to be sullen? View other people as annoying flies in their black bubble?

Cole sat beside me, his tray untouched and his notebook at his elbow. He didn't ask any of his questions after going over my schedule, circling classes we had together with a smiley face: homeroom, history, calculus, and English. But he didn't interrupt Amy's questions either when she got on a roll.

"So… y'all were living in that shack by Cole's house?" she asked. "No electric or nothing?"

I stabbed at my peas, trying not to withdraw or lash out, my usual MO. "Right."

"Like camping sort of," Deacon said between bites.

Camping. The word bit into my heart a little too hard. I nodded, concentrating on making sure my fork reached my mouth without incident. "Sort of."

"Where're you from? Originally, I mean." Amy shook her chocolate milk. "Somewhere around here?"

"Bluefield. My mama was from Poplar Branch, though." I sneaked a glance at Cole. "She grew up in the house we stayed in."

He smiled, unsurprised. Looked like Mim filled him in. Wonderful. Nothing better than feeling like a talking point.

Amy's green eyes then clouded with empathy. "Cole said you have a younger brother."

Enough. No more friending.

I dropped my fork on top of my food. "I do," I told her, my tone saying what my words didn't. *Shut up!*

"Oh." Amy bowed her head, cheeks flushing.

Silence overtook the table, leaving the background cafeteria chatter. I let it, not caring about school politics or social mores. *Hello, Mountain View, I'm Uncomfortable, ready to stir things up.*

Cole cleared his throat and opened his notebook, rifling through the pages. He didn't write in it or read his headlines. He used it like a sword, or maybe a shield? "Now that we've gone straight to Awkwardtown…"

I stared at my hands balled in my lap. "Guess I'm not ready to talk about things."

"You don't have to, Free," Amy said. "We can talk about other things."

I lifted my head. "I'm game for anything else."

"Okay." She gestured to my shirt. "Do you have any other clothes besides those jeans and that Pearl Jam T-shirt?"

"Christ, Amy! What's gotten into you?" Cole kept flipping pages without glancing at them. "Didn't expect *you* to act like a douche."

"Yeah, babe," Deacon added. "Kinda shallow."

"I ain't trying to be mean! I'm asking for a reason, if y'all would shut up for a second and listen." She enunciated the last word slowly.

Cole and Deacon might not like this subject, but I had no problem with it. A surface subject with an easy answer: "Nope, not really," I said. "Most things I owned got worn out pretty quick once we moved here."

Amy fiddled with her nose ring. "I have some clothes I don't wear no more if you want them. You can come over, or I can bring them here. Whatever's easiest."

"That'd be great. Thanks."

Amy offering clothes in better shape than mine was like Mr. Gifford handing over outdated groceries. Survival 101, plain and simple.

"No problem. They're just hanging in my closet doing nothing." She glared at Cole and nudged Deacon. "See? The word is l-i-s-t-e-n," she spelled out.

"Touché," Deacon said.

Cole pulled on the neck of his T-shirt, no longer "reading" his notebook. "Ah, sorry, about the douche thing."

"Well don't expect me to forgive y'all right away." She sat straighter. "Not every day a girl has two boys groveling at her feet."

The guys laughed and began joking with each other, both digging into their food as if the diffused tension gave them appetites.

Amy turned to me and mouthed, *We okay?*

I nodded and smiled at her.

My shell cracked a little. Maybe I wanted to be part of something else besides survival, even if it were only for three months.

The girl from Gifford's, the pretty one with perfect tan skin who always watched Cole when he wasn't looking, sat next to Amy. They greeted each other with nods, and the new girl mumbled something about being late.

"Hey," Cole said to her. "Where've you been?"

"Nowhere. Just finishing a story." She was all smiles and wide eyes. The kind of smiles and wide eyes a person wore when they were hiding frowns and tears.

Cole moved his chair closer to mine, the legs screeching against the floor. "You all right, Jess?"

Everyone watched them in silence.

"Absolutely. Pulled a *you* and didn't get it done last night." Jess held out her hand to me. "Hi. Jessica Hernandez. Jess, for short."

I shook her hand. "Freedom Paine." I grinned, at a loss for anything else. "Free, for short."

"You know who she is," Cole muttered.

"Freedom Paine, huh?" Jess asked me, ignoring Cole as she peeled a banana.

"My mama was sort of a hippie," I said. My mother's explanation after my first day of kindergarten, when a boy made fun of my name: *To be free you got to experience pain. I experienced an extra amount pain growing up in the holler, so I shared my abundance of freedom with you.*

"Must be nice," Amy said. "My parents are boring." She pointed at herself. "Amy. They gave it enough thinking time to give me *three* letters."

"What'd you want your name to be?" Cole asked. "Stardust? Lily Pond?"

"Well, yeah. Why not?"

"I love your name, babe." Deacon smoothed his thumb over her earlobe. "Amy's a hot chick's name."

"Impossible," Amy said, but she blushed and leaned in to kiss him.

Jess continued to watch me. "So, you—" She closed her mouth. Shook her head. And gathered her things while frowning at Cole. "No. I can't."

Cole sighed. "Jess, come on."

Tears floated in her dark eyes. "I can't, okay? And screw you for expecting me to."

No one said a word as she stormed out of the cafeteria.

Just a few days ago I took my father to the hospital, lost my brother, and was put in foster care. Now I was in school, hanging out with people who weren't my family, and dealing with a jealous girl. The transition from the former to the latter felt like whiplash.

I had no idea who I was anymore.

At least Cole was in English, my first class since California, along with Jess and Deacon. Deacon talked to me until the warning bell, introducing me to people I'd never remember and cracking jokes about one or two of them. Cole interjected himself into the conversation some, and Jess continued ignoring me. I nodded in the right places, shook my head in others.

Inside, I screamed.

Psychology went better. A waste of time, sure, but quiet, which I appreciated. Sarah was in the class, too. She didn't try to talk to me or get me to sit next to her when Mr. Jane said, "Pick a seat. There're enough empty ones."

I chose one in the back, near the window. Twelve kids were in the class. Most took notes and listened to Mr. Jane explain cognitive behavioral therapy. Sarah was like me: staring out the window with a frown that said "People like me don't need classes like this."

Cole met me at my locker at the end of class. He smiled as I walked up, and my heart did its usual flutter thing when he smiled at me. My shoulders relaxed, too. He was alone. Good. No new friends to deal with, no angry girl to ignore. Just Cole and his oceans.

"Hey," I said, clutching books to my chest.

"Hey." He opened my locker after I gave the combo and handed my backpack over. "Class go okay?"

I packed my books in the middle pocket. "If you mean, did the one class I had without you last forever, yes. Yes, it did." I didn't know where that came from or if it was bold or blurting. But when his smile deepened, I didn't care.

"Good," he murmured. "Look, about Jess…"

"It don't take a genius to see how she feels about you."

He rubbed the back of his neck, not meeting my eyes. "Yeah."

"Are you guys…?"

"No." He looked right at me then. "Absolutely not."

"It don't matter or nothing."

"It does to me." He peered over my shoulder and then behind him toward the exit to the parking lot. "Talk to me a minute, will you?" He took my elbow without waiting for a reply and led me down an empty hall. He didn't stop until we were at the end, near a boys' restroom. "I'm not ready to give you up yet."

I melted and formed again. Formed around his words. "What?"

"I don't want to go outside and have your foster mom breathing down our necks."

"Why? You have more annoying questions to ask?" I teased.

Oh, that smile. That smile, that smile. "As a matter of fact… I was wondering something."

"You're always wondering something."

"You got me there." He opened and closed his mouth. Then, "How're you getting to California?"

"Drive."

"No shit. But how? It costs money."

"I got a few bucks, and…I haven't figured it out yet." I glared down the hall. "Why do you care?"

"Are you serious?" His voice dropped to a whisper.

Dang it! He'd been there for me every time I needed him, and I still lashed out after hard questions. An apology sat on the tip of my tongue, but he spoke before I could let it go.

"When will you get it, Free? When will it sink into your head?"

"What're you talking about?"

He stepped closer. And closer. Closer until I felt his breath against my cheek. "I'm talking about you. *Everything* in my life lately is about you, and it's making me crazy."

"Why?"

He brushed a finger across my bottom lip. "Because you gave me cookies."

I shook my head, not able to think with him so close, so warm, and feeling so good in my personal space. "You're dumb," I managed.

He snorted, diffusing some of the tension, the good kind of tension I wasn't sure I wanted to go away. "Agreed." He backed up and leaned against the wall. "Now, as I was saying…"

I licked my dry lips and tried to recover as fast as he had. "You weren't saying anything. You were asking."

"Same difference. Money."

I leaned against the opposite wall. "Any suggestions?"

"Maybe one or two."

"Well? Are they secret suggestions?"

A grin. "Maybe one."

I groaned. "*This* isn't helping."

"First, you seriously gotta find a way to leave that house. You need a job."

"Had a job. Lost it."

He shook his head. "No, you didn't. I talked to Mr. Gifford and explained things…without explaining things."

My heart did its Cole flip. "You did?"

"Yep." He pushed off the wall. "You think that woman'll let you work?"

"Don't know." I bit my lip, already working out a way to convince Jolene to let me leave. "What's your second idea?"

"Not gonna tell you until we get the first step out of the way."

The way he stared over my head, avoiding my eyes, made me nervous. *What are you thinking?* "What if the first step don't work?"

"You'll make it work." He sighed and tipped his chin down the hall. "C'mon. Now's as good a time as any to try."

That night, after sweat and worry and stomach-twisting anxiety. After asking Sarah what I should do and after her answer to go for it. After hiding on my bottom bunk while the two younger girls, Kate and Shelly, played with broken Barbies. After stalling, stalling, stalling, running through Plan A, Plan B, Plan C, all the way to Plan Z, I found out it was easy as going into the living room and asking the question.

"I got a few rules first," Jolene said, sitting on the couch and smoking a cigarette. "Show me you can be trusted, I'll let you out starting Saturday. But you go to church with us every Sunday morning, be in this house by seven on school nights, and ten on the weekends. First time you break my rules, leaving privilege is cut off."

The last time I'd been inside a church was for Mama's funeral, but for a chance to leave this house and work? I'd make it right with Jesus for that.

"Thank you, ma'am."

CHAPTER 23

Cole

Mystery Girl: Math Genius

I waited for Free outside Callahan's office, pacing, sitting, and standing to pace some more. Every plan I'd hashed out rode on Free being able to make money.

Please have found a way to get out.

As soon as Free left Callahan's office, she beamed at me. "You waiting for me?"

"Absolutely." I held up my hands. "So? Jolene letting you out?"

"Starting Saturday." Free spouted off rules about curfew and church, but all I heard was yes.

"So you're free, then?"

She laughed. "Since the day I was born."

I loved her laugh. Loved it. "Smart-ass."

"I thank you." She mock-curtsied, her mood brighter than usual. "Anyway, Callahan let me call Mr. Gifford, and now I'm on the schedule this weekend…with you."

"Well, it's about time something goes right." I tipped my chin toward homeroom. "C'mon."

"*And*," she said on our way to class, "Mrs. Callahan also found out where my dad's going. I can write him letters, and she'll mail them for me. He needs to get me on his visitors' list."

My heart sank, but I forced the smile to stay on my face. "Day's looking better and better."

"I'd say so."

I didn't want to think about her being gone forever, so I shoved it from my mind for the rest of the week and watched her, talked to her. Considered the second part of the plan I had yet to tell Free, the part my friends convinced me was a good one. Jess even helped with the planning—probably to help get rid of Free as soon as possible.

But going to California would eat up my apartment money, giving me a longer stint in Poplar Branch. Could I do it? I was willing to give it a shot. I mean, why not play the hero like Free accused me of being? A man only had a few chances in life to prove himself worthy of more than what God gave him.

I wanted to wait until Saturday to break it to her, when we'd be alone. Maybe a cowardly move, maybe strategic.

It was surreal to see her every day, though, in this world separate from the holler. Here, I was Cole Anderson, senior and newspaper editor. Not Cole Anderson, white trash who lived in a dilapidated trailer.

Amy and Deacon treated Free as if she'd always been part of our group—and Jess would come around. I hoped. Amy also brought in those clothes she'd promised, as Deacon had been doing for me in secret since the sixth grade. For some reason, I felt closer to Free because of it, like she was made from the same fabric that constructed me. Except her fabric consisted of numbers where mine was sewn together with words.

Seriously, I'd never met anyone who loved math the way she did. Case in point:

Since the beginning of the year, Mr. Stuben put impossible equations on the board. He'd definitely watched *Good Will Hunting* too many times. Deacon and I always joked about his obsession with finding his own personal genius. Jason Hawthorne, the only junior in our class, was as close as Stuben had gotten, and it wasn't that close. We were convinced not one person in McDowell County was smart enough to decipher what those numbers, squiggly lines, and letters meant.

Then Freedom Paine walked into class.

"Hey, Free, ever see *Gifted*? *The Theory of Everything*? Any movie that has anything to do with a genius?" Deacon joked while we waited for class to start.

Free's brow furrowed in a way that made her more beautiful. "Huh?"

Deacon pointed at the whiteboard. "Stuben's on the prowl for West Virginia's most brilliant mind." He shot a thumb behind him, toward Jason's desk. "He's *numero uno* so far." The kid shot spit balls across the room and cackled when one stuck to the neck of a girl in front of him.

We laughed, thinking Free would, too. No, she focused on the whiteboard, her eyes shifting back and forth, lips pursed. The equation hypnotized her. Or relaxed her, maybe? Deacon hit my shoulder and mouthed, *What's she doing?*

I shrugged and watched the way her features softened as her mouth began to move with silent numbers. Was she…? No. She wasn't…

"Free?"

She blinked as if she'd forgotten where she sat and concentrated on me. "What?"

"You can solve that?" I pointed to the board without taking my eyes from hers.

"I think so."

"Yeah?"

She nodded.

Pride swelled my chest. It weirded me out, this warm glow bursting inside my rib cage at the thought of her doing what no one else could. I wanted to stand on my chair and declare to everyone, “She’s mine! She’s all mine.” She wasn’t. But I sure as hell wanted her to be.

I gestured to the board. “Well, go on.”

Her attention gravitated back to the equation as if it called to her, pleading with her to solve it. “I don’t think so.”

“Free.” I lowered my voice. “Go.”

“No.” She pulled a notebook from her backpack. “Not right now.”

The next day, she stared at the board again with her lips moving and eyes roving. I kicked her chair. “Get up there.” I raised an eyebrow in challenge. “I know you want to.”

She looked at me, the board, and then me again. “You don’t think he’ll get mad?”

“Who? Stuben?” I snorted. “Mad is not what he’ll get. Trust me.” He’d probably fall to my mystery girl’s feet and worship her.

“Maybe I’ll take a closer look.” She slowly went to the board, her cheeks flushing.

Deacon and I watched as she stared at the problem. The noise from kids around us quieted too, going from brain-numbing to whispers to nothing. Everyone concentrated on Free’s back as she stared at the equation, oblivious to everything else but those numbers and letters and squiggly lines.

Mr. Stuben came in as Free took a marker from the holder beneath the board and began to write. He gawked at her, the Styrofoam cup in his hand held frozen at mid-sip. The bell rang, but no one moved, especially not Stuben, awe erasing some of the wrinkles from his face.

Free wrote and wrote, stopping every so often to study her work before writing some more. When she finished, she snapped the cap on the marker and turned to me, beaming.

God, I wished I knew enough math to make her that happy all the time.

"Who are you?"

Free whipped around to face Mr. Stuben after he spoke. "I'm… Free."

"I know your name, Miss Paine. But who *are* you?" he asked again. He stared at her as if the star he'd wished on finally pulled through.

"I…" Free glanced at me, quickly capping and uncapping the marker she held.

I stood, always wanting to save her even when she didn't need it, but Stuben rushed to her side. He didn't fall to her feet, but he did worship her.

I slumped back down as Stuben and Free started talking in low, excited voices. He'd point at the problem, asking questions, and she'd nod or shake her head as she explained things, both ignoring the rest of us as if we didn't exist inside their genius dome.

Smiling, my chest so tight I could hardly breathe, I opened my notebook and flipped to the right page.

CHAPTER 24

Cole

Girl Meets Perfection

Hannah pounced as soon as I came home from work Friday night, waving a letter in my face. "You see this? *See*? And he swears he's gonna change, get himself a real job. Lying bastard."

I took it from her and skimmed the first few badly written sentences. My stomach tightened. *Oh, no.* Richie made parole. In "two weeks or so," he'd be out. His letter made him sound like the dickhead he was. God forbid he'd give us the exact date.

"It'll be fine," I said after reading.

"Dumb thing to say."

"Whatever. Mama asleep?" I asked, searching past her to the hallway.

"Passed out a while ago. She raved like a lunatic for hours." Hannah pulled at her hair. "Lucky you missed it."

"Yeah, lucky." I bunched the letter in my fist. "No sense worrying about this now."

"How can you of all people believe that, Colie?"

She was right. The *thought* of my brother scared the hell out of me, but the man in person? What I felt about that was stronger than something so pithy as "scared." No point in copping to it though. Hannah knew already.

I headed to my room, tossing the crumpled ball into the kitchen sink on the way. "Night, Hannah."

Saturday.

About time.

I shoved last night from my head because today Richie was still in jail, Mama was still sleeping, and Kaycee was singing a new song she'd learned in church last week while Hannah made her breakfast. Perfect.

After eating the toast my sister made me, I showered, shaved, and dressed in the nicest sweatshirt and pair of jeans I owned. Made sure my notebook, a blanket, and flashlight were in my bag, too. Then drove to the address Free gave me.

I tapped on the wheel while waiting for her in the driveway. A minute passed before she came out, wearing skinny jeans and a form-fitting green sweater I recognized as Amy's old clothes. Her dark hair twisted in a braid that hung the length of her back instead of the usual ponytail, the style making Free's cheekbones more pronounced.

On her way to the passenger side, she smiled at me as if I were one of her math equations.

Oh, man.

I had it bad. Really bad. When she opened the door and slid in with a "Hey, you," my heart dropped to the floor.

"You're beautiful," I told her.

She blushed as she fastened her seatbelt. "Stop. Don't be *that* guy."

"And what *guy* would that be?"

"You know," she said, tucking a stray hair behind her ear, "the kind who says those corny things he thinks a girl wants to hear."

I pulled out of the driveway before answering her. "I'm not saying it for you."

"No?" She switched radio stations until she found an Imagine Dragons song. "Then why say it?"

I waited until we were parked in Gifford's lot then turned to her. "To be clear, I've said those *corny* things and more in here." I took my notebook from my bag sitting between our seats. "Maybe one day I'll let you read the stuff that comes to mind when I think of you."

She narrowed her eyes at me. "I don't understand you, Cole."

"What do you mean?"

"Why *me*?"

"Why *not* you?"

"I…" She shook her head, watching a few people walk down the sidewalk.

Another something she wanted to avoid. Fine. Probably best to avoid it, anyway.

I put my notebook away. "C'mon, Will Hunting. Time to work." Deacon had started calling her that after calc on Thursday, and by the end of Friday, half the people we ran into heard what she did and copied the nickname. It made her smile then, as it did now.

Once we clocked in, the last thing on my mind while working was actually working. I spent more time hanging out at Free's register than stocking shelves and unloading crates. In his nice way, Mr. Gifford warned me once or twice to get back to work: "You might want to see about them potatoes, Mr. Anderson" and "Those cereal shelves look awfully bare."

Free laughed every time our boss caught me slacking. Her laugh…I wanted to find out everything she found funny, so I could make her laugh all the time.

Jess came in around noon, crazy talkative and giving Free her attention. I didn't trust her for a second.

"Are you going to Deacon's game?" Jess asked me.

"Nah, we got plans," I said, stacking some candy near the registers—yes, another excuse to be near Free.

Jess rested a hip against the counter. "We?"

She knew damn well whom I meant. I spared a glance at Free, who had a curious frown on her face. "Free and I," I said quickly.

I hadn't told Free we'd be doing anything after work. She didn't deny it though. She didn't say anything.

"Where're y'all going?"

"A surprise." I didn't peek up from my candy bars, afraid of both Free's and Jess's reactions.

"Huh, cool," Jess said. "Did you tell her about the other thing?"

I felt the color drain from my face as I gave her a warning look. "Not yet."

"What other thing?" Free asked.

"I'm sure you'll find out soon." Jess winked at her with the fake smile she wore when she wanted to cry. It made me feel like a lousy friend, like I cheated on her even though I'd never promised her anything. Man, Amy had better been right about Jess. I so wanted to get back to where we were before last summer.

By the time Free and I were ready to pack up this week's outdated food, the trouble with Jess disappeared from my mind. I was excited to leave. Nervous too. I'd never taken anyone to the cliff. Neither had Deacon until last year, when he brought Amy for the first time. I knew then he loved her because we'd sworn to keep it secret, even from the girls. But I wanted to prove to Free beautiful things existed in the holler.

Weird. Maybe I loved her a little.

"What's the surprise?" she asked, fidgeting with her shirt-sleeve.

"If I told you, it wouldn't be a surprise."

"What about the 'other thing'?"

Dammit, Jess! "Tell you *after* the surprise."

"Annoying," she mumbled, but she stopped pulling at the unraveling thread.

"Thanks." I gestured to the food. "You want any of this?"

"Plenty of food at Jolene's. You take it."

"You sure?" I'd have given her the entire pile, but I was glad she didn't want it. Bare cupboards plagued my house once again.

"*Yes*, Cole. I'm sure." She grabbed some bags and started filling them. "Don't just stand there, writer-man. Hurry up. I want my surprise."

I chuckled, bending down next to her. "Yes, ma'am."

She stuffed some boxes of spaghetti in a bag. "Jess was cool today."

I felt my face heat up. "Uh-huh."

"Maybe I should say something to her."

"Probably not a good idea."

"Why not?"

"She'll be fine, okay?" *I hope.* "Let's go."

On our way out, Free made a point to say goodbye to Jess. A genuine goodbye, one that shocked Jess enough to be even nicer to Free and invite her over to hang out sometime.

Oh, no. I definitely didn't trust her. But maybe…

Please be right, Amy.

We walked to the car, hands full. When I opened the back door, Free let out a small gasp. I had cleaned the bloodstains as best I could, but a brown tint still smeared the fabric.

I stepped toward her, and she held up a hand. “No. I’m fine. I don’t want to talk about it.”

“Okay, yeah, no problem.” I pointed to the bag in her hand, and she gave it to me. I tossed it in. “Ready?”

She went to the passenger side. “Sure.” On our way up the hill, she sighed one of those loud, irritated sighs. “Poplar Branch?”

“Trust me,” I said, laughing at her puckered lips.

When we passed my place, I craned my neck toward the front yard, my heart quickening. *Two weeks or so.*

“What’s wrong?” she asked me.

“Nothing. Why?”

“Because it looks like you wanna kill somebody.”

I let out a slow breath and loosened my grip on the wheel. “Do I?”

“Uh-huh. What is it?”

I concentrated on the muddy road, wincing when we hit a big pot hole. “My brother’s coming home soon.”

“And that’s bad?”

“Yeah.” I swallowed. “Yeah, that’s bad.”

“Why?”

What did I tell her? The truth? Hell no. “No major reason. It’s just he’s a dick, you know?”

She touched the hand I rested on the seat, and I felt the jolt all the way in my stomach. “Well, you can vent to me about him anytime.”

Wrong. “Thanks.” I turned off the road to the spot where Deacon usually parked. The small patch of dirt and rock was big enough for one vehicle, and only if the wheels overlapped the base of the mountain near the trail. “Ready?”

"No."

"You'll like this place."

"There's nothing I like about this place."

I cut the engine and grinned at her. "Not even me?"

"Shut up."

"Yeah, I'll probably never do that." I grabbed the bag I'd put chips and a couple bottles of juice in, along with my backpack. "Prepare to see paradise, Freedom Paine."

Her lips twitched upward. "Paradise? In the holler?"

"Uh-huh." I got out and climbed the ravine, strapping my backpack onto my shoulders. Behind me, Free grumbled about mud, sharp rocks, steep hills, and her sore foot, and after every cuss I promised that we were close. She continued to follow, thankfully. I always prepared for her walls to erect and her attitude to change right before she ran away from me.

When we arrived at the cliff, huffing and sweating from the climb, I put everything down and pulled the blanket from my backpack. I refused to look at her. To be honest, I was afraid she would hate it here and demand I take her home.

"What do you think?" I finally asked, spreading the blanket on a flat rock.

Silence.

Don't look up.

I made sure each wrinkle in the old quilt was smoothed out, then did exactly what I told myself not to.

Oh.

Her face glowed, as if the cliff connected with her, allowing her eyes and her mouth to be its mirror. Relief filled the air between us, and that space, only inches, became miles. My hand trembled as I captured her wrist, coaxing her to sit next to me on the blanket. When she fixed her eyes on me, it suddenly hit me that *I* gave this to her.

Me.

Idea 1083

Miracle Worker

"Thank you," she whispered.

"You're welcome." I wanted to kiss her. Taste her voice. "Deacon and I found this place when we were kids."

"Y'all were adventurers, huh?"

"Something like that." I snagged the juice, handed her one. "Mostly escape artists. The cliff is idea one hundred twenty-two on my list."

"Nice." She smiled and twisted the cap off her bottle. "What do you mean, though?"

I scratched the back of my neck, trying to find a way to explain. To make this rock and dirt and mile-long plunge to the valley sound as magical as we'd always believed it to be. "This place takes our problems from us. Like… it hides us from them for a while."

"How?"

"Mm, I can't explain it." I placed my bottle on the rock and stood. "Better if I show you." I took a deep breath and yelled as loud as I could, my happiness, frustration, and stress echoing back to me. After a breath and another yell at the mountains, I sat, heaving and smiling, then laughing when Free's wide-eyed shock targeted me.

"You lose your mind just now?" she asked.

I laughed harder.

"Seriously." Her voice was a blend of light and worry. "What's wrong with you?"

"Absolutely everything, which is why yelling at absolutely nothing feels so damn good." I pulled her up with me and situated myself behind her, standing so close my chest brushed her back. "Your turn."

She shook her head. "I can't. It's strange."

"Yes, which is why you should do it." I rested a hand on her hip. "Just try."

Her body hitched as she sucked in air, but she didn't move away. She didn't do anything for a while, just stared at the mountains, taking deep, shattering breaths.

She was a natural, though. Because then she screamed. Screamed until her body quaked and she went limp, with only my arms keeping her up. Her screams transformed to sobs.

I turned her in my arms and held her, stroking her hair as she cried. "It's okay," I said. "Everything'll be okay."

She buried her face against my chest, her walls disintegrating into nothing as she whispered, "I don't think it'll ever be okay again."

CHAPTER 25

Free

$$\bar{a} = \frac{\Delta v}{\Delta t}$$

Rapid Acceleration

Screaming at the mountains, crying to them—I understood what Cole meant. The cliff *was* an escape, a perfect one. I concentrated on his pounding heart against my ear, my own calm. I had screamed for Little. For Daddy. For the gaps separating us. For the fear I'd have to break my promise and end up trapped here in the holler like everyone else. Like Cole.

We stood there for a long time, quiet. And when he pulled me down to sit with him on the blanket, he didn't speak right away. His lips brushed my temple, touching me deeper than the surface of my skin.

"Are you cold?" he asked, his breath on my cheek.

I shook my head.

"Do you want to leave?"

Again, I shook my head. "I'm sorry."

"Don't be. Don't ever be with me."

We stayed at the cliff until the sun lowered and the air chilled. His notebook remained in his bag, and he only let go of me to shift positions. It was beautiful here, more so when bursts of red and orange bled into the fading blue sky. I'd never watched a sunset before, never stopped to appreciate the time when night came to relieve the day.

Our trek down the mountain wasn't as quiet. Cole slipped into his usual banter, guiding us with a flashlight he'd pulled from his backpack.

"I pissed myself up here once. Don't judge. It was dark and the real danger of getting bit in the you-know-what by a rattlesnake was pretty high."

Then: "What do you think the probability of getting molested by a boomer is right now? You're the math whiz, right? A good eight out of ten chance?"

I laughed, countering, "What makes you think a boomer would find you attractive enough?"

"What do you mean?" He covered his heart, and the flashlight glare bobbed in front of us as it bounced off his chest. "I happen to be quite attractive to rodents."

"Well, then I'd calculate your chances of a boomer humping your leg is highly probable."

"See?" He chuckled and moved a branch before it could smack me in the face. "Math genius. And just so you're aware, I need to interview you. Sheckler will kill me if I let your story go."

"I ain't so sure about any interview."

"And *I'm* not sure you'll be able to resist my awesome interviewing skills."

I smacked his shoulder, laughing. "Shut up."

"Already told you, probably never happen. The words inside my head would explode."

"You mean the questions."

He grinned. "Potato, patato."

We reached the car, and disappointment darkened my mood. I'd have to leave him and sleep in that house with seven other kids who didn't have a Cole Anderson to breathe life into them.

"What time do you think it is?" I asked when we got in.

"Can't be more than seven. Why?"

I drummed my fingers against my leg, afraid to ask. Afraid not to. "I don't want to go back yet."

He glanced at me with his crooked smile. "I don't want you to go either."

I felt my cheeks warm. "Good."

"You have a place in mind?"

"Mim's? I need to show her I'm okay, maybe ask about her car." Hopefully I could convince her to let Cole use some parts. The Buick needed fixing. No way did I want it acting up during the trip to California.

"All right." He focused on the road. "Hey, ah…"

I knew that tone, the I-have-questions tone. "What?"

"Don't get mad."

"I'm not. Just ask what you want to ask already."

"Okay, fine. How do you expect to make enough money? I mean, we don't make much, and—"

"I'll figure it out."

"Right, but what're you aiming to do once you get to California?"

I honestly had no idea. My promise stretched as far as being there. "Get a job, I suppose. Wait for Daddy to get out."

"Where're you planning to live until he does?"

"Lived in this car before; I can do it again for a while."

He rubbed the back of his neck. "Look, I got some money saved."

"I ain't taking your money."

"I'm not offering to *give* it to you."

"What're you offering?"

"I'm—Shit!" He slammed on the breaks as flashing headlights came up the road. "Goddammit." Cole pulled as close to the mountainside as possible, giving the truck barely enough room to pass. He honked then rolled down his window when the truck didn't move. "Go!" he yelled.

The truck stayed put, its lights shining into the Buick so bright they almost blinded me. Almost. I could still see, and because of that, the rage I'd released at the cliff found its way back.

I jumped out without a word and ran to the truck, the need to choke the driver making my fingertips burn.

"Free!"

I ignored Cole, no longer caring about anything but what I needed to do, right now, this second. "Roll it down, you coward!" I banged on Byron's window. "*Roll it down!*"

Byron, his watery eyes wide, shook his head and kept his hands on the wheel.

I slammed my palm against the glass over and over, echoing myself until Cole gripped my shoulders. "Stop. Please, Free."

I slapped Cole's hands off me. "Get out!"

Byron's lips thinned as he reached into his glove box, pulling out an old revolver before rolling down the window. "You best get the hell away from me, girl." He cocked the gun and aimed it at my forehead. "I ain't about to take no shit."

"Hey, hey, hey!" Cole thrust me behind him and held up his hands. "No call for guns, Byron. Put that thing away, for Christ's sake."

"Why? So y'all can jump me right here in the middle of the road?" He flailed the gun around. "Not a fucking chance."

"This is all your fault!" I clenched my fists. "*All* this is your fault."

Cole pulled a hand behind him and rested it on my hip, squeezing me in place every time I tried to inch closer to the truck.

"Nah, it ain't! I told him to stay away from Sloan, but the sonofabitch wouldn't listen."

Cole gasped and loosened his grip on me enough so that I barged forward. "*You* told him about Duffy! If you'd have never opened your slimy mouth, he wouldn't be in a hospital bed waiting to get sent off to the clink!" I punched the side of the truck, the sting from the contact waking me enough to pay attention to the gun.

"No, no, no! I just told him about the sang, and your daddy took it a step further." Byron spat out the window, a stream of brown chaw juice barely missing my shoe. "You ain't got nothing to be mad at except Landry's stupidity. Thinking we could take ten pounds of sang without anyone knowing…"

"*We?*"

"Listen." Byron set the gun beside him and spat again. "I ain't arguing with you. Fact is, Landry was dumb enough to get caught." He nodded to Cole. "Maybe you should school your jasper girlfriend on the laws of the holler, boy."

"Right, yeah, I'll do that." Cole's voice was the kind of polite that promised bad things. "By the way, Richie'll be home soon. You owe him money, right? I'll be sure to tell him I ran into you with your gun in my face. Laws of the holler and all that."

Byron's face paled. "The hell you say."

Cole pulled me flush to his chest. "God's honest truth."

"Forget all y'all," Byron said, voice shaky. He rolled up his window and gunned the engine, almost hitting the Buick as he ripped by it.

The only sound for a few moments was the Buick's struggling motor.

Then, "Duffy Sloan threatened you, didn't he?"

I nodded, watching Byron's taillights disappear.

"Holy hell," he whispered.

"They won't get away with it."

"There's nothing you can do."

I stormed to the car without answering.

Cole followed but didn't speak until we were close to Mim's. Finally, he said, "Please. Whatever you're thinking, don't do it."

I kept my eyes pointed toward my window, trying not to withdraw. Cole deserved better from me.

"Free?"

I closed my eyes.

Seven hundred sixty-two divided by three point four...

Times sixty-eight...

Fifteen thousand, two hundred forty.

Tell him!

"Deputy Smith wanted to know who beat up my father. Well, I'll be sure to inform him—on my way out of this hole. Maybe mention my uncle and his association with Duffy Sloan."

Cole stopped at the railroad tracks, quiet as the train chugged by. When the bar lifted, he said, "If you snitch, you won't be able to come back here."

I watched the train until it disappeared around the bend. "Good."

"How're you planning to convince me you haven't done lost your mind?" Mim asked.

We sat at her kitchen table, her boys wrestling in the living room with the TV blaring. Being in Mim's house calmed my heart rate, and the familiar furniture and noise relaxed me enough to think coherently. Byron wouldn't get any more headspace. He'd pay, and knowing I would make sure of it had to be enough.

"I haven't lost anything but my brother and daddy, Mim." I bounced my leg until Cole pressed on my knee.

Mim blew a stream of smoke over our heads. "You're just gonna pick up and go once you turn eighteen?"

"That's the plan." I kept my eyes on hers, her stare not intimidating me.

"Uh-huh, and all by yourself?"

I nodded.

"Do you have a driver's license?" Cole interjected, talking for the first time since we got here.

"A permit," I told him. "Not like that's important. I can drive without breaking the law."

"What if there's a checkpoint or something?"

"Chance I'll have to take." I turned to him, mostly to avoid seeing the smirk spreading across Mim's lips. "What? Not like you have a license."

He grinned and pulled out his wallet. "Wrong."

Shocked, I stared at the license he held up, his smile proud and his eyes bright.

"How the hell'd you manage that?"

He stuffed it into his wallet again. "I used to be Callahan's project, too."

"Huh?"

"Yeah. She helped me get it, and I agreed to take my SATs."

Cole, the boy from the holler whose primary goal was to graduate and rent a rundown apartment, had so many more secret angles. "How'd you do?"

"On what?"

I blew out an irritated breath. "Duh. You know what."

"Twelve eighty, I think. Point is, I got my license out of the deal."

"Wow, that's really good, Cole."

"Doesn't matter," he said.

I wanted to tell him not to let it go to waste, but that would've made me a hypocrite, and I didn't feel up to being a hypocrite at that moment.

"Hello?" Mim snapped her fingers. "We went off track here, didn't we? He's right; you don't got a license or money or a real plan."

I sighed and faced Mim. "What do you want me to say? I won't go? I'd be lying to you. I… I promised him."

Mim reached across the table and covered my hands. "He'll forgive you, honey. And someday, maybe you'll be able to go, but—"

"I'm going." I pulled my hands from hers. "With your help or without it."

She didn't answer.

But Cole did. "You have help, Free."

"What're you talking about?" I asked him.

"I'm talking about the second part of the plan."

"There's a plan?" Mim chuckled. "Oh, I gotta hear this."

I shook my head. *What?*

Cole grinned at her, a quick flash, then focused on me. "You need me."

"I don't."

"You do." He sat straighter. "I'm going with you."

"I ain't coming back, though."

He shrugged. "I'll get a bus ticket."

"What about food? Money?"

He rolled his eyes, waving a hand toward Mim with a do-you-believe-this flip. "You need food and money, too."

"But only enough for one person."

"Gas costs the same no matter how many people are in the car." He pressed a finger to my mouth when I opened it. "And I got a hundred forty bucks saved, plus we can stock up on food from Gifford's and store it here. Besides, you could use the help driving."

I pushed his finger away. "That money's for your apartment."

"Which will be here when I get back and save up some more. Crap apartments are a dime a dozen. How much money you have?"

Oh, this stubborn boy! "Like a hundred fifty."

"Good. We should be able to save at least a few hundred more by the time we leave."

"You ain't listening to me."

He leaned closer, his oceans inches away. "You're wrong, Free. I *have* been listening, and you don't need to go alone."

Our argument went on forever while Mim stayed silent, smoking with that smirk on her face. She finally stopped us with the permission to let Cole use the Olds for parts—if he went with me. I huffed, yelled, and ultimately agreed to shut them up.

But after he dropped me off with his promise of "I'll be waiting for you after church gets out," and after I tried to sleep, I realized something:

I *wanted* him to come.

CHAPTER 26

Free

$$\gamma = \frac{F}{\ell}$$

(More Than) Surface Tension

I went into Mrs. Callahan's office on Monday morning with one goal in mind: to barter.

"I hear you've captivated Mr. Stuben," Mrs. Callahan said after a sip of coffee.

"What? Oh, right." My leg bounced with impatience. "It was fun."

"We have a math club if you're interested. They don't compete like at your old school, but it could still be enjoyable."

No. "Maybe."

She set her mug by her keyboard and folded her arms on her desk. "How has your first week with the Mabry family been?"

My leg bounced faster. "Lived in worse places."

"So… good?"

"I guess."

"School going well?"

"Sure," I said around the tip of my index finger.

"Could you stop biting your nails?" She shuddered. "It grosses me out a little."

I folded my hands on my lap. "Sorry."

She winked. "Not your fault I have a weak stomach."

Without my nails, I had nothing to concentrate on except tugging the sleeve of another sweater Amy gave me. I loved the clothes, feeling sort of pretty when I wore them.

"You have a letter for your father yet?" Mrs. Callahan asked. "I could send it out in today's mail."

"Oh, please." I reached into my bag and handed her the letter I'd written last night. "He's gone, then? They sent him back already?"

"He was discharged Friday afternoon."

I nodded, leaving the sweater alone to dig into my thigh. He'd better take this time to figure out our next move, dream bigger than before. "I don't have an envelope."

She tucked the letter into her top drawer. "I do."

I closed my eyes for a second, putting Daddy in the back of my mind and forcing myself to remember what I wanted to ask of her. "Ma'am?"

"Yes?"

"I was wondering. Maybe…" I cleared my throat. "I got my permit in California, but… what I'm asking is…"

She smiled as I tried to force the words out, and when I gave up, she said, "You and Cole Anderson seem to get along well."

Ugh. "We do, I suppose."

"And I assume he told you I helped him get his license?"

"Sort of."

"Did he tell you what I asked of him in exchange?"

"Yes, ma'am."

She tapped her manicured nails against a notepad, the one she wrote in when I gave her more than one-word replies. "What would you be willing to do?"

I stared past her shoulder, swallowing the terrible things I wanted to say. "What do you want?"

She laughed. *Laughed.* "Don't look so scared, Freedom."

"I ain't scared."

"Good to know." She *tap, tap, tapped.* "If I help you get your driver's license…" She paused. "If I help you…"

It took every ounce of willpower not to scream, tell her I changed my mind. But then I pictured Little and his carrot hair and sweet face. Daddy being stuck in a jail, all alone.

Her lacquered nails stopped on the notepad. "Got it. I want you to fill out some college applications."

No matter how much my willpower begged me not to, I jumped to my feet. "Wait. Why?"

"That's the price, Freedom. Take it or leave it."

"I don't have no computer or nothing."

"No problem." She pulled out a stack of papers from a desk drawer. "You can fill them out the old-school way."

"I ain't going to college."

"I'm not asking you to go to college." She tapped on the papers. "Just to fill out the applications."

I took a step toward the door. "What's the point of doing one without the other?"

She tilted her chin toward my seat. "Sit down, Freedom," she said, her voice calm. "Listen."

I slumped into my seat, my leg now bouncing in overdrive. "Listening."

"Whether you believe me or not, my reasoning is this: maybe you aren't planning to attend college now, but what if you change your mind?"

"I won't."

She leaned forward. "You're an intelligent young woman; your transcripts show that. Your *exceptional* SAT scores. I see it, too, and Mr. Stuben can't stop raving about you. He's been emailing me, even calling me at home. All he wants to talk about is your genius and what we need to do about it."

Confidence warmed my chest, something I hadn't felt since California, when Mr. Jorden said close to the same thing. Then we lost our house and that confidence turned to vapor.

"I ain't a genius," I said, concentrating on my shirtsleeve. "Idiot savant, more like."

She chuckled. "However you want to classify yourself is fine with me—as long as you acknowledge it."

I sighed. "How're we doing this?"

"So, you're saying yes?"

"I guess so."

Mrs. Callahan turned to her computer and began punching in keys.

"What're you doing?"

"Holding up my end of the deal," she said. "Next, we'll call Mrs. Mabry, let her know when testing is available at the DMV, see if she can get a copy of your birth certificate. Where were you born again?"

I laughed, stunned. "Bluefield."

"Bluefield. Right." She kept typing.

"Just like that, huh?"

She nodded. "Just like that. As long as you keep your end of the bargain."

Jess and Amy waited for me outside Mrs. Callahan's office. "Hey, Free," Amy said with a wave. Jess looked up from her phone and smiled at me.

"Hey." Surprised, I stumbled into the doorframe and smacked my arm. "Ouch."

What is this?

"Cole said he meets you here." Amy yawned. "Sorry. Anyway, thought we'd beat him to it today." Her heavy makeup didn't cover the shadows under her eyes.

"Are you okay?" I asked her, stemming the urge to feel her forehead for a fever like I did with Little.

"Yeah." She yawned again, this time until her jaw cracked. "Just a little tired. I feel like I haven't slept in days."

"I tried to tell her to go home, but God forbid she misses a day with Deacon." Jess tucked her phone in her back pocket and blew Amy a kiss when she stuck out her tongue. "Come on. We'll walk you to homeroom."

"Okaaayyy?" I said, holding my backpack strap tighter to my shoulder. *Here it comes.* The "He's Mine and You Can't Have Him" speech. Totally hoped to avoid it.

Jess linked her arm with Amy's when she lagged too far behind. "Has Cole asked you to homecoming, Free? Only a few weeks left until the big day now. Amy and Deacon are shoo-ins for king and queen. We gotta go support them."

Amy rolled her eyes. "A moronic social gathering of teenaged Homo sapiens trying too hard."

"And you're their queen, so shut it with your nonconformist crap." Jess grinned and brought Amy closer to her.

I stayed quiet, wanting the power to blend in with the lockers.

"So?" Jess said to me. "Did he?"

"N-no. I doubt he will."

"Why?" She waved at people as we walked, her tone curious, not mean.

"Because—I don't know." We stopped at my locker. "Listen, you don't have to worry."

"What do you mean?"

"Cole and I, we're friends. Period." I stared at my shoes, needing something to focus on besides her. "I'm not into love triangles, okay? My life's complicated enough."

Silence.

I glanced up. "He doesn't li—"

Jess put her hand in my face. "Stop."

Oh, crap.

"There can't be a love triangle."

"You know what I mean." I turned away from her and opened my locker.

"Oh, I do, and you're wrong. There can't be one… because he only sees you."

My hand froze as I pulled out my American History book. "What?"

"I've known Cole since first grade, and he's never looked at anyone the way he looks at you." Her breath hitched. "I wish he did—look at me—but he never has."

I brought my book to my chest and faced her. "How does he look at me?"

"Like his world begins with you," Amy answered quietly for her.

I didn't want to feel hot and light. "I… I don't know what to say."

"Just be happy." Jess peered over my shoulder. "He's as close to perfect as I can imagine any guy to be. Moody, annoying, but the best friend anyone would be lucky to have."

"I—"

"There you are." Cole touched my arm. "Been searching all over for you."

I wanted to turn to see if he looked at me the way Amy claimed he did.

"You can't keep her all to yourself, Cole Anderson," Amy said.

"Well, I can sure give it a shot. Whoa..." His voice pitched lower. "You okay, Amy?"

She let out groan. "Why does everyone keep asking me that?"

"Because you sort of look like hell today. *Anyway.*" Jess stretched out the word until the syllables mashed together. "Free tells us you're a slacker, Cole."

"What?" He laughed. "She'd be lying."

His world begins with you.

I couldn't say anything. I just wanted to sink into Amy's words a while longer.

Jess leaned against the lockers and crossed her arms. "Why haven't you asked her to homecoming?"

"Told you I wasn't going."

"But why not take Free? It'd make it less boring if we all went. I'm going with Aidan Roberts. Dense as a rock, but he's gorgeous."

Nothing but silence came from Cole.

I twisted to find his jaw clenched. "It's fine," I said. "I don't have a dress, any—"

"I have a dress you can borrow," Jess interrupted.

I bit the inside of my cheek, waiting.

"All right, fine. *Geez.*" Cole raked a hand through his hair, those light brown locks in need of a trim. "Want to go?"

"Oh, aren't you a romantic?" Amy said.

Cole grinned at her over my head. "It's a dance. Not like I'm asking her to go steady or something."

"Asking her *to go steady*? This isn't the seventh grade—in 1952. Seriously, Cole." Jess sighed. "Hopeless. C'mon, Amy, let's give our clueless friend some privacy while he trips over his tongue."

They left us alone, laughing on the way to class while I tried to act "normal."

"So?" Cole said, raising his right eyebrow like only he could do. "You game?"

I smiled. "Sure. Why not?"

CHAPTER 27

Free

Pr (E ∩ F)
Occurring Events

For the next few weeks, I spent as little time as possible at Jolene's, and Cole didn't seem to mind hanging out with me.

Most days after school, if we weren't at Gifford's, Cole worked on the Buick at Mim's, using old tools from her shed. I sat on the porch steps and did homework or worked on those college applications while he tinkered under the hood. We talked about everything.

I told him about my mother's love for alternative music. Told how Laura had burned Little's hand before she disappeared. How Daddy had sold Mama's engagement ring to have enough money to come hide here.

Cole told me his birthday was September 2, the usual first day of school, which sucked for him when he was younger but didn't make much difference now. I found out about his mother. His sister and his niece stuck in the holler.

Stuck in the holler.

I hated the idea of *him* stuck there. Cole, this perfect boy with a perfect heart who was kind to everyone. He'd probably spend the rest of his life trapped in the iron-colored dirt of Poplar Branch. Mama told me that once the holler had you, it fought tooth and nail to keep you. Daddy battled it to save her, and I wished I had that strength to save Cole.

Tonight, I hung out with Amy and Jess at Jess's house, trying on dresses for homecoming, while Cole and Deacon went to a junkyard to find a heater core Mim's Olds didn't have. I hated to admit that I missed Cole entirely too much.

"Yes! That's the one. Don't even think of trying on another," Amy said. She lounged on the bed and stuffed pound cake Jess's mom made into her mouth.

"You think?" I studied myself in the mirror hanging on the back of the door and smoothed a hand down my hip. I'd already tried on ten dresses, and I was ready to combust. Thank goodness the short-sleeved black dress was The Dress.

"Great. I'll be the only one wearing color." Jess collected the discarded dresses off her bedroom floor and gestured to Amy with a red pump in her hand. "Lord knows your dark and dreary ass will be wearing black, too. Couldn't you have found a different way to piss off your folks?"

Amy shrugged and shifted to set her empty plate on the nightstand. "It suits me."

"Whatever." Jess threw the clothes into her closet then showed me a picture on her phone of her and Amy. "Amy before she turned into the bride of Marilyn Manson." Amy looked drastically different, with long blond hair and wearing clothes I now owned.

I handed the phone back. "I think the goth thing works."

"Thanks," Amy said, rubbing her stomach. "At least I got one friend with some fashion sense."

Jess rolled her eyes and turned me back to the mirror. "Neither one of you know what you're talking about." She held up her phone. "Now smile. I need to add some pics to Insta."

I studied our reflection as Jess made different faces for each picture she took. All of this was so normal. Normal and good.

I looked down at my folded hands. Did Daddy's fingers still hurt him? His ankle? What was Little doing while I tried on dresses? Was he scared? Did his grandparents keep Laura away?

Did he think life was better without me?

Shame slammed down on my shoulders, and it felt as heavy as always. The dress made it heavier, too. I pulled it off and found my clothes. "I'm not feeling good." I punched my legs into my jeans as anger for Jess and Amy clouded my brain. It wasn't their fault they made me feel normal, but I was pissed at them just the same.

"What's wrong?" Jess bundled the dress and dumped it into my hands. "I say something to make you mad?"

"No. It's just… I have to go." I forced myself to smile. "I just need to go, okay?"

"I'll take you." Amy got off the bed and moaned. "I'd don't feel great either. Too much cake."

"Thanks," I told her on the way to the door. I held up the dress. "And thanks for this, Jess. Really."

Amy drove me back to Jolene's, stopping at the train tracks to puke, which made me feel like garbage. Here she was, actually sick. The only thing making me ill was a heavy dose of shame, and the only remedy was time alone to feel sorry for myself.

I spent the rest of the night wishing the days would go by faster and telling myself I needed distance from everybody, especially Cole. I felt myself getting too close to him, almost like I needed him. I didn't want to need him. Or dream about him. Or fantasize about him and me and a future we'd never have. He was toxic, the kind of toxic that felt super good. A drug addiction.

The next day, I tried to avoid him. *Tried* being the key word. He cornered me at my locker after last period. "Okay, enough ignoring me. Look." He held up an early copy of tomorrow's paper.

The front-page headline? "Freedom Paine: Math Savant and Odd Lover of Grunge Music"

I tried not to smile. Again, *tried.* "That's… stupid."

Cole had begged me to do the interview for two weeks. After I said no a hundred times, he managed to talk me into answering his weird, funny questions last Sunday at the cliff—while he plucked the stitches out of my foot.

He grinned and handed the paper to me. "Nah. I'd say it's brilliant." His grin softened as he brushed his thumb across my bottom lip. God, I loved and hated when he did that. "Wanna tell me what's wrong now?"

I focused on the paper. And confessed my sin: "I feel like I'm not giving Little and Daddy enough of me."

"What? No. That's not true." He hugged me, whispering, "You're just letting yourself live."

He was too nice, too understanding. Too good for me. But I held onto him anyway.

"I need to get to Stuben's." I reluctantly stepped out of his arms. "See you in the library?"

Yes, I joined Math Club—only to eat up some hours between school and curfew. Luckily, Stuben was pretty awesome and made numbers as fun as the mathlete team was in Needles. We met on Tuesdays and Thursdays, and Cole waited for me in the library.

"Uh-huh. Sure you're okay?"

I walked backward, nodding. "Sure as I can be."

"All right, then. I'll be waiting for you."

His promise, whether he meant it to be one or not, hit exactly where I needed it to.

Once I got to Stuben's class, Jason Hawthorne waved at me from the back of the room. "What up, Will Hunting!"

I smiled at him. "Hey, Jas. Anything new today?"

"Duh." Jason pointed to an equation on the whiteboard.

"Awesome." My brain absorbed the numbers. They helped unravel the knots in my stomach Cole's promise had already loosened.

"Free, you wanna come over here a minute?" Mr. Stuben said from his desk.

I turned to him as Jason and the others made "you're in trouble" noises from their perch in the back.

"Shut it, heathens." Mr. Stuben was seriously the coolest teacher ever. "Look at the board, and we'll be with you soon."

"Problem?" I asked, sitting next to him.

"Nope. The exact opposite." He finished typing and shifted his laptop so I could see the screen. "Mrs. Callahan told me about those applications. Thought we could add one more."

MIT. The site I'd searched hundreds of times in California.

I frowned, returning my attention to Stuben's expectant face. "She also tell you I don't plan to go to college?"

"She mentioned it," he deadpanned.

"Well, then…"

"*Well, then* I like to play make-believe just like Mrs. Callahan, and I want to pretend my prodigy isn't planning to throw her talent away." He closed the laptop and stood. "I've already written my letter of recommendation, and I contacted Mr. Jorden to do the same. Keep it in mind, okay? Deadline is January 1, so you have time."

I concentrated on my shoes and followed him to the rest of the group.

No, I didn't have time.

When I met Cole in the library, I pushed Stuben's MIT idea out of my head. No way would I fill out that application. What if I got in? That would hurt worse than getting denied.

Cole's hair was messy and his smile huge, helping me forget faster. "I have something for you," he said, rocking on his heels with his hands behind his back.

His smile made me smile. "You do?"

"Yep." He wouldn't stand still.

"Let me see." I reached around him.

He backed up, laughing. "Patience, patience."

"Cole! You're driving me nuts." I loved every minute of it. "Tell me."

"Not a fan of surprises, are you?"

"Not even a little bit."

He moved so close I felt the heat wafting off his skin. "You don't even want to guess?"

I searched my brain for a sarcastic retort, something to lighten the pressure in my chest. Failing. "N-no."

"Fine." Cole pulled his hands from behind his back and offered me some folded papers. "Here."

I took them without looking down. I didn't want to take my eyes from his oceans. "What is it?"

"You do realize I'm awesome, don't you?"

"You have your moments."

"I'll take that as a yes."

"Take it any way you want." I could barely concentrate with him so close. "Just tell me."

A grin. "It's an itinerary."

"Itinerary?"

He lifted the first paper from my grasp and held it up to show a map, our route marked with blue and red color-coded stops for gas and rest areas. A big black X marked Needles like lost treasure. "I planned out our trip to take you home."

CHAPTER 28

Cole

McDowell County Captures More Victims

Her eyes filled with tears.

What the…?

"Why're you crying?" I pointed to the papers clutched to her chest "It's just directions and stuff."

"I'm not crying."

I bent until we were eye level and tipped her chin. "Usually, when water leaks from one's eyes, it's considered crying."

She snorted, a loud sound that made heads turn in our direction. "You're dumb."

"So you keep telling me." I collected my things from the computer table. "Let's talk outside."

At the bleachers, Jess consoled Amy, who sobbed into her hands.

Why the hell's everybody crying today?

Worried, I stepped toward them but stopped when Jess shook her head and mouthed, *One minute*.

What's wrong? I mouthed back.

Later.

I nodded with a sigh and gestured to the bottom row. "Guess we'll sit here for now."

"Is she okay?" Free asked, studying Amy and Jess.

"I hope so. Are you?"

She wiped her cheeks with the back of her hand. "More than okay. I can't believe you did all this."

I grinned, trying to keep my ego in check. "Thought it'd make you feel better. And all I did was Google it. Found the fastest route, where the rest stops are, gas stations too. Ah, there's no bus stations in Needles, but there's an Amtrak station. Be cool to take a train. Closest depot here's in Charleston, but Deacon'll pick me up. Anyway, I think we're set. All we need is more money."

"You're a Google expert, too, huh? Not just a question aficionado?"

"I'm a man of many talents. Maybe someday I'll show you a few more." I cringed as soon as I said it, especially when her eyes widened. *Geez.* "Hey, I didn't mean…" I made an awkward—dumb—gesture, showing that I was, in fact, being an unintentional perv.

"I get it. Put your hands down."

Shit. "Sorry. I seriously didn't—"

"Subject change?"

I forced myself not to fan my heated face. "Yes. Please, God, yes."

She smiled a little, folding and unfolding the papers. "You think my father's hands are better?"

"Hope so."

"I can't get the image out of my head, you know?" She shivered. "All that blood."

She wasn't the only one. "It's nothing I've ever seen before." I nudged her shoulder. "But I'm sure he's fine. Somebody would've told you if not."

"Yeah."

"And you'll be seeing him soon, right?" A sharp stab hit my gut. Regret.

"Right."

I nudged her shoulder again. "He's fine. Think positive."

She nodded and focused on the papers. "What if they don't let me see Little?"

"That's the opposite of positive."

"But—"

"They'll let you see him."

She lifted her gaze to the field when Coach Nate yelled at Deacon for overthrowing the ball. "I just wish I could talk to him."

Talk to him... Of course! Why hadn't I thought of it before? "Wait here for a sec." I ran to Deacon's truck and grabbed his cell from the glove box before returning to Free.

She peered over my shoulder as I typed while trying to catch my breath. "What're you doing?"

"Just practicing my expert Googling skills. What're the grandparents' names again?"

She gave the names, and I plugged them in. "There!" I held up the phone after a few moments. "This has the same area code as the Amtrak station, so I'm assuming..."

Free snatched the phone from me and stared at it. "That's them."

"Go on, then."

Her finger hovered over the number. "What if—?"

"No. Just call."

"I don't—"

I touched the number for her and turned on the speaker. It rang once, and again, then: *"The number you have reached is no longer..."*

"Sorry, Free," I whispered as she continued to stare at the phone, the recording starting over.

"I feel so far away from them." Her voice sounded small, almost nonexistent. Defeated.

I looked behind me to Amy, who still cried, then out to the field where Deacon yanked off his helmet to bitch at somebody for missing a catch. We had cliff plans, but—

Yes! *Got it.*

"C'mon." I took the phone from her and climbed down the bleachers. "I have an idea."

She didn't say a word on our way to Poplar Branch, not until I pulled into her old driveway. "No, Cole. No way. I'm not going in there."

"You don't have to."

"Then why'd you bring me here?"

"Because you need to remember what you're fighting for."

Her mouth bowed up a little. "Is this a tough love moment?"

"We can call it that." I brushed her bottom lip. "Just because we hit a roadblock doesn't mean we give up."

"What do you suggest I do, then?"

"About your brother? Facebook." I shrugged. "Twitter, probably."

"Seriously?"

"Well, yeah. You got friends over there? People who could maybe check in on him?" I pulled out Deacon's phone and clicked on his Twitter icon.

"Oh, um…" She aimed her attention at the roof. "A few, I guess. There's my mathlete team."

I laughed, couldn't help it. "Mathlete team? Numbers really do it for you, don't they?"

"They make sense." She paused, biting on her lip. "They're the only thing on the planet that has a definite solution."

Man, I wanted to kiss her.

I clicked on the search bar instead. "Give me the names of your geek friends, and I'll put my stalker skills to use."

She gave three names, and I searched them. One didn't have an account, but the other two did.

I fired off a quick DM, telling them who I was and what I wanted. "There, done. Now all we gotta do is wait."

She covered my hand with hers. "Cole?"

I didn't move, afraid she'd take her hand away. "Yeah?"

"Thank you."

One of the kids, Elena Han, DM'd back before we parked the car near Deacon's truck. Her response: "I'll keep my eyes open! Tell Free I said hey!"

Free smiled. "I miss her."

I typed that back to Elena and stuffed the cell in my bag. "C'mon. Deacon's probably freaking without his phone."

As we walked up the path, the desire to beg Free to stay almost took over my words. This Elena Han, and the other mathlete people, didn't miss Free like I'd miss her. But even so, she wouldn't give up her brother and dad to stay here. Why would she? For me? Yeah, sure. Some prize that'd be.

By the time we reached the cliff, Amy was already yelling to the sky. Without a word, we sat next to Deacon on his Steelers blanket, our feet dangling over the edge. We remained quiet while Amy released her misery. I hoped whatever pain festered inside her disappeared some.

After a few more minutes of screaming loud enough to rival Free's first cliff session, she sat on the other side of Deacon, who had his arm around her waist before her butt hit the blanket. He brushed dyed hair from her eyes and whispered in her ear as she worked to catch her breath, kissing her temple every time he stopped talking.

I started to say something to them a few times, give a lame "It'll be okay" or "It can't be that bad," but the way Deacon's eyes watered and his lips trembled…

Helplessness sucked.

I glanced at Free, who pretended to work on her college essay while sneaking glances at Amy, and pulled out my notebook.

Friends' Odd Behavior

- *Amy cries on the bleachers. (screams louder than usual)*
- *Deacon—bad practice (out of character). Abnormally quiet. (looks like he wants to cry)*

I felt like an ass as I wrote. Free took all my concentration today, and I hadn't paid attention to my friends. They were obviously screwed up over something.

"Okay," I said, closing my notebook. "Good stuff or bad?"

All three of them met my stare, Free the only one showing confusion. Amy and Deacon had guilt and fear and a whole mess of other things flashing on their faces.

"Well, Jesus. What is it?" I demanded. "Y'all rob a bank? Murder somebody? Whatever it is can't be that bad."

Amy burst into tears, and Deacon tucked her face against his chest, shaking his head at me. "You're gonna be pissed."

"Try me."

He just stared at me, his lips pursed.

Free put her things in my backpack and moved to Amy's side. She rested a hand on our crying friend's back, murmuring comforting words I'm sure she'd uttered to her brother a thousand times. Amy lifted her head, dark makeup smeared all over her cheeks, and moved from Deacon to curl into Free. "What're we gonna do?" she said against Free's shoulder.

Free held her closer. "We'll figure it out."

"Yeah, but we got to know what's going on before we can do that," I told Deacon. "I mean, what could possibl—"

"Amy's pregnant." Deacon stared straight into my eyes, scared, brave, and ready to bash my face in if I said anything he didn't like.

"Oh, shit."

"No, not 'Oh, shit.'" He stood and paced way too close to the edge. "Not 'Oh, shit,' okay?"

"Okay, okay," I said, covering my shock with the calmness I used when talking Mama down from one of her rants. "Just come away from the edge, all right?"

Deacon surprisingly listened, still pacing like a maniac. I didn't dare glance in Amy's direction, afraid I'd lose it and tell my friends the things they didn't want to hear: "Your lives are over!" and "How could you be so stupid?"

Instead, I blocked Deacon's path, forcing my calm onto him like a Jedi Master. "When did you find out?"

"Last night." He scratched the back of his neck. "She thinks she's like six weeks."

"All right. Okay." I crossed my arms over my chest. "This isn't the worst news ever."

"It ain't the worst anything, Cole. It ain't." His eyes went liquid like they often did when he looked at Amy. "The love of my life is pregnant with my child, and I'm… I… I don't know what I am, but we're both sort of happy but not. Terrified as hell, mostly. Ain't that right, babe?"

Amy laughed a little, her voice muffled against Free's flannel.

Nothing about this was funny. Nothing. My best friends succumbed to McDowell County statistics, and they'd be trapped like Hannah and others in our class who had dropped out for this reason.

"Have y'all told your folks?"

Deacon rubbed his forehead. "Not yet. We're trying to find a way to do it without my dad taking a swing or me kicking her dad's ass if he tries to put his hands on her."

"You think your daddy'll hit you?" Free asked Amy, her voice going high.

Amy stared up at Deacon, her trust in him shining bright in her teary eyes. "Deacon won't let him."

"Goddamn right I won't."

"What about college?" I asked.

He collapsed next to Amy, taking her into his arms. "I can barely get through high school as it is. College is for people like y'all. Not me."

"So, what? Go in the mines with your dad?"

"Hell no," Deacon said. "Join the Marines. Already talked to Callahan today. She said me and Amy can get married when we turn eighteen. She'll get military benefits and could even go to college later if she wanted on the government's dime."

I shook my head. "You've thought this through, haven't you?"

"Meet with a recruiter next week."

The shock of it weighed us down, and silence took over. Deacon, the guy who had the golden arm that held the golden ticket out of here, stumbled and fell at the finish line.

"Deacon, the soldier. I can see that," Free said, breaking the tension. She saluted him. "You're definitely a kicking-ass-and-taking-names guy. And you'll get to marry a hot chick with a nose *and* eyebrow ring and have little soldier-goth babies."

Deacon grinned and held out his fist over Amy's head. When Free gave it a bump, laughing, he said, "Ooh-rah, Will Hunting. Ooh-rah."

CHAPTER 29

Cole

Prison Systems Are Failing

Free didn't say a word on our way to her house, and I was too irritated to force a conversation.

Some people were destined to make it out of here, my friends being two of those people. They lived in decent houses, had semi-decent parents, and never worried about food or winter or if there was enough pilfered coal stored to keep them warm at night. Now, if the Marines didn't work out, chances were good they'd be my neighbors, living in one of the rundown apartment complexes in Welch, surviving.

I parked at Free's house and cut the engine. She didn't get out, which was perfect because I didn't want her to leave.

"You okay?" she asked.

"No, yeah, I'm fine." I faced her, wishing I had the courage to pull her to me. "I'm not the one about to be a daddy."

"True. But…they seem to have a plan."

I tucked hair behind her ear, letting my fingertips linger on her neck. "You more than anyone should get how plans can end up."

She shivered under my touch but didn't move away. "Isn't that the gospel if I ever heard it. Still…"

I let my hand drop. "I thought they'd make it. Out of everybody, they were gonna leave McDowell County behind."

"Right." She adjusted the radio station from country to her stuff, avoiding me and this conversation.

I knew why: *she* was leaving. I didn't want to talk about it either. "So, you ready for Saturday?"

Free peeked up from the radio. "Maybe. You?"

"Yes, ma'am. Got my suit and tie already picked out."

She bit her lip, the action not hiding her grin. "I can't picture you in a suit and tie."

"I've never worn one, so it'll be a surprise for both of us." Of course Deacon had loaned the clothes without me having to ask.

"Right, well, I best be getting in there. Don't want Jolene mad at me." She collected her things from the back. "See you at school?"

"I'll be waiting for you outside Callahan's." Same thing I said to her every night when I dropped her off. Same thing on the weekends, too, just varied: *Waiting for you bright and early* or *Waiting for you after church.* Always waiting for her.

"Good." She opened her door. Hesitated. "Cole? I got no idea what I'd do if…"

I shook my head when she didn't finish. "Funny, because I have no idea what I'd do 'if,' either."

Free cupped my cheek, sending jolts to the pit of my stomach. "What does that make us?"

Perfect. Happy. Amazing. "Desperate."

She sighed. "I suppose you're right. Night."

On the way home, our words repeated inside my head. Why did I have to say desperate? Why not something cooler, less honest?

We *were* desperate, though, for entirely different things. I desperately wanted her to stay, and she desperately wanted to leave and never look back. I was a necessity to her now. A tool she needed to meet an end.

Yes.

I was exactly that: a tool.

Surprisingly, Hannah *and* Mama were awake when I walked through the door. Mama even seemed moderately sober. Sober and scared, like my sister.

"What's going on?" I asked them as I dropped my bag by the door.

Hannah came into my arms, her thin body shaking. "It's Richie."

Dread slithered inside me, speeding up my heart. "What about him?"

Right then, the toilet flushed. My brother came out of the bathroom looking stronger and healthier than before. A smile curved his lips, showing teeth surprisingly intact despite the drugs he'd put in his system. "Hey, little brother."

Cold only the threat of Richie created seeped into my stomach, freezing everything but my fear. *He's home.* I wanted to turn around and never come back, but my feet wouldn't work.

"Well, don't just stand there!" Richie wrapped his arms around Hannah and me. He was my height, but I felt suffocated with him so close, his stale breath hitting my cheek.

I found Mama over his shoulder, her face stark white, and hated her for the millionth time. She could've made him leave, find a different place to live, but she didn't. She let him come back to flip our lives upside down again.

I stepped away from my brother and retrieved my bag. "Where's Kaycee?"

"Sleeping," Hannah said. She slipped from Richie's hold and sank down next to Mama.

"She tried to stay awake with her Uncle Richie, but the poor little shit's all tuckered out." Richie rested a heavy arm over my shoulders. "She's damn cute, Han. You done good with her."

"Thanks, Richie." Hannah's voice hitched on his name. "We, ah, we missed you a bunch."

"I should hope so!" He pulled me closer, his arm tight against the side of my neck. "But me and Cole need to catch up, if y'all don't mind."

"'Course not, baby. I'm sure your brother's got a lot to say," Mama said, her shoulders sagging with relief. "Me and Hannah are going on to bed now. Long day."

For the first time in my life, after all she'd put this family through, I wanted to bloody her nose.

To save herself, she fed me to the wolf.

Idea 1084
Vanishing Artist

The next day during lunch, I laughed too loud when Amy made a lame joke, asked Jess what she was wearing to the dance on Saturday, and talked football with Deacon even though I had no clue how to play the game. Maybe that last one had given me away.

Deacon punched me in the shoulder as soon as I finished asking how many "scores" he got during last week's game. "What's going on?" he asked. With all his issues, he could still see right through me.

I rubbed my shoulder and peered at Free sitting next to me, who frowned like everyone else at the table. "Nothing. I'm fi-ne."

"Don't believe you," Deacon said.

"It's not a big deal, really. Don't worry."

Jess stabbed pear slices with her fork then waved them in my face. “You see, that’s precisely the reason we’re worried—because you’re telling us not to worry with worry on your face. Stop being obtuse; it’s not cute.”

Amy rolled her eyes, being herself today, except for not wearing her usual makeup. She looked younger without it. Too young to be a mother. “As flawed as our friend’s logic is, she’s right. You’re hiding something, Cole Anderson.”

“I’m not,” I said, pissed that my voice cracked.

Free squeezed my thigh. “Cole?”

Ah, damn. “Fine. It’s honestly nothing, just… Richie’s home.”

No one said a word. They just drilled me with concern so thick I could almost feel it clogging my pores.

I pushed my tray away. “What? Stop looking at me like that.”

Deacon leaned forward. “If he touches you…”

“My God,” Free whispered, and squeezed my leg harder. “He hits you, Cole?”

Great. Now she knew everything.

I couldn’t look at her. Her pity would’ve chased me under the table. “Sometimes.”

“Well, he ain’t hitting you again,” Deacon said, making all this worse. I hated that I couldn’t do what he could.

I glared at him. “Yeah, I’ll make sure to let you save the day.”

“Hey, I didn’t mean—”

“I know it.” I stood and reached for my things. “See y’all in class.”

CHAPTER 30

Free

Pr (E) = 0
Impossible Odds

"You look like a movie star." Sarah sat on her bunk, eating chips I'd brought home from Gifford's. Kate and Shelly sat on either side of her, eating and nodding as I smoothed my hands over the front of the black dress.

It was too pretty, too expensive to be covering my body, but I loved how I felt in it. Amy let me borrow her straightener, and Jess gave me some makeup, which Sarah helped me apply. By the time I straightened my hair, now brushing the edge of my hips with the curls tamed, I didn't even look like me.

"You sure are pretty all right," Kate said, wiping her greasy hands on her pajama bottoms. Shelly nodded again, never one to talk much.

The four of us had gotten closer—not close enough to hang out outside our bedroom, but friendly. I asked Sarah one night why she never spoke to me in school. She said, "No point in making friends."

Since then, I made sure to sit by her in psychology and force her to talk to me. Everyone needed at least one friend.

Cole taught me that.

"Thanks. But I'm positive I'll be falling on my face before the night's over." I twirled on my borrowed heels, stumbling and eliciting giggles from the younger girls.

"Just don't walk much," Sarah said, taking another handful of chips.

"How am I supposed to not walk at a dance?"

She shrugged. "Never been to a dance before."

"Me either."

"You can always take your shoes off," Sarah said. "It'll probably be dark, right?"

"Guess I'll find out."

"And…" Sarah hesitated, concentrating on the chips. "You get to go with Cole Anderson. If I were you, I wouldn't complain much."

I started fussing with my dress again. "We're friends."

"I wish I was his 'friend.'" She air-quoted the last word. "He's cute."

"Don't matter how cute he is." I went to the door. "See y'all later."

Jolene and Kenny sat in their usual spots on the couch, Jesus on the television, as I came downstairs.

"You look nice, Freedom," Jolene said when I told them I was leaving.

"Thank you, ma'am." I fiddled with the tips of my hair, smiling when Kenny gave a nod before returning his attention to the TV.

Jolene grabbed a bag from the coffee table and stood. "But curfew's still ten, understand? Here." She pulled a black cardigan from the bag, one that appeared new and surprisingly my size. "Got this for you the other day. It's awful airish tonight."

"I…Thank you," I said, accepting the sweater from her.

"Welcome." She pointed to the wall clock. "Ten on the dot."

Cole pulled up the same time I was wobbling on my heels down the driveway. Instead of waiting in the car, he got out and met me in his suit and tie.

Sarah was wrong. He was more than cute.

"Told you," he said, lifting a hand to smooth my hair.

"Told me what?"

"You're beautiful."

I bit my bottom lip to prevent a sigh from escaping. "Shut up."

He took my hand with a grin. "C'mon."

On the way, I watched his face as the moon and streetlights bounced shadows across his cheeks.

"What?" he said, smiling and without looking my way.

A protective surge rushed inside me as I kept staring at him. "Is everything okay… at home?"

His smile disappeared. "Yeah, sure."

"Cole…"

He reached over and squeezed my hand. "It's fine, okay?"

"Okay." I held his hand tighter when he tried to pull away. At least his smile came back.

When we arrived at the gym, the dance was already loud. Kids danced, congregated near a table with a large punch bowl, sat on the bleachers, and huddled in corners. A few teachers patrolled the happenings, tapping on shoulders of people making out or dancing too close. Jason Hawthorne nodded to me as he bounced around the dance floor to a Drake song.

We stood by some tables, Cole as lost as I was, when Jess skipped toward us with Aidan Roberts. "Hey! It's about time you made it!" She looked gorgeous in her red formfitting dress and hair piled atop her head in dark ringlets.

"You look great," I said, gesturing to her dress. "Red's your color."

"Ain't you sweet?" She patted her curls. "But I know it."

Cole laughed and nodded to her date. "How's it going?"

"Cool, man." Aidan bobbed his head, his attention on the dance floor.

"Y'all clean up pretty good too, by the way." Jess turned to her date. "I'm thirsty."

Aidan groaned. "Fine, but we're dancing after." He left without waiting for an answer, dodging gyrating bodies and vigilant chaperones.

As soon as Aidan was out of earshot, Jess stopped smiling. "Amy wanted me to tell you..."

"What?" Instantly, Cole wore the same scowl Deacon had when Cole told us about Richie.

Jess stepped closer. "Deacon and Amy ain't coming."

Cole narrowed his eyes. "Why not?"

"Tonight's the night. They're telling their folks. Didn't want to wait any longer."

"Shit." Cole peered at the exit. "Maybe we should go to Deacon's."

"And that's why they wanted *me* to tell you." Jess stood directly in front of Cole. "This isn't for us to get involved with. So, y'all should dance, have fun. And we'll go to Deacon's first thing tomorrow."

Cole raked his hands through his hair, clearly wanting to leave. "Do I have a choice?"

"Absolutely not. Have fun—Amy's orders." Jess patted her hair again. "Now, I'm gonna make Aidan dance with me, and you two should do the same."

"This is crazy," I said as we watched Jess meet up with her date.

Cole grunted in agreement. "Can't believe they picked tonight."

"We can go if you want. Maybe they won't mind."

He stayed quiet for a moment then took my hand. "No, Jess's right."

I didn't move as he tugged, his focus on the dance floor. "I don't know how to dance."

"Neither do I," he said and raised his eyebrow, "but aren't you brave, Free?"

"No." I took off my shoes and cardigan anyway, leaving them on the table next to us, and let him guide me to the middle of the floor.

"Now follow my lead—or lack of leadership or whatever." He rested his hands on my waist and started shaking his hips awkwardly, making me laugh and eventually join in. After a few tries to find a groove and failing, my inhibitions eased up. Who cared if we couldn't dance? It was fun to move and act like everyone else on the floor.

We spent the night dancing in our weird, uncoordinated way, even to slow songs like Ed Sheeran's "Perfect." And right after they announced homecoming court, when Deacon and Amy won king and queen but didn't show to accept their crowns, Cole put in a request for Stone Temple Pilots.

"For your mama," he whispered when the song started.

Good memories flooded in of my mother twirling around the living room with my father. I touched Cole's cheek. "Thank you."

I loved how he smiled even as his cheeks reddened. He started shaking his hips again. "All right, now. Let's see what you got."

Then we jumped to "Vasoline," laughing and making total fools of ourselves. Jess joined in, dancing with more grace. Aidan bopped along next her, doing that I'm-too-cool thing boys did when they didn't know how to dance. Jason and his date joined our circle when the DJ switched from Stone Temple Pilots to Velvet Revolver. We swayed in the middle of the floor, singing at the top of our lungs to "Fall to Pieces." By the end of the night, I was sweaty, my hair and makeup messed up—and I was perfectly happy.

Forgive me, Little.

Cole and I were making fun of each other's singing when he parked in front of my house. "See? I'm not the only one obsessed with good music," I said, and proceeded to sing a few bars of "Fall to Pieces."

He laughed and reached for my mouth. "Stop! My ears are bleeding."

I dodged him, and then howled the words as loud as I could.

"All right! You win." He managed to cover my mouth. "But would it hurt to sing a little Blake Shelton or Carrie Underwood?"

Challenge accepted.

I started in on a muffled version of "Before He Cheats" behind his hand.

"No, no, no! I take it back!" He released my mouth when I burst into laughter while holding my hands up in surrender.

After we quieted down, we smiled at each other, both of us opening our mouths to say something, laughing, and doing it again. When I gestured for him to go ahead, he said, "Did you see Sheckler's face when he announced the homecoming court?"

I brushed tangled hair from my eyes and nodded. "He stared right at you when Deacon and Amy didn't come up on stage."

"Yeah," he said, his eyes softening as he watched me. He slid his thumb across my bottom lip, making my stomach shoot electricity to my heart. "I'm sure he'll want me to write about it."

"You think they'll be okay?"

"If I know Deacon, he's got everything under control." Cole dropped his thumb from my face, and I had to swallow the disappointed moan in my throat. "I'm more worried about Amy's dad. He's sort of a prick."

"Will he try to hit her?"

His shrug didn't camouflage his concern. "He hits her mom, but… Deacon won't let him do anything."

"I hope you're right."

"I am." His smile returned. "You have fun?"

I couldn't look away—didn't want to. "It was great."

"Good." He touched my neck this time, one soft glide of his calloused index finger across my throat. His touch had the same kind of magic as his words.

I squeezed my eyes shut. No. We couldn't do this. *I* couldn't. I searched my brain for something to say, something to make us laugh again. Nothing. I opened my eyes to find him closer.

I licked my lips. "Um…"

He leaned in until I felt his raspy breaths against my lips.

"Cole?"

"Yeah?" He came even closer, his eyes wide open.

"Don't, okay?"

He pulled away. "Oh, uh..." He wiped the corners of his mouth and stared out the windshield. "Sorry."

All the good feelings between us vanished.

"No, it's okay, really. Just, I'm leaving soon, and—"

"I know you are." He started the car.

"Look, we—"

"It's almost ten. Better get in there before she comes out here."

"See you tomorrow, after church?"

He nodded, his attention still on the windshield. "I'll be waiting for you."

"*I'm* sorry. I wish…" What? What was I supposed to say?

"Night, Free."

After a heavy sigh, I got out. Before I shut the door, he whispered something so soft the grinding motor almost hid his words. But I heard them.

"*I* wish I didn't love you."

CHAPTER 31

Cole

The Holler Welcomes Back Local Man

D*id* I love her?

Yes, dammit! I loved her, and didn't that just complicate everything?

I'd make this up to her, though. Tomorrow. I'd just claim temporary insanity. A major lapse in judgment.

Why the hell did I try to kiss her?

Stupid, stupid!

But, man, I really wanted to kiss her.

My chest tightened when I pulled into my driveway, and all thoughts of kissing Free cut off with the engine. Cars littered the yard and lined the berm in front.

Sonofabitch.

Since Richie had been put away, only Shad invaded our trailer to sell Mama her pills and collect his "payment." Tonight I walked into a full house, with bluegrass streaming from an old CD player and people lounging anywhere they could plant their asses, holding beer cans or taking their turn on a communal pipe. Of course Mama was right in the middle, smoking, drinking, and high as the sky. All the while, Hannah held Kaycee at the edge of the couch. My niece absorbed what my brother brought into the house with wide, scared eyes.

Only a few days back and Richie's promise to change already showed its cracks.

"Hey, little brother!" He staggered over, and whatever was in his red plastic cup sloshed over the edge. "Don't you look spiffy?"

The urge to choke him made it hard to catch my breath. "Thought you were changing."

He finished his drink and crumpled the cup in his fist, tossing it to the floor. "Can't a man have a get-together with close friends and family?"

"No, Richie. He can't." I shoved past him and lifted Kaycee off Hannah's lap. "Come on, silly. Time for bed." I gestured for Hannah to follow and headed to my room.

Richie blocked me.

"Hey, now, she wants to hang with her Uncle Richie." He tried to pull Kaycee from my arms but stopped when she screamed and clung to my neck. "Well, what the fuck's wrong with her?"

Tension formed around us as thick as the smoke polluting the air. Hannah pressed a hand on Kaycee's back, saying nothing. She knew better.

I scanned the room, my eyes stopping at the corner by the coal stove.

Jackpot.

"Hey, Byron," I said, avoiding Richie's death stare, the one saying trouble wasn't far behind. "You tell Richie about the other day?"

Byron's eyes narrowed. "Me and your brother done patched our differences."

"Is that so?" I bounced Kaycee to hide how my arms shook and stared into Richie's dilated pupils. "While y'all were patching things up, did Byron mention the gun he held to my head?"

"That's some bullshit if I ever heard it!" Byron stumbled over. "I was only trying to—"

"He pointed a gun at you?" Richie interrupted.

This was my brother's sense of family loyalty: he could beat me up, no one else. "Yep, with an old-as-hell revolver he keeps in his glove box. Go see for yourself."

Richie nodded. "I think we'll do that." He backed up to the door, holding the now-screeching Byron by the collar. "Someone turn down the music," he yelled over the noise. "People are trying to sleep."

I let out a breath. "Thanks, Richie."

He saluted me with a wobbling hand.

The party didn't slow down after we shut ourselves in my room, the music loud and the dickheads littering our living room louder. Every time Mama laughed, or Richie told anyone willing to listen that he was "the fucking man," I covered Kaycee's ears, even after she fell asleep.

Idea 1085
Find a door to an alternate dimension

I waited until Mrs. Anvil came to get Hannah and Kaycee for church, and then headed outside, exhausted, anxious, and feeling the full weight of Richie's return. I'd had to maneuver around a few people polluting the living room floor with their stink. Mama slept in there, too, with Shad, his arm draped around her waist as they lay on the couch.

"Where're you going?"

I cowered at the sound of Richie's voice, dropping the keys in the mud.

Dammit!

"Nowhere, just out," I said, not turning around.

"Byron says this car belongs to his kin." He sounded tired, hung over, and maybe still high on whatever he'd taken last night. "What you doing driving around in it?"

"Told you it was my friend's."

"Your friend's Byron's niece?"

"Yeah." I plucked the keys from the mud and turned, not wanting him to sucker punch me. Better I see it coming. "So what?"

He held up his hands, smiling around a cigarette dangling from his mouth. "I don't care who you bang, little brother. Asking an innocent question is all."

His face was scruffy and gray, and deep circles surrounded his eyes. But at least he appeared somewhat sober, and a sober Richie was a safer one.

"I'm not banging anybody."

He took a deep hit, and said on the exhale, "Shame."

"You want something, Richie?"

He smoked his cigarette to the filter and flicked it toward a pile of casings in the yard. "Need a favor."

"What?"

"I gotta see some people about some things."

I held the keys tighter. "I'm not letting you take the car."

"Damn, Cole, never asked to take it, did I?"

"What, you want me to be your chauffeur?"

"Yep." He said it so final, like denying him wasn't an option.

It wasn't.

If I said no, he'd take the car. And he could, even with a hangover. Pissed me off, my helplessness. *Mental note: Sleep with the keys and ignition coil wire from now on.* Thankfully Dad's mechanic lessons never stuck with Richie. The idiot didn't know a motor from a spare casing. "How long's it gonna take?"

"Not too long." He headed into the house. "Lemme get dressed."

Not too long ended at 9:16 that night. I swear I drove him the length of Poplar Branch and stopped at almost every house. He'd go to the door, come back sometimes an hour later, wiping at his nose, showing me money people owed him, or bitching about people who didn't have money to give. After one house, he came back to the car with bloodied knuckles. I dared to ask him how his job hunt was going after a stop at Duffy Sloan's, and all he'd said was, "You're looking at it."

Well, shit. After Free set the law on Duffy, a huge war would break out up here. Everybody who worked for the old bastard would be on a mission to find the snitch, and after what I did to Byron last night, he'd sing for whoever wanted to listen about my association with Free. Wonder if Richie would fight for me then?

By the time we made it home, Richie went straight to bed. I had no idea how long he'd been awake, but it must have been at least twenty-four hours. Mama was on the couch, tired-looking and acting as if she wasn't a total piece of trash.

"Where'd y'all go?" she asked as I scrounged for food.

"All those assholes ate everything I brought in here!" I yelled, ignoring her question. I slammed the fridge, its empty shelves a good excuse to let go of my anxiety. "What the hell are we supposed to eat?"

"Some peanut butter on the shelf," she said, not even flinching from my outburst. "I get my foodies in a couple days. Calm your ass down."

"Great, Mama. Perfect." I stormed outside, saying over my shoulder, "You're as bad as he is."

I wanted to get to school early, cut Free off on her way to Callahan's, but Richie…

He bitched after I refused to let him take me to school so he could use the car. I almost didn't make it out of the house, but he gave up, saying, "I'll just take it when you come back."

No he wouldn't, not without the ignition wire.

As soon as Free came out of Callahan's office, I stepped in her path. "Hey."

Apprehension shadowed her face. "Are you okay?"

Oh, man. She felt sorry for me. I'd never wanted a do-over more than I did at this moment.

"I'm fine, really. About yesterday," I started. "I had every intention of coming over."

"No, yeah, forget it." She stared at her shoes, both of us ignoring the noise in the hall. "It's no big deal."

"It *is* a big deal. I meant to come by, apologize for being a dick."

"You weren't."

I tilted her chin until her eyes met mine. "I was, and I'm sorry. No kissing."

"It's not like I don't want to kiss you."

What? I had to tamp down the hope before it got carried away. "I guess if I can't kiss you, that's the next best thing." I gestured to the hall. "Let's go before we're late."

"What happened? Yesterday, I mean," she added quickly as we headed to homeroom.

"Family stuff."

"Your brother?"

I nodded. "But nothing to worry about outside of him being annoying as hell."

"You'll tell me if it gets more than annoying, okay?"

I didn't answer.

"Cole? Promise me."

I stopped at our lockers and tried to smile. “I promise.” Of course I wouldn’t tell her or anyone else. They didn’t need to know how bad shit was getting, or how powerless I was to do anything about it. Some hero I made.

At lunch, the missing king and queen told us what happened.

As of homecoming night, Amy was living with Deacon—after her dad kicked her out. The situation was fine with Deacon, who said, “My family belongs with me, anyway.”

“He’s right,” I whispered to Free when Jess and Amy started talking about babies. “Some people belong together.”

“I know.” She concentrated on her tray. “Which is why I’m leaving.”

CHAPTER 32

Cole

Anger Erupts Over Ideological Differences

On Saturday morning, Richie's whisper blared louder than any alarm clock. "Your car won't work."

I jolted awake and scooted to the back of my mattress, fingering the ignition wire tucked behind it. By the way the drugs made Mama and him sweat so much, our entire place smelled like week-old roadkill. That smell turned my stomach more than usual, fear never a great ingredient to mix with anything.

"H-how would you know?" My voice shook too much. So did my hands.

He threw the keys at me. "How do you think?"

I glanced at my backpack, everything in a pile on the floor. *Brainless!* Hide the wire but forget the keys? I stood on weak legs. "Strange. I'll take a look before work."

His left eyelid twitched. "You done something to it."

"No, I didn't."

"You think I'm some type of idiot?"

I waited too long to answer—and that was all it took.

Richie elbowed me in the lip, hard, and I went to the ground. "You ain't got an answer for me, boy?"

"Dammit!" Metallic blood filled my mouth, and I spat on the floor, trying not to break right there in front of him like a scared little kid.

"You think because you drive around in a car you ain't sharing and hang out with those fancy friends and wear their *fancy* clothes that you're anything special? You're forgetting something, little brother." He jabbed my nose with his middle finger. "You were born from this dirt just like me, and you'll die in it, too."

He punched the rotting wall with a yell, leaving a hole behind, and stomped out. Seconds later, the front door slammed shut. I just sat there, forcing myself to breathe.

Idea 1086
Transform to Fluid

When I pulled up at Free's after work, she was waiting for me outside. She got in before I even shifted into park, holding up her shiny, new driver's license and smiling the same way she had in her photo, kind of lopsided and not ready. "I'm legit now."

"Yeah, awesome."

She tapped her license on my shoulder with a snort. "Don't sound so excited. I only sold my soul to get it."

I tried to smile. "No, sorry. Good job. Really."

"Hey." She brushed her index finger across my cut lip. "What happened?"

"Cut myself." I shifted into reverse and backed into the street.

"Liar."

"It's fine."

"Cole—"

"Don't, all right?" I gripped the wheel tighter as I drove to Mim's. "Trust me when I tell you it's not a big deal."

"Did your brother hit you?" Her words were low, scared.

"Nah, I…I had a few beers with him last night though. Tripped going into the house." I hated lying to her, but I hated the idea of her knowing the truth more.

"You don't drink."

"A few beers don't make a habit."

She leaned up to give me full view of her frown. "I know you're lying, so stop. Don't be that 'I slipped and fell' person because it just sounds dense, especially coming from you."

"What do you want me to say, then?" I whispered. "Nothing you can do. Nothing *I* can do, either."

"We can use your half of the money to find an apartment." She paused. "I can go to California alone."

"Absolutely not."

"You can't kee—"

"It's not enough, anyway." I parked in Mim's driveway and turned to her. "Look, it was one time." I held up my hand when she opened her mouth. "And I can handle him. Handled him all my life."

She just stared at me, pinching her thigh. Then, "You shouldn't have to *handle* him, Cole."

"I won't have to for forever. Chances are he'll be back in the jailhouse after his first dirty piss test. His parole officer warned him about it already." Another lie I hoped she wouldn't call me on. "Don't. Worry."

"You need to tell Deacon."

I threw my hands in the air, smacking the roof with my fingertips. "So I should sic my best friend on my brother, have him fight my battles for me? Besides, even *if* I wanted him to,

Deac's got the baby—*a real baby*—to think about now. He doesn't need to be worrying about my problems."

Silence. A whole lot of it.

She opened her door. Hesitated. Then said, "If it happens again, I'm telling him."

Ouch.

Deacon: one

Ego: zero

Later, we had Mim's house to ourselves after she and her boys left for choir practice. We sat on her bed, eating a box of outdated snack cakes while studying our route and counting our savings, money we kept here. By now, reviewing our itinerary became more habit than anything; we both knew the directions to California by heart.

I tossed my last wrapper in the pile of cellophane wrappers between us and pulled my notebook from my bag. "What prison they send your dad to again?"

She rattled off the name around a mouthful of chocolate cake as she stacked the money. "Wrote him another letter the other day," she added after taking another bite. "Hope he doesn't procrastinate and puts me on his list."

"Yeah, hopefully." I wrote the prison name, pressing the pen too hard on the page.

"Oh, hey. You hear anything from Elena?"

"Don't you think I'd tell you?"

She fidgeted with a few dollar bills. "Just asking, Cole."

Shit. "Sorry."

"Forgiven. Anyway, we saved almost five hundred bucks. Five hundred! Can you believe it?" She reached across the pile of money and wrappers to steal the notebook from my hands. "Stop writing and celebrate with me."

"It's great, Free."

She must've heard how *not* great I thought it was, her smile faltering some as she handed my notebook back. But she wouldn't dig too far, not after I tried to kiss her. She'd acted careful around me since then, like I'd crack if she said the wrong thing. And after seeing my lip? She'd probably start acting like I was made of wet paper.

She went to the other side of the room where I set the bags of food I'd gotten from work today and divided it into the three usual piles: our trip food, food for Mim and her boys, and the rest for me to take home. "You think this'll be enough for you?" she asked, pointing to the biggest pile on top of Mim's dresser.

I nodded and got up to put my portion back into some bags. "It should get us to next week easy."

"Good." She collected our money from the bed and tucked it into the nightstand drawer, along with the folder filled with our map and stuff. "How much money do you think we'll need to spend before leaving?"

We'd only spent money on gas, the heater core from the junkyard, and what little I gave Mama to help out. "Maybe a couple hundred or so?"

"So, five weeks' pay minus..." She did her math thing and calculated our paychecks. "We should have like eight hundred dollars!" she said. "I've never saved that much in my life."

I hated how excited she was. Hated it.

"Well, you'll need all the help you can get, seeing as you'll be living in a car."

Her smile fell as she gathered the food spread on the floor she'd set aside for Mim. "You can have half of what's left. I'll manage."

"Manage in your car?" I winced when my tooth scraped against my cut lip, pissing me off more. "Great plan, Free. *Really* great. Escape this *fucking* place to live in a *fucking* car somewhere else."

She threw a box of macaroni at me, just missing my head. "That's *exactly* what I'm doing. Escaping!"

Everything escalated too fast, her anger and my misery. "You think your brother wants you to live in a car? You think your dad wants that?"

"It won't be forever."

"Oh? Until when? Until your dad gets out of the jailhouse and decides to do something else idiotic?"

"Shut up, Cole."

I yanked my fingers through my hair. Tried hard not to give in to the urge to punch a hole in the wall like Richie had done this morning. "You say your dad's a dreamer? Christ! What do you think you're doing right now?"

"Shut up!"

"You're being just as ridiculous as he is. Don't you see that?"

Her lips pursed as she stood stock-still in the middle of the room, her arms pressed hard against her sides.

And I kept right on tearing into her. "This whole asinine plan…I can't believe you…Living in a goddamn car, Free? How is that not as bad as living here!"

Nothing came out right. Nothing.

"What do you think I should do?" Anger dripped from every word she said, burning me. Making me madder. "Stay here, work at Gifford's forever? Maybe waste my life writing *stupid* escape plans and live in Poplar Branch with you?"

"Why not? Huh? What's so wrong with that?" Everything. Everything, everything was wrong with that.

And she let me know it. "Because the last thing I want to do is end up like you! The smart kid who has no plans to do *anything* but graduate high school and rent a crappy apartment."

"*End up like me*?" I laughed, a snarling sound. "No, hey, don't end up like me! I mean, you're right. Graduating high school is such a *stupid* fucking idea!"

"Yeah, it is! Oh, and let's not forget letting your brother beat the hell out of you until you do manage to graduate and find your shitty apartment!" She covered her mouth and gasped, regret darkening her eyes. "I-I'm sorry. I didn't mean it."

My insides turned to vapor. "You did." I gathered my bags. "Fuck this, Free. Seriously. Fuck this."

"Cole, I—"

"And you *do* have options, a hell of a lot more than I have." I pointed to the applications on the nightstand and the half-written essay she wouldn't let me read. "You're just too damn scared to admit it, *smart kid*."

"Wait!" She followed me out the bedroom door. "Will you just wait."

"I'm done waiting for you." I ran down the stairs, stumbling on the last one.

"Cole!"

I stopped and turned to her.

"Please. I'm sorry." Her chin trembled, and tears traced paths down her cheeks. "Let's…I don't know."

I could take her anger. But her tears? No.

I brushed a trembling finger over my sore lip. Looked everywhere but her face. "I think I have to…" I swallowed when my voice cracked. And cracked. And cracked. "I'll see you tomorrow, okay? Just…Yeah. I'll see you later." Without another word, I took off.

And didn't stop until I made it to the cliff.

I screamed until my voice disappeared, then slumped onto the cold rock. She was right. About everything, she was absolutely right. But so was I. And what the fuck, anyway? I mean… What the actual fuck was I supposed to do?

I collected pebbles and tossed them over the cliff. It'd be cool if one crashed into my trailer and the impact blew it up. Idea 1087—

Oh. Right.

I dropped the rest of the pebbles and rubbed my hands together. Free was definitely right about me. And fighting with her was pointless. She never lied to me, never told me things I wanted to hear to save my feelings. She just made me love her. Not her fault.

After four days of apologizing to each other and trying to pretend Saturday never happened, we splurged the night before Thanksgiving and went to the movies with Deacon and Amy. It didn't really make up for our fight, but hey, it was something.

I hated that we wasted four whole days walking on eggshells with each other, especially because we only had thirty left. I wanted the power to slow down time, make each day longer, like days on Venus. Idea 1088. But no, thirty ordinary Earth days were all I had until I never saw her again.

"Sucks not being able to see you tomorrow," I said as soon as I cut the engine in front of her house. Jolene said Thanksgiving was a holiday for staying home, so Free had to stay. All I'd be doing tomorrow was avoiding Richie and Mama and anyone else who came over to party.

"It's only one day, right?"

I stared at the wheel. "Right."

"Hey." Free captured my chin and forced me to look at her. "What's wrong?"

"Nothing's wrong. Hate missing a day with you is all. We only have so many."

"I know." She wrapped her coat tighter around her. The first snow of the year decided to start while we sat in the theater. She also avoided the topic, changing to a familiar one: "Has your brother done anything else?"

"Told you it's fine."

"You're not acting fine."

"Live with two addicts and you wouldn't be fine most of the time either." I rubbed the back of my neck. Prepared to grovel for the millionth time this week. "Sorry."

"Don't be." Another subject change: "You think Amy'll be okay?"

"What do you mean?"

She brushed hair from her eyes. "Well, Deacon'll be gone for a while after graduation. She'll be alone with his folks and a new baby."

I bowed my head and whispered, "She won't be alone."

A pause. "Y'all love each other, don't you?"

"'Course," I said. "Thought it was obvious."

"It is. Um… so, I'll see you Friday?"

"Yeah." I smiled at her, not feeling it at all. "I'll be waiting for you bright and early."

She opened her door. "I'll be waiting for you, too."

CHAPTER 33

Cole

Assault Over Thanksgiving Dispute

No turkey roasted in the oven Thanksgiving morning. Not at *my* house, where people slept off last night's party on the living room floor. Holidays were different when I was younger and my dad still worked at Janson's Auto in Davy. Mama would cook a whole mess of things, and she was good at it. We were happy once, and that made days like this worse.

Last night, I packed food, blankets, and a couple of notebooks with plans to spend the day at the cliff. If I couldn't be with Free or my friends, the next best place was there. It'd be cold and snowy, but a hell of a lot better than staying here.

When I opened the front door, I found Richie standing at Duffy's truck window with the old bastard talking and pointing at Free's car. "Take it, then," he said. "He owes me that and more, anyway."

Shit!

I shut the door and searched the bodies on the floor for a cell. Nothing.

Shit! Shit!

Maybe this wasn't a big deal, maybe Duffy was just talking garbage. *Maybe, maybe…*

Kaycee came out of her room as I searched the last person, who grunted and swatted my hand away. "What's wrong, Colie?"

Her innocent voice tightened the panic in my chest. She'd been a baby the last time she saw Richie put his hands on me, but now she'd have to witness what was coming and be old enough to remember it. "Go back to your room, okay? Tell your mama to lock the door."

"But I'm hungry."

I took off my backpack and pulled out a box of crackers. "Here." I picked her up when she took it and carried her to the room. "Don't come out."

Hannah woke up, groggy and rubbing sleep from her eyes. "What's going on?" Her cheeks paled when her hands dropped and her gaze lifted to my face. "What is it?"

"Richie's gonna try to take the car." My whole body went numb as I said it. "Just stay in here."

"Give him the car, Colie!" Her voice pitched high, making her sound as young as Kaycee.

"No."

Mama woke too, a hangover clouding her face. "What're y'all going on about?"

"Richie's gonna hurt Cole!" Hannah jumped from the bed and took Kaycee from me. "Give him the car!"

I shook my head, my words tangling in my throat.

"Give it to your brother, baby." Mama sat up and held her hand out to me, tears in her bloodshot eyes. "It ain't worth it."

"N-no. Keep the door locked."

I shut them in and went to my room, taking the ignition wire and keys from my bag. Where to hide them? Where? I lifted my mattress and pried a board loose, stuffing the keys and wire in there as the front door opened. "Cole! Where you at?"

I swallowed a scream and prayed this wouldn't be too bad. That he was more tired than high and would give up after the first hit like last time. His footsteps came closer to the room as he yelled my name again. And when he forced open the bedroom door, the lock not strong enough to keep him out, I had to lean against the back wall so my watery knees wouldn't take me to the ground.

"There you are." He came in, cracking his knuckles, anticipation in his dilated eyes. "Mr. Sloan says that car belongs to him."

"He's a damn liar." I wished the wall would swallow me up. "It's Free's. Her dad did him wrong, not her."

He came closer. "Not how he sees it, and it ain't how I see it neither. Kin's got to pay for kin mistakes."

"Tell him to take it out on Byron." My voice sounded like Hannah's. "That asshole's the one who told Free's dad about the sang in the first place."

He nodded. "I'll make sure to tell Mr. Sloan, but I'm going to be needing those keys."

I shook my head, my lips too numb to form more words.

"No?" He shut the bedroom door. "Well, now, we're about to have a problem." He dumped everything from my bag, pulled my clothes out of the dresser, and ripped the pictures off my wall. "Where're the keys, Cole!"

"Fuck you!" I ran for the door, and he swung at me. I dodged and tried to hit him first.

Missed.

"You little bastard!" He tackled me to the ground, swinging at me, relentless, brutal.

I covered my face, his fists coming fast. "Stop!" I screamed, curling into a ball.

"Give me the keys!"

"No!"

He kept hitting and hitting, throwing in kicks to my stomach and ribs. I tried to breathe between each blow to my gut. But after he slammed an elbow to my temple, I zoned out, my mind doing its Richie-escape. I pictured myself floating above, watching him lose control over my prone body, not feeling anything. No pain. No fear. My life hovered between the holler and Heaven. Someday, God would take me. Someday, He wouldn't make me go back.

Someday.

CHAPTER 34

Free

$Pr(E) = \frac{a}{a+b}$
Unfavorable Odds

Friday came and went.

No Cole.

I tried not to worry as I lay in my bunk Friday night, talking to Sarah about Jason, whom she apparently had a crush on. I gossiped with her and told myself Cole would be here to pick me up in the morning. We had work, and no matter what was going on at home, he wouldn't miss it.

He did.

Fear coated my skin like hot wax as I rushed downstairs and found Jolene in the kitchen. "Can I use your phone?"

"For what?" She didn't look at me as she fed a baby in the high chair.

"M-my friend, he was supposed to get me for work."

"Maybe he didn't want to come get you."

"No, no, he wouldn't do that. He…" My voice broke, getting her attention.

"Now, you calm down. I'm sure everything's fine. You hang out with that boy from Poplar Branch, don't you?"

I nodded, holding a fist to my mouth.

"You need to expect this kind of thing from those white trash fools. They do what they please." She set the jar of food on the table. "I'll take you to work. Lemme get Kenny to finish here."

I didn't argue with her. Maybe she was right, maybe Cole had had enough of me. *Please let that be it!*

When I got to work, he wasn't there.

"Did Cole call in or anything, Mr. Gifford?" I didn't give him a chance to give me his usual greeting.

"Can't say he did, Freedom." Concern marred his brow. "Is everything all right?"

"No, I… No. I have to go, okay? I need to see if…" I didn't finish before I was outside and on my way to Mim's. I skated on the slushy roads, falling twice, the dirty snow soaking my jeans.

Something's wrong!

"Can I use your phone?" I asked as soon as Mim opened her door.

"You're sopping wet." She frowned past my shoulder, opening the door wider to let me in. "Did you walk here? What's the problem, honey?"

"Don't know yet." I went straight to the kitchen and dialed Deacon's number.

When Deacon answered, I dug into my thigh. *Don't cry. Don't break.* "Have you seen Cole?"

"Haven't seen him since Wednesday night with y'all."

What if his brother—*No! Please, no.* "I think we should see if he's okay."

"You haven't seen him either?"

The tears came no matter how hard I tried to keep them in. "Not since the movies. We're supposed to work today. He… he never showed up."

"Where are you," Deacon said, his voice shaky.

I gave him Mim's address.

"Be there in ten."

We didn't talk on the way to Poplar Branch, Deacon driving as fast as he could on the slick roads up the mountain. I shivered, the cold soaking me to the bone.

Two thousand, eight hundred, fifty—

Please be fine!

I jumped out before Deacon turned off the truck, racing for the cinder blocks.

"Free! Wait, damn it!" Deacon reached my side and took my arm. "Richie's no joke."

"What if we're too late?"

Deacon led up the blocks to the door. "He ain't dead. Probably beat up real bad, but not dead. Wouldn't be the first time."

"How many times, Deacon?" The tears wouldn't stop.

"Too many." Deacon knocked. "Stay behind me."

The door opened, and I peered around Deacon to see Cole's sister, her face pale.

"You shouldn't be here," she said.

"Where is he, Hannah?" Deacon's low voice made her flinch.

"You're doing him no good by coming," she whispered desperately. "He'll be fine in a few days. You know how it is."

"This ain't right."

"I understand that better than you." She glanced behind her. "But it's best you stay out of it."

"I'm done staying out of it." Deacon took a step forward as Richie staggered to the door and pushed Hannah out of the way.

"What the hell you want?" Richie said to Deacon, his eyes glassy.

My stomach twisted with hate. Richie, the person Cole feared the most. I wanted to kill him.

Deacon beat me to it.

"You sonofabitch!" He clocked Richie, knocking him to the floor, and then crouched low to keep pummeling him.

"Get the fuck off me!" Richie tried to fight back, but he didn't have a chance against Deacon, who dragged him outside into the snow by his bare feet.

"Find Cole!" Deacon yelled to me as he slammed his fist into Richie's face again and again.

I rushed into the house to find Cole's mother, sister, and niece huddled on the couch, crying and hugging each other. "Where is he?" I demanded, my own tears falling as fast as theirs.

Hannah pointed to the short hallway. "First door on the right."

I took off, trying to block out the cries from Kaycee, her tiny sobs finding my heart. But when I opened Cole's bedroom door to him curled in the fetal position, everything else faded into the background. "Cole!"

I fell to his mattress and pressed against his shoulder until he opened his right eye, his left too swollen. "What're you doing here?" he asked through puffy lips.

"You're leaving." I took stock of his torn-up room. His things. I had to get his things because he was never coming back here. "You're *fucking* leaving this place."

I found his backpack and an empty canvas bag and filled them with his notebooks, clothes, shoes, anything I knew was his. Without looking at the couch, I went outside long enough to throw Cole's things into Deacon's truck.

"Hurry up!" Deacon had Richie's face smashed into the mud and snow with one hand, his knee on the older guy's back. Weird, strangled cries came from Richie, inhuman and dark.

I nodded, wheezing as I ran back to Cole, who sat at the edge of his mattress, trying to tie his boot laces. I lowered to do it for him, my fingers shaking so much it took two tries. "Can you walk?"

He groaned but stood with my help. "Y-yeah, but…" He leaned heavily on me, his weight as dense as lead. "We need the wire."

"What?"

He pointed to the mattress. "L-lift it."

I used my foot to tip it on its side. "What now?"

"The floorboard." He pointed to a skewed board by the wall. "Underneath."

I let go of him long enough to lift the board and snatch a wire and the keys.

He leaned into me again when I went back to him, and said, "Get me out of here."

Absolutely.

His mother ran to us and caught Cole by his hoodie sleeve. "Where you taking my boy?"

"Let. Go." My voice came out strong, threatening. I was a bear protecting her cub again, just as I'd been for my brother.

She stood there for a few seconds, her eyes wide. "Sorry, baby. I'm so sorry."

"Me too." Cole bent to hug her. "But I'm done, Mama."

Yes, yes, he was.

"Deacon! Let's go!" I yelled, inching closer to my car.

Deacon eyed Cole as we slogged by him. "Holy shit, man."

Cole grunted. "S'okay."

Deacon gave Richie one last punch to the temple then stood and spat on his unmoving back. "Asshole."

"Wait." Cole lifted a hand when Deacon rushed to us. "Lift the hood."

Deacon did as he asked.

"The wire," Cole said to me. He took it from my outstretched hand and stumbled to the Buick's engine. In seconds, he backed away, holding his stomach. "Shut it."

I closed the hood and fumbled with the keys as Deacon helped Cole into the car.

"Where we going?" Deacon asked as he clicked Cole's seatbelt in place.

I started the car, and gave him the only answer I had: "Mim's."

CHAPTER 35

Cole

The Good Folks of McDowell County

If someone had ripped open my skin, poured gasoline on my organs, and lit them on fire, I wouldn't feel any worse. Everything hurt. My face, my ribs, my pride. Nothing I hadn't dealt with one time or another, but now I had to deal with it in front of Free.

"Careful. Take it slow," she whispered, guiding me to Mim's porch steps, holding me tighter when I slipped on ice.

Deacon followed as we climbed the stairs, his heavy, angry breathing loud in my ears. It didn't bother me to be beaten up in front of him; he'd seen it before. But I was pissed. He'd kicked the shit out of Richie—something I couldn't do, and my bruised face and tender stomach proved it.

"What in the name…?" Mim held the door open, wide-eyed. "Which one of them hillbilly assholes done this?"

"His brother," Free told her.

"My God in heaven…" Mim reached for my other shoulder and helped guide me to the couch.

Her boys crowded around us, quiet for once. "He gonna be all right, Mama?" her oldest asked.

"'Course, baby. But I need y'all to be good while we take care of him." Mim gathered her kids and herded them to the stairs. "Get some ice for those boys, Free."

Free ran into the kitchen, and I could hear her opening the freezer and slamming ice cube trays on the counter. Ice wouldn't help much; the bruises were a good two days old. She came back to the couch and sat on the edge while Deacon stood at the end of it, holding the towel filled with ice she'd given him to his right knuckles. When she pressed another ice-filled towel to my left eye, I recoiled with a hiss.

"Shh, it's okay," she cooed, touching the towel gently to my face. "Jesus." Her voice cracked. "Jesus." It cracked some more. "Jesus…Jesus…"

Her tears prompted mine, and nothing I could tell myself stopped them.

"You're safe now, man." I felt Deacon's hand on my leg, his voice hitching. "You're safe."

Mim came down and hugged Free from behind while placing a hand on my chest as we continued to sob. Another weakness Free had to see.

Another failure I had to live with.

When I managed to pull myself together, I nodded to Deacon, gingerly wiping my cheeks. "You finally got to thump him."

A struggling smile lifted the corner of his mouth. "Felt pretty damn good."

"I bet." I shifted to rest my head on Free's lap, the effort shooting dull pain up my side, and wrapped an arm around her thighs. "Thanks for coming to get me."

She brushed my temple. "What happened?"

"Got my ass kicked."

"No, that's not what I mean." She threaded her fingers through my tangled hair. "*Why*, Cole?"

I licked my swollen lips. "He wanted to take the Buick."

"You should have let him take it!" she cried, her tears dripping on my skin.

I pulled myself closer to her. "Not my car to give."

"Un-fucking-believable!" Deacon dropped his towel on the coffee table, the ice crackling against the wood. "Why the hell would they give him parole, anyway?"

"Well, he ain't getting away with it." Mim went into the kitchen and picked up the phone. "We'll see how he likes it when prison comes calling again."

"No, Mim, don't." I struggled to sit with Free's help. "You call the law and everybody'll think I did it."

Mim stared at me for a long time, the receiver cradled between her neck and shoulder. "So, he don't have to answer for what he done?"

"I don't have much choice," I said.

"Goddammit." Mim hung up the phone and rested her forehead against the wall next to it as we watched her without moving. "You eighteen, Cole?"

"Yes, ma'am."

Her back heaved before she lifted her gaze to mine. "That settles it."

"Settles what?" Free asked.

Mim hugged her arms to her chest. "I can't afford to do much, but I can certainly give you a couch to sleep on and food in your stomach until we figure things out."

Stunned, I stared at her, tears again threatening to steal away my dignity. "I don't expect you to do that."

"No one said you did. You kids…The things you have to go through." She nodded as if answering a silent question in her head. "You're coming here—end of discussion."

Free jumped up and hugged her. "Thank you, thank you, thank you!"

"It's the least I can do for y'all. Wish I could do more."

"W-we have money," Free said. "Over six hundred—"

"Wait, no." I pushed off the couch with more willpower than strength. "As much as I want you to stay, it's not gonna be because I got in your way."

"You're not in my way." Free shook her head. "How can you *say* that?"

"Because I—"

"I ain't taking one red cent from y'all." Mim pulled away from Free and grabbed her cigarette case off the kitchen table. "Your mama would turn in her grave." She lit a cigarette and inhaled before continuing, "You're like my own daughter, Freedom, *my own blood*."

"Are you sure?"

"Have I ever said something I ain't meant?"

"But..." I held out my hands. "How am I supposed to repay you?"

"You're a good boy, Cole." Mim tapped her cigarette ash in the ashtray on the counter. "Nothing like your daddy or good-for-nothing brother, you understand? And you can repay me by showing every soul in the entire holler that you got out. That you beat it."

I nodded, my mind already working on how to achieve that. "Yeah, okay. I can."

"And I believe you." She took another hit, and said, "I hope you don't mind noise. My house is full of it."

"I don't mind it one bit."

"Well then. Welcome to the Alcott Zoo."

CHAPTER 36

Free

$V_g = \frac{Gm}{-r}$
Potential

I made Cole chicken soup while he showered.

And argued with him when I tried to feed it to him after he dressed, losing.

I also bribed Mim's boys with chips to stay out of the living room while he dozed on the couch. Every time he moaned in his sleep, I pressed my hand against his chest to check his breathing as I had when Little was an infant.

When he awoke and held his arms out to me, I curled against his side without a word.

Mim left us alone mostly. She called Mr. Gifford, too, let him know a version of what happened. When the afternoon leaked into evening, she brought us blankets, turned out the lights, and went to bed.

Cole stroked my back, moving his fingertip along my spine as we lay in the dark. "You're gonna get in trouble."

I shifted closer to him. "I don't care."

"You should."

"Why?"

He sighed, his chest inflating and deflating against my cheek. "You have a little over three weeks, Free, and we still need money. You gotta work."

"We have enough to get there and for your train ticket back."

"Yeah, but you'll need to eat until you find a job."

"We have plenty of food to take already."

"It won't last forever." His finger stopped in the middle of my back. "You need the money."

"I can't drive my car home," I said, digging for any excuse to stay. "What if Jolene tries to take my keys?"

"I'll drive you."

I sat up to inspect his bruises in the moonlight. "You can't."

He grunted as he stood, wobbling a bit before holding a hand to me. "I got beat up, not shot. I can hack it."

"You could barely stand this morning."

"But I can stand now."

I studied his left eye. "You swear?"

"May God strike me dead." He ducked a little when he said it, making me chuckle.

"Always joking…" I grabbed the keys off the coffee table. "Let's go."

"Right behind you."

Once I made it home, I shifted into park and left the motor running. "I'll walk over tomorrow morning, skip out before Jolene makes me go to church."

"It's five miles."

"You saying I can't do it?"

"It's a long walk."

"I'm walking."

"Well, all right." He managed his crooked smile. "Wake me up as soon as you get to Mim's, hotshot."

"Maybe I will, maybe I won't." I leaned over and kissed his cheek, causing him to wince and suck in his breath. "Oh, crap. Sorry."

"Pain's worth it."

He always said the right things. Things I shouldn't love to hear. *You're leaving, remember?*

Leaving…

Excitement rippled inside my chest. Or maybe it was anxiety.

I cupped his cheek, careful to avoid bruises. "Stay with me."

"What?"

"When we get to California." I leaned closer. "*Stay.*"

"Free… What about school?"

"What about it?"

He brought my hand down to the seat. "The only goal I've ever had was graduating high school. It's not much, but it means something."

I swallowed. "You…We can figure it out there. They have schools in California, too, Cole."

"I don't know." He smiled a sad smile. "Maybe."

I nodded, my throat tight and aching. Maybe was better than no. "Be careful," I whispered as I opened my door. "See you tomorrow."

"I'll be waiting for you."

I woke up before any of the other girls and tiptoed into the bathroom to shower and brush my teeth. Then I *almost* made it out the front door.

"Where you think you're going?"

I froze. "Um." I turned to face Jolene, who stood at the kitchen sink. "Work."

"Not before church." She had her hands on her hips and a cigarette hanging from her mouth. "And not after either."

"About last night, I…" I moved away from the door. "I'm sorry. My friend, the one I told you about? He got hurt."

"Your friends ain't my concern." She puffed on her cigarette from the side of her mouth. "You're staying in today, going to church with the rest of us, and cleaning for punishment."

I glanced at the mountains of laundry near the bottom of the stairs and to the dishes piled in the sink. "I have to…" I couldn't meet her shark eyes and say a full sentence.

"You got nothing to do but spend the morning with the Lord and cleaning after."

Crap. "Just today?"

She puffed and stared, one eye squinting to avoid the smoke billowing around her head. "What'd I tell you about breaking curfew?"

"It was only fifteen minutes!"

"Late is late."

I stepped forward with my hands out. "Wait, I—"

"I'm a one-strike woman, and you done swung your last swing. But…" She flicked her ashes in the sink. "You clean this house, show you're sorry, and I might be persuaded to forgive you this one time." She turned her back on me and shuffled toward the coffeepot. "You go on and get them girls up."

Ugh. "Yes, ma'am."

I spent the entire day after church cleaning, doing laundry, and whatever else Jolene could find for me to do. While I scrubbed, I showed off my math skills to some of the younger kids, and they *oohed* and *aahed* when Sarah checked my answers on a calculator. I also finished my essay and the rest of the applications, and I actually felt accomplished after.

The main reason I didn't go crazy being stuck in the house was my call to Mim. Sarah kept watch as I sneaked into Jolene's room and found her cell phone.

"He's fine," Mim promised. "He hasn't been up since last night, except to use the bathroom and eat a bit."

"Good." I squeezed the phone. "Do you think he'll be going to school tomorrow?"

"He's insisting he is. Says he has things he needs to do there."

"O-okay. Tell him…Tell him I'll be waiting for him."

The next morning, relief loosened my muscles as the Buick chugged into the student lot. I hurried to Cole's door before he finished parking. He looked better, still bruised, but the swelling in his lips had gone down, and he didn't appear so drained.

"It's about time," I said, opening his door.

He gave his crooked smile as he got out, slower than usual, and wrapped an arm around me. "Thanks for waiting."

"You're late," Mrs. Callahan said as I took my seat.

"Yes, but…" I pulled papers from my bag as she stared me down. "Maybe these will make you forgive me."

Surprise lit her face as she reached for the paperwork. "You finished?"

"Deal's a deal. Got my license, and you got a bunch of useless applications and a messy, handwritten essay on why I want to go to college." My leg started bouncing, and I had to refrain from biting my nails to avoid grossing her out.

"Glad you're as honorable as you are frustrating, Miss Paine." She skimmed the applications with a smirk until she found the essay at the bottom of the pile.

I gave Mrs. Callahan everything in that essay. Gave her Mama's death, Daddy's dreams, Little's birth, and my promise to him.

"Oh," she whispered.

If my leg bounced any faster, it'd propel me to the ceiling. "It don't matter or nothing, but if I were going to college, I'd write exactly that."

She glanced up. "This is beautiful, Freedom."

"Now you see why I have to go. My brother needs me."

"But wouldn't it be great if you could give him the future you promised in this essay, one with an education?"

I stopped pretending with Mrs. Callahan a while ago. She knew what I had planned after she read the first letter I wrote to my father.

"No. I…No. I told him I'd be there, and I will be."

"Oh, you should go. But only to see that he's fine with your own eyes. Then come back, turn in these applications. Finish school."

"What if he's not fine? What if his mother's there and she's hurting him?"

"You said she's not allowed near him."

"But what if she is?"

"And what if she isn't, and he's in school and happy with his grandparents?" Her voice stayed calm, contrasting the panic in mine.

"What about my father?"

She sighed. "Do you honestly think he'd want you to give up the opportunity for an education? There are resources, scholarships, programs to help people like you. *I can help you.*"

"No." I pulled my fingers through my hair, yanking at the roots. "I ain't leaving Little alone."

"But he's not alone. He's with his grandparents."

I gathered my things and stood. "I…Can we stop?"

"Yes, of course." Mrs. Callahan always stopped when I asked her to, something I loved about her. She went to the door. "See you tomorrow morning?"

"I'll be here."

Cole still waited in the main office as we came out, a notebook tucked under his arm. "Mrs. Callahan?"

She lifted her gaze to him and smiled, only to dip into a frown. "My Lord," she whispered under her breath.

"It looks worse than it is." Cole, always trying to make other people comfortable.

She moved with her arms out to him but stopped. "What happened?"

"Got jumped is all. No big deal. But, I was wondering… Can you maybe give me some of those college applications?"

"I—Yes. Yes! Absolutely." She covered her anger like a pro. "Why don't you come in and we can talk."

"Yeah, okay. Thanks." He turned to me after Mrs. Callahan went into her office.

"When did you…?" I wanted to be happy. To jump up and down and hug him.

He's not going to stay with me.

Cole slid his thumb across my bottom lip. "I promised Mim—and you were right."

"Right about what?"

He pulled out his Escape Plans notepad from his back pocket and showed me the last page.

Final Idea

Go to College

"I'm never escaping Richie or anyone else up there, not unless I do something real." He shrugged. "This is the best something I came up with."

"Cole, this…" *Don't cry. Don't be sad.*

"I can't stay with you, Free," he whispered.

His oceans. Eyes I knew I'd drown in one day.

I just never thought it'd be this painful.

I nodded.

He tucked the notepad into my hand. "Here, I don't need it anymore."

CHAPTER 37

Free

D = rt
Distance

Christmas morning at Jolene's was sort of nice. Kenny passed out presents, and Jolene recorded it. Sarah got a winter coat and some clothes, Shelly and Kate opened Barbies, and I didn't see what the other kids got, but they were all happy. I unwrapped a new duffel bag, a thick blanket, and a gas card.

"It's pre-loaded with fifty bucks," Jolene said as she videoed me opening it.

I held the blanket and card to my chest. "Why?"

She set her phone on the end table in exchange for her cigarette case. "You ain't our first kid to turn eighteen, Freedom. Knowing your circumstances, I'm guessing you'll be long gone come tomorrow, maybe to find that brother of yours." She took a hit, and added on the exhale, "You'll be in my prayers, girl."

I ran my fingers over the soft fleece. "Thank you, Jolene."

"Be safe, you hear? And if you change your mind, you got a place with us until you graduate." She picked up her phone. "Choice is yours."

I nodded.

But I didn't wait until my birthday to leave. I packed my things and Little's into my Christmas present that afternoon, and Jolene didn't stop me on the way out. "Good luck," she said as she rolled out pie crust with some of the kids, including Sarah. She wiped her hands and came over to me.

I dropped my bag and hugged her. "I'll miss you."

"I liked being your friend, Free."

"I liked being yours, too." I pulled away and grabbed my bag. "Bye."

Cole waited for me out front, like he'd promised last night.

"Merry Christmas," I said as I got in. I threw my stuff in the back, on top of blankets, pillows, and his notebooks. He'd already packed for tomorrow, and I wouldn't analyze why that upset me. "You've been busy."

"Didn't want to waste time doing it in the morning." He shifted into drive after backing out then covered my hand with his. "And Merry Christmas. Jolene give you a hard time?"

"No, she expected it. Gave me a new bag and everything."

"Good deal."

When we got to Mim's, Deacon, Amy, and Jess were there. I shrieked when I saw them at the door waving like lunatics.

"Surprise," Cole said, smiling his crooked smile.

I smiled back and cupped his cheek, skimming a finger over the faded bruise under his eye. "Thank you."

Later, we hung out in the living room by the tree glowing with multi-colored lights and homemade ornaments. Deacon whispered to Amy on the couch as he rubbed her slightly swollen belly, while Jess took pictures of us as she talked to Mim, who was busy setting the kitchen table. Cole kept the boys occupied, wrestling with them in front of the TV.

While I watched, curled up on the old recliner, all I wanted to do was cry.

After supper, Jess and Amy hugged me, and when they cried, I finally did too. "I'm going to miss y'all so much."

"I wish we could've known you sooner," Jess said. "And I wish it didn't have to be California."

"Make sure you find a way to keep in touch—Snapchat, Twitter, whatever," Amy added, wiping her eyes.

"I'll try," I told her as they put on their coats.

Deacon and Cole talked near the door, with Deacon handing Cole his cell and a small box. Cole's face flamed red as he glanced at me, the box, then Deacon, shaking his head and trying to hand it back. Deacon pointed to Amy, me, then held up his hands, shaking his head, too.

"What was that about?" I asked Cole when they left.

"Nothing I plan to tell you."

"Why not?"

"Because." Wow, his face could get red. Almost purple, even.

Interesting.

"Seriously, it's stupid. Anyway." He showed me Deacon's phone. "He let us borrow it, just in case."

"Nice." I tilted my head and crossed my arms. Gave him the same stare I gave Little when I thought he was lying to me. "What's going on?"

"Nothing." He waved a hand in the air and totally avoided eye contact. "It's all good."

"Is it?"

He nodded, still not looking me in the eye.

"You're avoiding something…"

"No."

"Liar."

"Can I have few minutes with my girl here, Cole?" Mim stood by the tree, holding a package with blue wrapping.

"Yes! I mean, yeah, sure. No problem."

"Coward," I muttered.

"Yep." He smiled at me and headed to the stairs. "I'm gonna take a shower."

When the bathroom door shut behind Cole, Mim came over and smoothed my hair. "If you ever want to come back…"

"I know." *This isn't supposed to be so hard!*

"Good." She kissed my forehead and handed me the package. "Happy birthday."

"You didn't have to get me nothing."

"It ain't much, just something I found while going through old pictures and such." Mim tipped her chin to my hands. "Open it."

I slowly unwrapped the paper to reveal a framed picture. "Mama," I whispered.

"It's the day she brought you home from the hospital. See how tiny you was? Just this fragile, gorgeous child." She brushed a finger across my mother's face. "She was barely nineteen, too young to know any better, but she knew for certain you were the love of her life."

I held the picture to my heart. "It's perfect."

"Just like you." She hugged me and sniffed. "I promised myself I wouldn't cry."

I squeezed her tighter. "I'll be fine, and I'll keep in touch, I swear."

"You better." She pulled away and wiped under her eyes. "Now, I'm going to bed and dream Santa put a sexy fireman under the tree."

I grinned. "Night, Mim."

A half hour later, Cole lay in a sleeping bag on the living room floor, insisting I take the couch. He wrote in a leather notebook while I stared at the tree lights blinking on and off, holding my mother's picture.

"Free?"

"Yes?"

He closed his notebook and frowned up at me. "I need you to do something for me."

Anything.

Almost anything.

"What?"

"Don't tell Smith about Duffy."

"Why?"

"It'll start things." He hesitated. "Things that might get back to me."

"How would it get back to you?"

"Just know it will."

I shifted to my side. "He'll keep doing what he does to people."

"And he'll *keep* doing it even if you tell. About everybody up there protects him, whether out of fear or the fact he employs a ton of people."

"Employs people to sell drugs."

"Money's money. Doesn't matter to most folks how they get it."

Could I do this for him? Yes, of course. "Okay," I said after a few seconds.

"Okay?"

"If that's what you want."

He let out a sigh and opened his notebook. "Thank you."

"Welcome."

The sound of his pen as he wrote was like a lullaby, soothing me. But when the clock on the end table chimed at midnight, his pen stopped. "Free?"

"Hmm?" I said, my eyelids heavy.

"Happy birthday."

Smiling, I closed my eyes.

CHAPTER 38

Cole

Road Trip

Free and I sat in the Buick, waving at Mim standing at her screen door.

We did it.

Holy shit.

"You ready?" I asked, staring out the windshield and still waving like an idiot.

"We're really doing this, ain't we?" Disbelief colored her voice, even as her excitement crackled inside the car.

And damn, it was contagious. We were *leaving*, just the two of us. My scalp tingled, and warmth seeped into my body despite the cold morning.

Just us.

Smiling so wide it hurt, I said, "Hell, yes, we are."

"So crazy."

So freaking crazy. "Yeah."

"Cole?" She clasped my waving hand, bringing it to the ignition. "Start the car."

I nodded, my fingers actually shaking as I turned the key. The radio came on with the roar of the engine, and Free cranked it, Red Hot Chili Peppers filling the space around us.

She grinned and shook her head.

I pulled out, paying more attention to her than the road. "What?"

"Californication." She pointed to the radio. "It's fate."

"Nah, that's not fate." I gestured out the window to the run-down houses surrounding Mim's and lining the steep road, filled with McDowell County lifers. "*This* is fate, and we kicked its ass."

"Yeah, I guess we did." She started singing along then, low and soft.

"Oh, no…"

Louder.

"Not again."

Even louder.

"No singing!"

And then at the top of her lungs.

I laughed, and when the chorus came on, I joined her. *We actually did it!*

We drove through McDowell County, and then left it behind. And for every song that blared on the radio, we sang so off-key it hurt my ears. I thumped on the wheel, and Free danced in her seat. The song didn't matter. We sang it. Yelled it. I didn't know the words to most, so I made them up. She covered her ears and beamed as she belted out the right ones.

My voice grew too hoarse to keep it up for long, and Free quieted as well, now tapping her leg and humming. As I drove, I sneaked glances at her, and every time she caught me, we'd smile like we shared a secret no one else knew.

But when we made it to the Kentucky border, I skidded to a stop on the berm and stared at the blue sign: Welcome to Kentucky: Birthplace of Abraham Lincoln.

"Why'd you stop?"

I turned to her as cars whizzed by us, a mashup of feelings swirling inside my gut. Nerves, fear, and a ton of exhilaration. "This is the first time I've ever left West Virginia."

"Really?"

I nodded.

"Well, then." She pulled Deacon's phone from the glove box and yanked open her door. "Come on. Selfie time."

"Lame." I got out anyway and smiled all goofy, sticking my tongue out as she put her arm around my waist with one hand and lifted the phone with the other.

"There," she said, showing me our picture. She stuck her tongue out too, but man, she was beautiful. "Now you have proof."

The snow Mim had warned about before we left didn't come until late in the morning. By the time any flakes fell from the sky, we were well into Kentucky. We kept the radio on, and Free tracked the storm with Deacon's cell.

"Twenty-eight hours to go," Free said as she studied the directions. "And it looks like the storm won't hit us too bad, so we're golden."

I nodded as I passed a few cars on the KY 114. "Awesome. Ah, turn the phone off, all right? We won't be able to charge it until the rest stop."

"Good idea." She turned it off and stared out the window.

The plan was half today and the rest tomorrow. Our first real stop besides gas stations—places I made sure had restrooms—wasn't until Oklahoma. If all went right, we'd be in Needles, California in less than two days.

Only two more days.

"How long before the first gas station?" she asked.

A grin tugged at my lips. "You're not gonna be asking every five minutes, are you?"

"No. It's just this ride's *soooo* long."

"Well, let's think of something to pass the time."

"Sing?"

I rubbed my sore throat. "Definitely a hard no."

"Fine," she mumbled, and put the phone into the glove box. "What, then?"

"Questions."

She propped her feet on the dash. "You and your questions."

I glanced over to find a smile tracing her lips.

God, I'd miss her.

"You have any better ideas that don't involve singing?" I asked. "Want to perform math tricks? Use your big brain to entertain me?"

"No, I like the question thing."

"Yeah, you sound really enthused."

"Let me clarify: I like the idea of asking *you* dumb things. Let me be the annoying reporter for a change."

"Hmm…I don't think you got the chops for it. Annoying people is an art that requires years to perfect."

"Oh, I can surprise you."

I switched lanes. "You definitely can."

"Okay, first question: Mr. Anderson," she said, using a weird, not-quite-British accent, "what are your future aspirations?"

"See? You suck at questions. Stick with numbers, kid."

She sat up, giggling as she smacked me on the shoulder. "Be nice!"

"That was me being nice."

We settled back into our groove, getting to that place where we could laugh, like we weren't on the verge of never seeing each other again. She asked the most absurd questions possible, taking a page from my book:

"If you were a sea monster, which ocean would you want to rule and why?"

And: "When you become president, will you allow all birds to migrate south or will you call for our aviation friends to acquire passports?"

So stupid and so perfect and I answered every single thing.

We stopped for gas before we got on I-64, time flying, unfortunately. "When do I drive?" she asked, eating chips and drinking pop as I pulled back onto the interstate.

I dipped my hand in the chip bag. "Four hours or so. You should get some rest."

"And leave you alone without questions?"

"Yes! Please, God, yes." I stuffed chips into my mouth and laughed as she tossed some at me.

"And you didn't think I could be annoying," she said.

"Totally mistaken. You have annoying down to a science."

"Ha-ha, funny." She turned to the back. "But I ain't tired."

"You barely slept last night. You're tired."

"How would you know?"

Without taking my eyes off the road, I smoothed a finger under her eye. "Because you have circles darker than a crow's ass."

"Gross." But she handed me the chips and crawled over the seat. "The back seat's pretty comfortable, big enough for two people. Little and I slept here when—" Her breath hitched.

"When y'all lived in here?"

She was quiet for a second more. "He would snuggle as close as he could and tell me stories until he fell asleep. The things he comes up with…" A pause. "I can't wait to hear his voice, Cole."

I gripped the wheel tighter. "I know."

CHAPTER 39

Free

$m_1 * \Delta v_1 = -m_2 * \Delta v_2$
Exploding Momentum

Cole's snores filled the car, and I had to concentrate on that sound to keep my mind off the very real danger of pissing myself. The gallons of pop I'd consumed didn't help keep me alert, just engorged my bladder to bursting.

"Oh, thank you, sweet Jesus," I whispered, moving to the right lane when the rest stop entrance appeared. As soon as I parked, I ran into the restroom.

When I came out five pounds lighter, Cole was outside and stretching. "How long was I out?" he asked, yawning his last few words.

He'd spent the first part of his break writing in two different notebooks, the leather one he had last night at Mim's and one of his older ones, until the pen fell from his hands and his eyes closed.

"Three hours or so." I copied his stretches, trying to get the kinks out of my back. "Got quiet without you scratching a pen across those pages. Seriously, how do you come up with so much crap to put on paper?"

He laughed and headed to the restroom. "What I write's not remotely close to crap. More like Pulitzer-prize-winning journalistic brilliance."

I rolled my eyes, trying not to smile. "Whatever. Hurry up."

I waited for him outside, not ready to get back into the car. Three others were parked in the personal vehicle area, and a long row of semis lined up across a grassy divider in the commercial lot, their diesel engines humming.

I hugged myself, the air chilly. We had scheduled five hours to rest here. Five hours with both of us sleeping in the same spot.

As two of the cars zipped back onto the interstate, Cole came out, blowing into his hands and speed-walking in my direction. He wore a T-shirt and sweats, having taken off his hoodie before conking out. I liked seeing his arms. Liked knowing exactly how it felt to be held by them.

The first thing he did was get Deacon's phone from the glove box to text Amy. As soon as he turned it on, the thing buzzed with at least twenty messages. Cole grinned as he read some of them to me:

"When am I supposed to get you from Charleston?" and "Why do I give you a phone if you're gonna shut it off?" and "If you ain't dead, I'm killing you at the train station" and "Amy here: our boyfriend's worried about y'all."

While he read, I felt an ache. My friends, miles away.

"We need to charge this before we leave," Cole said, shutting it off after he texted an "everything's okay" message and putting it away.

"Right. So," I started, gesturing to the back.

He did his eyebrow trick. "What?"

"Where do you want to sleep?"

"You said the back was big enough for two, didn't you?"

"Well, yes, but—"

"And we can't leave the car running, waste the gas." He reached around me and opened the back door. "Only option: body heat."

"Oh."

He was so close, and even after being in the car for hours he smelled good, like himself. A smell I could only compare to what strength and honesty smelled like.

"What're you afraid of, Free?"

"Nothing. I—Nothing." I got in to avoid more of his questions.

Surprisingly, he didn't ask any as he lay on the outside, pushing me into the back of the seat. He pulled two blankets, including the one Jolene had given me, over us. I shivered against him, feeling his chest against mine, his breath in my hair. I wanted to crawl inside him, get as close as I could to his fast-beating heart.

"Free?" he whispered into my hair, sending a tingle down my spine.

"Yeah?"

"What's it like in Needles?"

I laughed a little. "Hot."

"That it?"

"It's… peaceful, I guess. Quiet."

"Sounds nice." He buried his lips in my hair, not kissing me, just breathing his warm breath against my scalp. "I hate that you'll be living in this car."

"I've done it before, and it ain't bad in Needles. No snow. No crazy hillbillies." I splayed my fingers against his chest, too scared to pull him closer. I wanted to, though. "Why didn't you ever ask me to stay?"

"Because it would've been selfish, and you'd have said no anyway."

I didn't deny it. How could I? He did everything right without telling me I was doing everything wrong.

"Can I tell you something?" I asked, no longer afraid.

"Anything."

"After the dance, when you tried to kiss me…" I pressed on his chest, feeling his skin, his pounding heart. "I regret it. More than anything, I regret saying no."

His heart beat faster against my palm, his breathing quicker against my scalp. "What would you do if I tried to kiss you now?"

I leaned back far enough to see his perfect face. He was nervous, his mouth open and his body quaking, exactly like mine. "I'd let you."

"You would?"

I nodded and touched his cheek. Everything inside came to life, like sun and fire and starry nights.

Cole leaned in until his lips touched my forehead. I inhaled, the touch soft, scorching me. He moved to my cheek, featherlight and powerful. My temple. My nose.

My mouth.

His lips were warm, and I sank into them, bunching his T-shirt in my hands, bringing him closer, moaning when his tongue pushed past my teeth. Still, our bodies trembled, like if our lips separated we'd scatter into pieces.

Too soon, he broke away, his heavy breaths blowing against my skin. "We have to stop."

"No." I laced my fingers through his shaggy hair and tried to bring his mouth back to mine.

He resisted. "Please, Free. I…I think we should stop, before…before…"

"Don't. Stop." I said each word slowly, hoping he'd understand so I wouldn't have to say it.

He inched backward. *Shaking, shaking, shaking.*

No. I wanted to have this moment to think about during the long nights ahead without him. For the days I'd be struggling to glue my family back together, trapped in survival mode. I *needed* this one slice of perfect before it melted away.

I pushed against his chest until he gave me enough room to sit up, and without taking my eyes from his, I lifted my sweat-shirt over my head. Then my T-shirt. My bra. "I want you to be my first. I…I want to give you…"

He stared at me, his eyes liquid blue in the flashing lights of cars and semis and lampposts. We were no longer in the Buick at a rest stop in Oklahoma. We were at our cliff, alone and un-afraid.

"Are you sure?" His voice dipped as he wiped the corners of his mouth.

I nodded, feeling exposed in the best possible way, naked from the inside out.

"O-okay." He reached for his bag on the floor and pulled out the box Deacon had given him yesterday. Condoms. His face reddened as he opened them, palming one before giving me back his oceans.

Then he touched me.

Finally.

CHAPTER 40

Free

You > Me

I forgot how dry Needles was, even in the winter. Definitely not like West Virginia, with its cold and trees and mountains—and cliffs.

"You're beautiful," Cole said as I came out of the bathroom. He waited for me beside the vending machines, the leather notebook and a pen in his hands. We'd stayed here last night, at the rest area outside Needles. Cole wanted me to give him one more night, and I agreed before he finished asking the question.

One more night in the back of the Buick with Cole next to me.

"You think so?" I twirled in the spring dress Amy had given me. We'd taken the time to "bathe," using the sinks to clean up and wash our hair. Mine still dripped down my back, soaking the peach fabric.

"Know so." He tucked his notebook under his arm and pushed off the pop machine.

"What if they don't let me see him?" Again my fears weighed down my shoulders.

And again, Cole said the right things to combat them: "You're not gonna let a no stop you, are you? Not my Freedom. No way."

"You're right." I stood on my toes and kissed him. "Ready?"

He brushed his thumb across my bottom lip. "No, but don't let that one stop you either."

We drove around the familiar neighborhood, searching for the right house. I had no idea what the address was, but I remembered the adobe walls, the desert-inspired front yard, the pretty white fence. Sweat dampened my hairline when I found it, the place Little now called home.

"There!" I pressed my index finger against the window, pointing toward a flesh-colored house.

"Are you positive?"

I nodded, and Cole pulled out Deacon's phone and snapped a picture of the house.

"What're you doing?" I asked.

He took another picture after stopping. "Think about it, Free. After everything we've done to get here…this place is *real.*"

I shook my head, my breath coming out faster. *Why is he smiling?* Why couldn't I?

"Hey." His lips turned down as he set the phone between us. "What's wrong?"

Breathe, Free! "I…Can we drive around once?"

"Yeah, definitely. This is your show." Cole pressed on the gas, leaving the house with its sensible car in the driveway and cacti in the middle of the yard.

My breath came out too quick and sweat poured from my scalp. This was it, all we had planned for. And I was too scared to follow through with it.

"Calm down, Free. It'll be okay." Cole rubbed my hunched back as he drove slowly around the block. Once. Twice. Three times.

"Everything feels different now. So different."

Cole didn't answer, just drove and kept his hand on my back.

I had no idea what "different" was, but the change from three months ago was never more acute in my mind. *I* was different.

No.

No matter how much I'd changed, one thing hadn't: my love for Little and the promise I desperately wanted to keep.

"Okay," I said, after the fifth turn around the block. "Okay." My breathing slowed as I concentrated on the feel of Cole's hand. On the sweat-drenched hair against my temples.

"Do you want me to stop now?"

I nodded, keeping my face covered with shaking hands.

The car stopped a moment later, and Cole pulled me into his arms, kissing the top of my head. "You can do this, Free. You can."

"What if he doesn't want me here?"

"He will."

"But what if he doesn't?"

Cole gently pulled my hands away from my face. "He will." He kissed me and repeated, "*He will*, Free."

I wanted to latch onto his oceans and float in them until everything righted itself again. "You'll be here after I'm done?"

"Yes, ma'am, down the street a bit. Go."

I kissed him once more, stealing some of his strength. "Thank you."

"You need to stop thanking me," he said against my lips. "Go."

I hesitated, gathered Little's silver book and his calculator from the dash, and got out. I didn't look back when the Buick's motor grumbled away, my focus on the cement porch and the tan door. Little was in there, maybe still sleeping, maybe reading a book. Maybe waiting for me.

I knocked, my fist so shaky it barely made a sound.

I knocked again.

A few locks clicked—and I held my breath.

Little's grandmother opened the door, her eyes wide. "Freedom?"

"H-hi, um…Hello." I clutched Little's book closer, concentrating on the weight of it, hoping my knees wouldn't give.

She peered around me, searching the street. "What're you doing here?"

"I—My friend and I, we—" I stepped forward. "Can I see him, ma'am? Can I see my brother?"

She crossed her arms over her chest, glowering at me with the kind of distrust one saved for politicians. "He's doing well, Freedom. Going to school, making friends…"

She wasn't going to let me see him.

"He's really happy…"

Let me see him!

"…but all he talks about is you and how you'd be here after Christmas. Even sleeps with that turkey picture under his pillow. Said it's magic."

Hope sparked in my chest. I lifted my head. "I promised him."

She tapped her manicured nail on her shirtsleeve. "I can't have you taking him again."

"I would never," I said so fast the words tripped over each other. "If he's happy, I'm happy. I just want to be a part of his life. *Please*."

She studied me with eyes the same crystal blue as Little's. "All right." She moved to the side and opened the door wider. "I'll wake him."

Relief made my knees weaker, and I stumbled into her living room, the silver book and calculator almost slipping from my arms. "Thank you. I…Thank you."

"I'll be watching you the entire visit."

"Yes, ma'am."

She gestured to a flowered couch on the way to the hall. "Have a seat."

I couldn't sit if I wanted to. Excitement, anxiety, fear, every emotion that shot adrenaline through my system, wouldn't allow me. I put Little's things on the coffee table and concentrated on the hallway, listening for sounds. For his sweet voice and the pattering of his feet. When he came out, holding his grandmother's hand and rubbing his sleepy eyes, the bad feelings melted away, replaced with one. Love. Complete and absolute.

"Little." My voice sounded foreign, choked.

But he heard me.

He didn't say anything. He just ran into my arms. I fell to my knees, crying, stroking his carrot hair, loving him with every fiber of my being.

His tears soaked my cheek, and his thin arms shook around my neck. "Hi, Sissy," he said in his small, brave voice.

I cried harder, holding him tighter, as he cuddled in my lap on the floor. He felt exactly right. My missing piece.

We sat alone in the living room, Little snuggled against my side on the couch playing with his calculator. Holiday scents, cinnamon and pumpkin, wafted from candles lit on the end tables, and a small, fake Christmas tree with white lights and toys underneath took up the far corner. This place felt like a home.

Little spent the last hour telling me about school, what he got for Christmas, his new friend Alex who came over to play. He gushed over his grandparents, kept saying how nice they were, how they let him eat ice cream before bed, how his granddad read to him from the "big books" kept on "a thousand" bookshelves in the den. I listened, stroking his hair, taking in his scent, absorbing the cadence of his voice, and answering the occasional math problem he'd give me in between his stories.

"Are you still camping, Sissy?"

My fingers stopped in his hair. "I…I don't know."

He tapped numbers into his calculator and moved closer to me. "Maybe you can live with me."

As he said it, I noticed his grandmother in the entryway between the living room and the kitchen. The subtle shake of her head answered his question. "I don't think there's enough room."

"Will you sleep in the Buick again?"

"For a little while."

"With Dad?"

I hesitated. "No. By myself."

Little tapped numbers faster. "I don't want you to live in the Buick."

"I know."

He gave me another multiplication problem.

I answered it.

Then, "Are you in school, too?"

"I was."

"But not now?"

"I'm here now."

More numbers tapped into his calculator. More quiet. He wasn't as thin as three months ago, his skin not as pale. Health glowed on his face. His grandparents gave him everything Daddy and I couldn't.

"Has she been here?" I asked.

Little shook his head. More tapping. "You should go to school, Sissy. You should do numbers."

"If I do, I won't see you every day."

"You can visit." He reached up and cupped my cheek. "I'll always keep my hand out."

I tickled him under his chin as tears burned my eyelids. "So I don't get lost?"

"Uh-huh. It worked, see? You're here."

"You're right, Little." I kissed the top of his head. "You're absolutely right."

His smile even looked healthier, stronger. "So, you'll do numbers?"

I reached for his book—and avoided his question. "Will you read to me?"

He nodded. "Sissy?"

"Yes?"

"You're my favorite."

CHAPTER 41

Cole

Girl Abandons Boy

D*id she change her mind?*

Not the first time Deacon had texted me this question, and after every message, my answer remained the same: *No.*

Deacon: *Think she will?*

Don't know. Talk to you soon.

I turned off the phone and shoved it into my pocket. Weird, me not wanting to deal with questions.

Shifting, I scanned behind me for the billionth time. She'd been in there for three hours, a good sign. Obviously their reunion turned out okay, her fears thankfully unfounded. But in a dark part of my mind, I hoped this would go bad, that she'd have no choice but to come back with me. I wasn't proud of myself.

Sighing, I grabbed my current notebook.

Best and Worst Night

- *She let me kiss her*
- *Touch her*
- *All doubts erased (I love you, Free)*

I almost caved and changed my mind about staying here with her, especially after the other night. But my staying would only make it easy for her to never go back, never finish school or go to college. Never escape.

Funny how the best way to escape McDowell County—for both of us—was to go back to it. Because the holler followed Free here, and it would live in the car with her while she struggled to find money and food and a place to live.

Yeah, funny…

I stuffed the notebook in my bag and unwrapped another peanut butter sandwich with a quick glance in the rearview. Finally, there she was, her focus on her shoes as she walked to the car. I turned for a better look and dropped my sandwich to the floor. "Shit."

Was she sad? Happy? I wiped excess peanut butter off my hands to my jeans and watched her.

Hurry up.

When she got in, she wouldn't take her attention off a piece of paper in her hand, a phone number.

"How'd it go?" I asked, trying to sound like my heart wasn't ripping from my chest.

"Good."

"Just good?"

She shrugged. "Great."

"You're not gonna elaborate?" I touched her cheek, and she flinched away.

Instantly, my insides felt dark and heavy as if my body began to mourn her. Forcing myself to turn the key, I started the car. She hadn't changed her mind, and I had no clue why that hit me so hard. Never once did she say anything to make me think otherwise.

At the first stop light, Free spoke: "She gave me their new phone number. Said I could call anytime I wanted."

I turned left without a word to her.

"I can see him almost every day if I want, two hours right after school and Saturday afternoons."

Stopped at the next light and studied the directions to the Amtrak station.

"When Daddy gets out, I'm gonna make sure we stay close. Maybe he can get his old job back."

I made a right when the light turned green.

"Little's doing real good, too, making friends and eating. He looks better, healthier."

I nodded, biting down on the inside of my cheeks as I pulled into the Amtrak station.

The next train to Charleston was tomorrow morning. I checked while Free visited her brother and had been happy because that meant another day with her. Now all I wanted to do was run as far away from her and this car as possible.

I cut the engine and sat there, staring straight ahead.

"Please don't hate me." Her voice carried as much misery as I felt.

"Impossible to hate you."

"This doesn't need to be the end." She shifted closer. "It doesn't."

I bowed my head. "You're delusional, Freedom. You're so delusional." Then I moved to open the door.

Wait.

I turned to her. "Come back with me. *Please*. I'm begging you. *Come back*."

"I-I can't leave him."

"You're not leaving him, not permanently. Finish school, go to college. *Make* something of your life and come visit him until then. Hell, I'll drive you here every month if I have to."

"You don't understand." Her voice heightened as tears filled her eyes. "He needs me."

"No, *you* need *him*, and that's not fair to either of you! He wouldn't want you to just *survive*."

"You don't know." She broke then. Shattered. "You don't know *anything*."

All the desperation drained from my body, leaving me empty. If I didn't stop, I'd break her more.

So I kissed her.

And took my hand off the door handle.

Without taking my mouth from hers, I said, "Let's go somewhere."

"But your train—"

"—doesn't leave until tomorrow morning." I pulled away just enough to see her eyes. "Just… *be* with me."

She rested her forehead against mine and nodded.

We ended up near a playground a few miles from where Landry lived, and I held her as we sat on a bench under the warm sun. Neither of us said much as we watched parents push their kids on the swings and some guys our age shoot hoops at the basketball court. As we sat there, I absorbed every breath she took, every move she made, the smell of her flowery shampoo, cementing her and this moment in my mind.

That night, Free spread a blanket on the sand by the swings after the last few people left the park. "We used to bring Little here." She pressed a hand to her heart as she kneeled on the blanket. "When we lived in the Buick, we'd come every day. He thought it was so great, you know? He trusted all our lies."

I sat next to her, refusing to give any false comforting words. We were past empty "It's okay."

"I'm scared, Cole."

"I'm scared for you, too." I tilted her chin to see her face and how the moon's glow brightened her skin, another something I needed to imprint on my mind. "What're you gonna do now?"

"Get a job somewhere, I guess."

"How? Where?"

She shook her head. "I… I don't know."

"Free—"

"I don't want to think about it now, okay? Not when we only have a little time left."

I nodded, keeping my mouth closed, and lay with her on that blanket under a million stars. And when she fell asleep, I went to the car and rummaged through my bag until I found the leather notebook, writing my very last entry before locking it into the trunk.

The next morning, after parking at the Amtrak station, I faced her and her tears, and I had to swallow a thousand times to keep mine inside. "Free…" My voice broke. How the hell did I let her go?

She cupped my cheek.

I turned into her hand and gave all I had left. "The way I love you…it's desperate."

"I…love you, too." She pressed harder on my cheek. "I do."

I squeezed my eyes shut. Love shouldn't hurt this bad. "I'm telling you this… I'm saying it because I sort of get it, what you feel for your brother. But even that kind of love shouldn't be an excuse to stop your life." I opened my eyes. "Because I'm not stopping mine, despite how I feel about you."

Then I kissed her for the last time.

Grabbed my things from the back.

And left her there.

I didn't look behind me on the way into the station. But after I bought my ticket, I waited, staring at the entrance.

Hoping.

I should've known better.

Deacon's phone vibrated in my pocket, and I pulled it out.

She change her mind?

I pursed my lips, fighting to keep the sound in, and texted him back.

CHAPTER 42

Free

a + b = c
Finally

The sun beat against my back, hot and unforgiving. Needles weather felt nice the first day, but after five, especially living in the Buick, I missed West Virginia's cold. Winter needed snow. But today, I didn't let the heat bother me as I watched the door, just like others who occupied tables next to me.

So this was jail.

I wished I could say it wasn't bad, but after sitting here for five minutes, surrounded by guards and high fences, I couldn't wait to leave.

When the door opened, some people ran to whomever they were here to visit. Others remained seated, watching as the men in tan jumpsuits came out. Some of the prisoners appeared happy, some sad and defeated.

I was one of the people still sitting—until I saw him limping into the yard. Clean-shaven, shorter hair, and looking almost exactly as he had before Mama died.

"Daddy!" I ran to him, laughing, crying, saying his name over and over.

Daddy held his hands out, beaming as I plowed into him. He twirled me around, hooting like he wasn't in jail but watching me hit those rusted cans on my eleventh birthday.

"I missed you," he said, kissing the top of my head and smoothing my frizzy hair.

"Missed you, too."

"C'mon, baby. I gotta sit." He held my hand and guided us back to the table, limping worse, his foot in a hospital boot.

"Why do you still have that thing on your foot?"

"They busted it pretty bad. Had a few surgeries on it, one just last week."

We sat across from each other, and I caught a glimpse of his fingers before he curled them into his palms. Some nails were growing back, but they were thick and knotty. "Do they hurt?" I asked, pointing to them.

"A bit." He gathered my hands in his. "Let's not talk about how beat up your old man is, okay? Tell me everything."

"Didn't you read my letters?"

He shrugged. "I wanna hear it from the horse's mouth. You fared all right? They send you somewhere okay?"

I told him, as I had in the two letters, about Jolene, Kenny, and the kids. My friends and Cole, my voice hitching on his name. How Mim helped us. I told him about my driver's license and the college applications. At the last part, he laughed and said, "You sure played that woman, didn't you?"

For some reason, his laughing irritated me. I hadn't played Mrs. Callahan, not really, and I missed her, as odd as that sounded.

"You see your brother?" He rubbed his index finger across my thumb, intent on every word I said, watching me like Mama used to watch him. Like I was his only person in the world.

"Y-yeah, a few times." I squeezed his hands. "He's real happy. Misses you."

He bowed his head. "I miss y'all more than anything."

I let go of his hands and picked at some loose stone on the table. "And Laura's not around. Mrs. Killian swore she wouldn't let her near Little. They're good people."

"I know."

I swallowed, and swallowed again, then gave him the truth. "We should have never taken Little away. We… we used Laura as an excuse to be selfish."

He nodded and gathered my hands again.

"What about you, Daddy? What happens… after?"

"I got eighteen months left. Thought maybe you and I could drive up the coast, try our luck in San Francisco. We could make a few bucks, come back to Needles, maybe find a place. You still got the Buick?"

It took all my willpower not to explode. To not scream at him in front of these people. "I'm living in it, have been for five days now."

"Good. Maybe find a part-time job. Keep yourself going until I get out of here."

I had expected outrage from him, at least some guilt after I'd told him my living situation. But no, he still wanted to live in his fantasy world. "What's in San Francisco?"

He smiled, his eyes exhausted. His body was tired of being in his fantasy, too. "Won't find out until we get there, but I got a good feeling."

"You're willing to start another chapter on *another* good feeling? Like the ginseng?"

He shook his head. "Now, that was a solid idea. If I could've—"

"No, Daddy."

"What do you mean, *no*?"

"I can't do it. Not anymore."

"Can't do what, baby?" His voice was soft as if he already knew what I was going to say.

"I can't live in your dreams." No tears came, not one. I had already made this decision—after Little pleaded with me to do numbers and after his granddad said I should "Seize the day!" and after his grandmother swore to never keep him away from me.

For all these reasons, I decided Daddy's reasons couldn't matter anymore.

He sighed, his shoulders sinking low on the exhale. "I don't know what else to do."

"I'm not here to ask you to figure everything out." I breathed in the dry air, pausing as I watched prisoners hug young kids or kiss crying spouses. "I'm here to tell you goodbye."

"What? Goodbye?"

I met his eyes so he could see my conviction. "I…I'm leaving, Daddy. I'm going back home."

He leaned forward, his dark eyes worried. "To West Virginia? Baby…There ain't nothing there."

"That's where you're wrong." I went to his side of the table and kneeled in front of him. "There's Mim and my friends. A chance to make something of myself, make you and Little proud of me."

"I *am* proud of you." He cupped my cheek. "I've *always* been proud of you."

I kissed his palm before standing, letting him go. "But I want to be proud of me, too."

Daddy peered at me, searching for something he'd never find again: my willingness to follow him, accept his dreams as mine. "Are you sure?"

"It's time I chased my own dreams, Daddy."

I didn't look back on my way to the Buick a half hour later, and I still didn't cry. Because I was done with just surviving, and nothing about that thought created sadness. I had every intention of living and—as Little made me promise—doing numbers. A promise I was more than ready to keep, especially after his grandmother promised to bring him to West Virginia to watch me graduate.

I started the car and turned up the radio, Judah & the Lion crooning through the ancient speakers. On the passenger seat rested some money, Jolene's gas card, food—and the gifts Cole hid in my bag. Directions back home starting from the prison's parking lot and the leather notebook. The notebook he copied everything he'd ever written about me in his messy, slanted way, our history embedded into every precious word.

First entry: **Mystery Family Moves into Mumford's Shack**

Last entry: **I'll Be Waiting for You**

Acknowledgements

I'd like to thank my agent, MacKenzie Fraser-Bub, for taking a chance on me and this book—and finding it the perfect home with Owl Hollow Press.

To the amazing people at Owl Hollow Press, you all are rock stars! Thanks so much for being supportive and showing love for *Into the Hollow*. Working with each of you has been a wonderful experience, and you've all made this book shine brighter than I could have ever hoped.

No writer has better critique partners than I do. Sunniva Dee, I don't know what I'd do without all your encouragement, support, and expertise with the virtual red pen. This book wouldn't be what it is without you. You're amazing, and I'm so lucky to have you in my life. Judi Lauran, I'm so grateful you came into my writing world! I rely on your advice, and I especially value your friendship. Angela McPherson, we started out in this crazy writing world together, and I'm so glad we're still trucking along and helping each other out. Jenn Wescoat and Sarah McCracken, thank you for being my faithful beta readers who will read anything I give you. I love you guys!

Finally, Steve, Tori, Katie, Olivia, Rhys, Mac, and Kody, thanks for putting up with me. I know it can be hard to live with a writer, but all of you have made it possible for me to realize this crazy dream with your love and support—and heavy doses of sarcastic wit.

Lynn Vroman

was born in Pennsylvania and spent most of her childhood, especially during math class, daydreaming. Today, she spends an obscene amount of time in her head, only now she writes down all the cool stuff.

With a degree in English Literature, Lynn used college as an excuse to read for four years straight. She lives in the Pocono Mountains with her husband, raising the four most incredible human beings on the planet.

Lynn writes young adult novels and is the author of The Energy Series and *Summer Confessions*. She is represented by MacKenzie Fraser-Bub of Fraser-Bub Literary.

#IntotheHollow

Find Lynn online at LynnVroman.com
Instagram & Twitter: @lynn_vroman

Made in the USA
San Bernardino, CA
07 November 2018